The Lady's Refuge

Belanger Family Saga Book 1

Naomi Rawlings

This is a work of fiction. Names, characters, places, and incidents are either a product of the author's imagination or used fictitiously. Any resemblance to actual persons, living or dead, actual events, or actual locations is purely coincidental.

Sanctuary for a Lady/The Lady's Refuge: © Naomi Mason 2012, 2021

Cover Design: © Clarissa Yeo 2021
Cover Photographs: Shutterstock.com
Editors: Elizabeth Mazer; Melissa Jagears
Formatting: Polgarus Studio

To My Husband,
For believing in me and supporting me. May I show you the same type of support, encouragement and love you show me.

Chapter One

March 1794, Picardy, France

Silence surrounded her, an eerie music more haunting than that of any chamber players. It soaked into her pores and chilled her blood.

Isabelle surveyed the shadowed trees of northern France, so different from the wide fields she'd grown up with in Burgundy. The woods lay still, most animals caught in winter's slumber. Her breathing and the crunch of her shoes against the road formed the only human sounds amid acres of forest and earth and animals—or the only human sounds of which she knew.

She clutched her cloak and glanced behind her. Did someone follow?

Her feet stumbled over the hard dirt road, her body trembled with cold, her gloved fingers stiffened until they nearly lost their grip on her valise and her vision blurred. Fatigue washed through her like waves lapping higher and higher on a shore. The long periods of dark through which she had traveled stretched into one another until the ninth night seemed no different from the first but for the growing blisters on her feet and cramps in her arms. *One more day.*

She was close, so terribly close. If she could just survive tonight, she'd nearly reach her destination.

1

A whisper. A crackle. The hair on the back of her neck prickled. *Something's out there.*

A rustle in the bushes ahead.

Isabelle reached to her waist, clasped the handle of her dagger and unsheathed it.

Was it an animal? A person? Please, no, not a person. The bushes rustled again.

Her hands slicked with sweat. Low to the ground, two reflective eyes appeared in the brush.

A wolf? She held its gaze, her heart pounding a savage cadence for each second the creature glared back. Fear licked its way into her chest. She sped her pace and clasped the dagger so tightly her fingers would surely leave imprints on the leather handle.

Her hand began to shake. She'd kill him if he rushed her. She must. But where to stab him?

As suddenly as the eyes appeared, they vanished.

Dropping her valise, she clutched her throat with her free hand and forced herself to take a breath.

She wiped her damp forehead, then groped for her elegant cross pendant and slipped it from beneath her dress. The silver glinted in the moonlight, but the shadows turned the emerald at its center a sullen black. Like her, the pendant survived, the only remaining fragment of her life before the *Révolution.*

In her mind, she could still see the light from the stained-glass windows that had slanted down on her six years past, when her father presented the cross for her sixteenth birthday. Even now she could feel his thick fingers as they fumbled to fasten the clasp at the back of her neck.

But was He still there? The God of the cross she wore?

"Holy Father? Give me strength?" More a question than a plea, nevertheless she uttered the words into the night. There had been a time, before the *Révolution* started five years ago, when her words would have been strong and sure. Now they floated into the gloom, a glimmer of hope swallowed in an abyss of doubt.

Through the wind's filter, a distant noise teased her hearing. A trickle of voices? She turned her head. The faint sound whirled and dissipated. She scanned the road toward the west and then the east.

Silence. Only the primitive night surrounded her.

Then a group of men burst from the woods, the four or five soldiers sprinting toward her.

Father, no! Don't let them catch me. Not when I'm so close.

"Look, there's a girl," a voice rang out.

A hot explosion of fear seized the base of her spine and spiraled upward. Enacting a plan she'd rehearsed thousands of times in her head, she gripped her bag and ran into the woods opposite the men.

"Stop, in the name of the Republic."

She sped toward the darkest places within the shadowed forest, seeking a large fir tree, a thick clump of saplings, anywhere that might shelter her for a moment. Perchance her pursuers would lose sight of her or trip over a log.

She didn't want to die. Not here. Not at the hands of those who'd already killed her family. She could die the moment she reached her destination. A carriage could run over her or an illness take her. She'd accept death by another means, but not at the hands of the *armée*.

Her bag caught on a branch. *Leave it,* her mind screamed, but she couldn't let these beasts find, tear through and claim her belongings. They had no right to her bag, no right to her.

"Stop, you vixen, or we'll make you pay."

"Come here. We want to tittle-tattle, that's all."

The shouts rang closer. Her pursuers' panting grew louder than her quick inhales. The men stumbled over rocks and saplings she evaded. They trampled the dead leaves across which she flitted. But still they gained.

She tripped on a rock, twisting her ankle. She cringed and bit back a cry as pain seared up her leg and her shoe gouged into a blister. Still, she pressed forward.

"Quit running, wench! We won't hurt you."

She veered to the right, following the thickest trees. Surely she could duck into some spot and let the beasts run past her. But the ground here was flat and barren beneath the trees. Not even a fallen log to hide her.

"Get her, fool."

"Where'd she go? I can't see her."

"By the tree."

Heavy footfalls from behind sounded as though they would trample her. Or was that her heart thumping its erratic rhythm? Hot breath teased her neck and ear. No. They couldn't be so close. It must be the wind swirling her hair.

"Faster. If she escapes, I'll send you all to the guillotine."

Isabelle burst into an unexpected clearing. Moonlight illumined her movements as she raced toward the nearest trees.

"We have you now!"

Something pulled her bag. She turned to wrench it free, but one of the men gripped the handle. He sprawled on the ground, as though he had lunged for her, only to catch the bag instead.

"Come here, sweetheart," he growled. His forearm, the size of a young tree trunk, rippled as he clenched the leather.

Let it go. They'll find the money and be happy.

Defiance surged like a flood inside her. She'd not surrender so easily. She yanked the handle. The lock sprang, her bag yawned open and her clothes spewed upward, raining down like her shattered life.

"You get her?" a man called out.

Isabelle glimpsed the silhouettes of others running toward her. Releasing her bag, she screamed, though it sounded like little more than a gasp for want of air, and stumbled forward toward safety. If she made it to the stand of firs ahead, she could lose the men in the thick branches. Seven more steps. Then five, then four.

An arm, strong as an iron band, clamped across her waist and pulled her back against a hard chest. She screamed and fought and kicked. Her captor tightened his hold, pinning her arms against her breast so forcefully her necklace dug into her flesh.

"Let me go!" Waves of hair spilled across her face. She scratched and twisted, but the more she fought, the firmer her captor's hold grew.

"That's right, girl. Fight until you're spent. We can wait." A second man towered before her. He jerked his chin, his leadership of the band evident in the simple movement, and the five men formed a circle around her. The *soldats* all wore bloodred liberty caps and those horrid tricolor cockades.

The leader stepped closer and yanked a handful of her hair, forcing her head back and her teeth to grit against the pain.

"What do you think?" Her captor spoke from behind her. "Is she an aristocrat?"

Aristocrat. The word burned fear into her gut.

"Does it matter?" Someone sneered. "We got her. Only one thing to do with her now."

The soldiers hooted in laughter, and gooseflesh rose on her arms.

The leader seized her wrist, ran his finger over her hand and grunted. "No calluses, but not smooth, either."

Isabelle shrank away, but her back met the solid wall of her captor's chest, leaving her no choice but to stare at the leader. The man possessed arms and hands so burly he could snap her in half. A thin scar twisted around his right eyebrow and bunched into an angry

NAOMI RAWLINGS

fist, and his powerful chest, clothed in an ill-fitting blue National Guard coat, rose and fell with each heavy breath.

The other soldiers crouched on the ground, searching her clothes and tattered bag.

Isabelle blinked back tears and lifted her chin. She'd been so close. One more day to the Channel. "Please, let me go. I've done nothing wrong."

"Nothing wrong? Now, that depends on whether you're an aristocrat. Where are you from?" Even in the gloom, malice shimmered in the leader's eyes.

"Arras." It wasn't a lie. She and Marie had lived there since her family's massacre five years earlier. "I'm a seamstress."

"A seamstress?" The leader's eyes ran slowly down her body, lingering so long her cheeks grew warm. "And what would a seamstress be doing alone? At night? So close to the shoreline?"

"I'm visiting my aunt. In Saint-Valery-sur-Somme."

The leader laughed, a chilling timbre that sent fear into her heart. "Sure you are. Everyone travels in the dead of night when visiting an aunt."

Isabelle licked her lips. "She suffered apoplexy, and we just received word. She needs someone to care for her. I'm traveling as quickly as possible, even at night." She'd rehearsed the story a hundred times, even told it a time or two during the course of her journey. So why did her voice quaver?

"Hah. A likely story." The leader's gaze darkened. "She's an aristocrat, men. Has to be."

Isabelle dropped her gaze and clutched at the hard arm around her chest. "*Non*, please!" They had to believe her. It wasn't a lie, not all of it. She *was* a seamstress. She *was* from Arras.

The leader smirked and took a strand of her hair between his fingers. Isabelle stiffened, bile churning in her stomach as he toyed with a curl.

6

"Pretty as you are, you're not worth the trouble of dragging to a trial." The leader separated her hair into little sections between his thumb and middle finger and stroked it. "We'll take care of you here."

The breath clogged in her throat. So they wouldn't cart her to the nearest guillotine or to Paris. They'd kill her in the middle of the woods with only the trees as spectators. Better than the alternative. But if she could get free somehow and make it to the shrubs, she could still hide in the tall grass. All she needed was a distraction. Something to make her captor lose his hold. But what…?

The arm around her middle loosened. Her captor's hand slid up, and he brushed his thumb along the base of her rib cage. "We got time to have this one before we kill her. She'd be worth it."

The air left her lungs in one hard whoosh. *Please, Father, don't let them rape me.* After five years of prayers falling on deaf ears, if there was any prayer God deemed fit to answer, surely this would be it. She didn't move or even breathe as she focused her eyes on the man in front of her.

If You've any shred of mercy, Father, spare me. Her hands, still held against her chest, sought the familiar outline of the cross beneath her dress.

The leader's eyes darkened, yet the fury embodied there shot past her and speared the man who held her. "You've a wife at home, Christophé."

She tried to suck in a relieved breath, but her captor's arm cut so tight she couldn't inhale.

A low growl escaped from the throat behind her. "You never let us—"

"I said no!"

The arm around her vibrated with tension, though the man remained silent. But the leader's attention slipped back to her.

"Who are you, wench? Truly?" The massive *soldat* pinned his eyes to hers, as though he already knew the truth.

"I told you."

"Don't feed me another lie about Arras." He dug the heel of his boot into the ground. *"Quel est votre nom?"* He wanted to know her name? Her eyes fought the malevolent black of his gaze. *Isabelle Cerise de La Rouchecauld, second daughter of the late Duc de La Rouchecauld, Louis-Alexandre. And after my sister was captured last week, all the province of Artois is searching for me.*

The words burned inside her, though why after years of hiding she should desire to confess her identity to a band of *soldats,* she didn't know. Her jaw trembled as she opened her mouth to recite the familiar story. "Isabelle Chenior. The daughter of a cobbler traveling to Saint-Valery to see her aunt."

Her chest grew tight. What if he forced the true answer from her? The man carried enough power, he could make her talk. And if he learned of her heritage, he'd take her to Paris, where she'd be executed before the raucous mob. With her ancestry dating back to the tenth century, the crowd would be wild for her blood.

As the mob must have been for her sister's. A sob welled in Isabelle's chest, but she shoved it down. She'd not think of Marie now, nor of her role in her sister's death.

The leader snorted. "Isabelle Chenoir, daughter of a cobbler? You lie again, but your name matters not. You all end up at the guillotine."

Yes, let him think her name didn't matter.

One of the soldiers trotted over. "Found the money." The leader held out his hand for the pouch of coins and bundle of *assignats* she'd hidden in the secret pocket of her valise. Her stomach clenched. Five years of her seamstress's wages, and the man palmed it as though she'd earned it in an hour.

Even as he took the money, the leader's gaze never left hers. A silent battle raged between them. Isabelle refused to drop her eyes. He was waiting for that very thing, it seemed. Her final surrender. If only her stare could fend him off forever.

He released the hair he'd been fingering and touched her cheek. She resisted an instinctive flinch as his cold skin pressed against her face. "You know what gave your identity away? That stare. A seamstress wouldn't look at me as though she were a queen."

He backed away. "Kill her, boys."

With the first blow to her kidneys, she couldn't stifle her scream.

⸗.⸗.⸗.⸗.⸗

Michel Belanger surveyed the land before him as the early sun painted the bare fields golden. He drew in a deep breath, smelled the earth and cold and animals.

His eyes traveled over the small, tree-lined fields as they did every morning.

Thirty-six acres. The land had been his for four years, seven months, and thirteen days.

And he loathed it.

He'd promised to care for the farm when his father died, but the obligation choked him, forever chaining him to northern France.

His neighbors were fools for thinking a declaration from the National Assembly freed them. True, the August Decrees four and a half years ago liberated land from the *seigneurs* and Church. But before, a man could leave a farm and seek work elsewhere. Now peasants like him owned their land. And the ownership only tied them to the monotonous work. Shackled their children and grandchildren to the unforgiving earth.

In the sweat of thy face shalt thou eat bread, till thou return unto the ground; for out of it wast thou taken: for dust thou art, and unto dust shalt thou return. It was a verse he'd rather not have memorized. Michel's eyes roved the fields yet to be planted and rested on the stone and half-timbered cottage that sat at the field's edge. He knew every bump and crag of the chipping wattle and daub, the manner in which sunlight slanted through the windows, the way shadows played in the corners of the two rooms. He came into the world in that house, and despite his dreams, he'd leave the world in that same structure.

But a promise was a promise, and he would work the land until it drained the life from his blood, as had happened to *Père.* The Belangers hadn't worked for three generations only to have the eldest son turn his back on the land. He would work hard. He would tame the land and add to it. And one day, he would pass it to his son. And mayhap that son would love the land as his late father had, as his brother still did, despite Jean Paul's decision to leave home.

But the day for heirs and inheritance lay distant, the only flicker of hope against a broad, dark horizon.

Until then, he would work.

Fishing pole in hand, Michel turned his back and followed the deer path through the woods to the pond he'd fished for the past twenty-one of his twenty-seven years. He and *Mère* hadn't much meat to grace their table. That should've changed with the *Révolution,* and had—for a time. Then last summer the beshrewed Convention in Paris said bread in the cities cost too much, so they imposed price controls on grain.

His grain.

Now a sack of wheat brought hardly enough to care for his mother. Let alone cover the cost of his seed.

Michel scratched the back of his neck. Five years, and the *Révolution* that promised liberty, equality, and fraternity had given him nothing.

The four-kilometer path was as familiar to him as the texture of field dirt in his hand, his feet so used to the twigs and stones that the feel of the earth alone underfoot could have guided him. Tilting his face toward the sky, he let the budding light warm his skin. Another month and the sounds of birds and frogs would serenade him while squirrels chased one another up beech trees. A stick cracked beneath his boot, and the noise sent a startled woodcock flying from the brush with its distinct whirr. He smiled, his eyes following the flight of the brown bird into the sky. Then he glimpsed something foreign in the familiar sea of earth and tree trunks and logs. A scrap of blue fabric. He veered from his path, took a step closer.

Cold sweat beaded on his forehead. Three meters past a ripped valise and the discarded dress that first caught his eye, a body lay facedown on the forest floor.

Chapter Two

A mass of wild black hair covered the back of the girl who lay before Michel. Her dress was torn and stained with mud and filth, one sleeve shredded and bloody with a thorny branch still entangled in the crude linen.

The flurry of footprints surrounding her told the story of her struggle. And struggle she had, against what looked to be a gang of four or five men.

Michel scanned the familiar trees, his fingers aching for the worn wood of his musket. Were her murderers still here? No movement caught his eye. No palpable tension raised the hairs on his neck. Most likely her attackers had dragged her from the road, brought her to the clearing to rob and rape, then killed her, abandoning the body immediately after.

He hoped her death had been swift. No one deserved such a painful and humiliating end.

He picked his way through the scattered clothes and neared the girl. Was there family to notify of her death? A father searching for his beloved daughter?

He crouched to touch her hand, and swallowed back a sudden surge of bile at the sight of her left forearm twisted at an impossible angle.

Whoever would treat an innocent girl such deserved death. Laying his fishing pole in the dirt, he ran his fingers over her hand. Cold, but not icy, not stiff. Could she be alive? Using both hands, he gently rolled her onto her back.

And stilled.

A fairy-tale princess. She must be. Dark curls of hair fanned beneath her head and rippled like waves on a pond. Her creamy skin looked as though it had never seen a day under the sun. A curtain of dark eyelashes fell against her high cheekbones. But no deep red hue stained her lips. Instead, a deathlike white clung to their shapely form.

Still, her features seemed too perfect, too delicate, to be from his world. As if, like Sleeping Beauty or another tale from his school days, a kiss could breathe life back into her.

Michel smoothed a strand of hair away from her cheek. If only the world would be so simple that a kiss could save a woman's life.

Instead of pressing his lips to hers, he covered her nose and mouth with his hand. A faint exhale of air tickled his skin.

Alive!

He touched her forehead and cheek, then ran his hands down her torso and legs as he searched for injuries. When he touched the left side of her rib cage, she inhaled sharply and groaned.

Michel sat back. The girl would require care: a place to rest, a doctor, medicine. He could bring her home, but he couldn't provide her with much. Would it be enough? Leaning forward, he bent his ear to her chest in search of a heartbeat. His ear bumped something hard beneath her dress. Frowning, he placed his fingers over the spot, and finding a chain, he fished the necklace out from beneath her fichu and chemise.

A heavy cross emerged from her neckline and fell into his palm. Silver vines curled around a gold cross and at its center sat a large square emerald. It was beautiful, a relic from times past, not like the jewelry sold every day in the market. And it was authentic. If the weight didn't give its genuineness away, the mesmerizing gleam in the center stone did.

He dropped the cross irreverently.

The woman was no beggar. No traveler.

Perhaps she was a member of the *bourgeoisie*. The wife of a Parisian accountant or lawyer. That would explain the expensive adornment.

Michel stood. Then she wouldn't be traveling alone, dressed in coarse wool and linen. She'd have a finer dress. *Non.* She could only be one thing: an aristocrat disguised as a peasant and seeking escape. She'd made a good attempt by getting within twenty kilometers of the shoreline. Most aristocrats had already fled the country or met the guillotine, but she apparently survived—until now.

He gritted his teeth. To think he'd felt sorry for the wench. It mattered not whence she came or how hard her journey. Her class had grown rich off his sweat and deprivation. Perhaps the fools in Paris set the price of his grain, but they hadn't stolen from him the way the aristocrats had. They took half his crop in taxes and then taxed the money his crops brought in. They played games while he worked, frolicked while he plowed both his fields and their land. Then they banned him from hunting and fishing the woods for food while they did so for sport and left animal carcasses to rot in the sun.

Michel stepped back. He wouldn't help her. He couldn't.

He surveyed the trees for movement yet again. Was she a trap? Had roaming soldiers attacked her rather than thieves? Did they watch to see if anyone helped?

He took another step away. Judging by her skin's temperature, she would die soon, and being unconscious, she would feel no pain. There would be no cruelty leaving her where she lay. He grabbed his fishing pole and turned toward the pond.

I was naked, and ye clothed me.

Michel halted as Father Albert's words from a Sunday long past scalded his mind.

But the girl wasn't naked. And he couldn't help her, not even if he wanted to—which he didn't. He'd be guillotined if he took her in and got caught.

He strode toward the pond. Besides, Father Albert had been talking about clothing the orphans in Paris, not the rich who had dressed in silks at his expense.

I was hungry, and you gave me meat.

Oui, and he wouldn't have any sustenance for himself if he didn't get to the pond and catch something. He quickened his pace.

I was thirsty, and you gave me drink.

Michel sighed and cursed himself for memorizing so much scripture. "She's not asking for water," he mumbled.

I was sick, and you visited me.

This counted as a visit, didn't it? He'd bent down, touched her, contemplated helping her. And turned his back the second he realized she was an aristocrat.

Michel straightened his shoulders. He wouldn't feel guilty. She'd have done the same to him under the *Ancien Régime.*

If you have done it unto the least of these, my brethren, you have done it unto me.

He stopped walking. "She's not the least of these, Father. She's the greatest. She's lived her entire life off the backs of me and my kin."

In prison, and you visited me.

"And prison's exactly where she deserves to be." He turned to take a final look at the girl. "Waiting for the guillotine."

I was a stranger, and ye took me in.

He huffed a breath. He threw down his fishing pole and stormed back to the girl. Assuming he took her in, what would he do with her? Nurse her? She'd probably die regardless.

But what if she lived?

He couldn't nurse her and hope she'd die. Cross-purposes, to be sure. He ran a hand through his hair and paced beside the body.

He wouldn't be able to eat tonight if he left her. Or look at a church. Or wave at Father Albert in the market. Or pray tomorrow when he went fishing.

Sighing, he set his fishing pole down, bent and hefted the burden into his arms.

She weighed no more than a bale of hay, but he felt as though he carried his own cross to Golgotha.

~.~.~.~.~

Light, voices, shadows, whispers swirled around her, eluded her, like a dream she chased but couldn't catch. Grass, matted and thick, tickled her fingers, back, and legs. Tall strands of it waved in the wind while dandelions turned their golden heads toward the sunlight.

Overhead, two birds chased each other.

Isabelle looked up from the field she lay in and raised herself onto her elbows.

The *Château de La Rouchecauld* towered before her, its triangle of red brick walls kissing the brilliant sky as it had for seven centuries. No garish chars from a fire marred the windows. No broken furniture littered the ground. No grass and flowers lay trampled by the mob. No gate demolished by angry peasants.

She was home.

Someone touched her forehead. Mother?

"Oh, *Ma Mère!* It's been so terrible. You should have seen…"

The hand pressed harder. Too large. Too rough. Not Mother.

Father, then.

"*Mon Père,* how did you escape the mob? I thought they..." The hand left her forehead. Cold! A frigid cloth replaced the warm touch. She reached up to move the rag. Pain whipped through her hand and down her arm. She groaned and shifted her limb.

"Well, well," said a deep voice. "She lives." The cloth left her forehead.

Isabelle cracked one eye, but the blistering brightness of the room forced it shut again.

"Wake up, woman. I've a farm to run."

Temples throbbing, she turned her head toward the impatient voice. "Who are you?" Her vocal cords, gritty from disuse, ground against each other.

"The man whose hospitality you've enjoyed while lying delirious with fever for these two weeks."

Two weeks? She opened her eyes again, slowly fluttering her eyelids until the burning sensation stopped. The only light in the room spilled from two open slits in the bare wattle-and-daub wall. A man, dreadfully familiar, hulked over her.

His broad chest strained against the two buttons at the top of his undyed linen shirt. While the material gathered at the neck, shoulders and wrists would accompany much breadth of movement, it ill hid his wide shoulders and thick forearms. Light brown hair in desperate need of a trim fell against his forehead and curled around his neck. His chest tapered down into a lithe waist, with his lower body encased in brown woolen trousers. In one hand, he held a worn, uncocked hat by its brim.

It's him. The soldier. The leader of the band that attacked me. The shoulders, the height, the massive arms were all painfully familiar.

She screamed, shrinking into the bed and clutching the quilt. Her bandaged arm shook with pain, but she cared not.

Why had he brought her here? Surely he wouldn't make her endure another beating. She shut her eyes and heard the jeers, saw the men standing over her, felt their blunt boots connect with her lower back, her rib cage, her abdomen.

She should be dead. Oh, why wasn't she dead? He was making sport of her.

"Calm yourself. I'll not hurt you."

At the sound of his indifferent voice, her breath caught. *That* certainly wasn't familiar—his voice had been full of loathing in the woods. She opened her eyes and gulped, pulling the quilt up with her good hand until she could barely peek over it. The stranger shifted his weight and paced the small confines of the room.

"I don't believe you." She stared at him, measuring his movements, comparing him to the man who haunted her memory.

He tunneled a hand through his hair and set his wide-brimmed hat on his head. "It would better serve you to believe the man who brought you home, kept you warm, and fed you."

This man walked differently than the soldier, and his hair…was lighter, shorter. His stature smaller. She let out a relieved sigh. *Oui,* this man resembled the soldier from the woods, but was not the same person.

Hard lines and planes formed a face weathered by the elements, but not altogether uncomely. His straight nose and strong jaw made him appear rugged rather than harsh. The leader of the soldiers had a hardened look that this stranger did not possess.

"Had you no part in the attack?"

Annoyance flashed, but no malice. "I don't rape women and beat them nearly to death, if that's what you ask."

"They didn't rape me." The words rushed out before she could check them. The man turned to face her fully. No scar curled around his eyebrow. *Oui,* he was innocent.

And he had nursed her for two weeks. 'Twas a long time to care for a stranger, although he couldn't know she was of the House of La Rouchecauld.

She bit the side of her lip. He'd shown her kindness, and she blamed him for attacking her. Furthermore, she brought the threat of soldiers, arrest, and the guillotine to his door. She'd naught have helped him were the situation reversed. "I'm sorry to accuse you falsely."

He crossed his arms over his chest and nodded. "You're forgiven."

His simple words washed over her, offering comfort and security. "*Merci.*"

Though he watched her intently, her eyes drifted shut. Oh, to go back to that place she found while sleeping, where she was home, her family still lived, food filled the table and death didn't stalk her. But she wasn't in Burgundy, where a mob killed her parents and little brother outside the gates of their home. She and Marie escaped only because they took a different route to England, parting ways with her parents at Versailles and heading north via their aunt's estate near Arras. News of their parents' deaths had taken months to reach them.

Then Marie died anyway.

Her fault. Isabelle clutched her throat. All her fault. "Are you having another spell?"

She opened her eyes.

The man stood close now.

"Just leave me be." The words fell quickly from her lips. He didn't understand who she was, that his kindness would sentence him to death if soldiers discovered her. She snugged the quilt tighter around her and rolled away from him. Pain seared her ribs, and her breath caught. But she didn't roll to her back or shift to ease the discomfort. Instead, she stared at the bare, uneven texture of the daub wall. Her family was gone now, even her sister. When she was running, she hadn't time to think about Marie or the way she'd betrayed her sister. But now she had time. Too much time. Why had she been the one to live and Marie the one to die? A tear slid down her cheek. Marie should still be alive, not her.

The peasant's feet crunched against the floor, telling her he lingered in the room, likely watching her. She inhaled deeply as her eyes drifted shut. She hadn't strength left to face him.

⁓.⁓.⁓.⁓.⁓

Michel stared at the beautiful woman lying in his brother's bed and rubbed his hand over his chin. She hadn't awakened long enough to get some broth or water in her. And now she lay still, drawn into a little ball as though defending herself against something he couldn't see. He took a step closer, ran his eyes over her.

The quilt rose and fell ever so slightly along her side.

At least she breathed. At least she hadn't curled up and died on him.

What's your name? Where are you headed? Is someone expecting you? Questions warred inside him, but she wasn't awake to ask.

He walked to the dresser and pulled open the top drawer. Her silver-and-emerald pendant lay atop her neatly folded clothes. He reached in and held the precious metal against his palm until the necklace heated with his touch.

If only the thieves had found and taken the pendant.

If only he didn't know about her heritage.

The woman sighed, and the hair on the back of his neck prickled. He dropped the necklace and waited for the words that were sure to come. Mumblings and shouts about someone named Marie and soldiers, a mob and parents.

And then the tears of delirium.

He turned toward the girl, but she didn't move. Only sighed

again. Mayhap the dreams were done haunting her now that she'd awoken for a bit. *God, please keep the dreams from her.* She may be an aristocrat, but she'd suffered through enough dreams during the past weeks to last the remainder of her life.

Leaving the girl, he went into the main chamber and found it empty. *Mère* must still be in the yard. He ladled some broth from the soup simmering over the fire and poured some water before going back to the girl and setting the tray on the bedside table.

The sturdy bed frame didn't so much as creak as he sat beside her. She groaned but didn't wake when he rolled her toward him and propped her head and shoulders against his arm.

Her body felt slight in his embrace, as though her bones would shatter if he squeezed too tight. Her eyelids rested peacefully, and she breathed deep and evenly, not with the erratic, shallow breaths that plagued her when he first brought her home.

Unable to resist, he wiped a tendril of silky black hair from her brow, then jerked backwards.

What was he doing holding her, smoothing away her hair? He laid the girl back on her pillow and raked a hand over his hair. He had managed to bring her back from death, and nurse her to health. But that was no reason to grow soft over the girl. It mattered not whether she was beautiful or helpless. She deserved a taste of the misery her kind had caused him and his family.

Didn't she?

Oui, of course she did. Her ilk had been taxing and oppressing people like him for centuries.

The girl writhed on her bed. "Marie! *Non,* don't take her. Take me instead. It's my fault. My fault."

The familiar words washed over him, then dissipated into silence. How many times had she cried something similar over the past weeks?

He stood and tightened his jaw. Whatever she dreamed, whatever she remembered, he had to get her well and on her way before anyone found her. But he couldn't send her forth before she healed. Not after how he found her in his woods. Not when God told him to take her.

But his obligation to restore her health didn't explain his urge to run his fingers down the slender column of her bruised neck. To smooth away the fading green and black splotch on her cheek.

He stalked from the room, leaving her broth and water on the bedside table.

Better to let *Mère* feed her. He'd get himself into trouble if he stayed any longer.

Chapter Three

Isabelle's life spun before her in traces and glimpses, impressions and feelings. Faster and faster the scenes swirled. She tried to latch on to the pleasant memories from before the *Révolution* arrived—to catch that last view of Christmas with her family, to relive the day *Père* gave her the pendant, to remember the walks she and *Mère* once took in the dandelion field.

Instead, she stood in the shade on a warm summer day, lush with the scent of wildflowers and earth. Sunlight filtered through the rustling oak leaves and bathed the world in its warmth.

"This is for the best, Isabelle." Marie didn't look up as she plunged the shovel into the earth beneath the tree. "If someone discovers us, the money will be hidden far from the cottage, and we can still escape to England."

Isabelle bit her lip. *England.* Reaching that land seemed little more than a wish. Even as Tante Cordele awaited them in London, they lived in the broken, leaking groundskeeper's cottage on their aunt's ruined estate.

"Here, let me dig." Isabelle reached for the shovel, clasping a palm over Marie's dry, lye-scarred hands. "I wish you'd found different work."

Marie shrugged off Isabelle's hold. "I haven't your hand for needlework. Besides, my job as a washerwoman is only for a time. Once we reach Tante Cordele, I'll soak my hands in scented water for a month. They'll be soft as new."

Marie was right. They needed money. Now. After they'd earned enough for two passages to England, they could stop their backbreaking work.

Marie rested the shovel against the tree and reached for the box Isabelle held, but Isabelle clutched it to her chest. The simple wooden square held no resemblance to the elaborate ivory jewelry box she'd left at Versailles, but inside rested the few earnings they'd scraped together and the coins she had hidden on her person before they'd been stranded.

Laying their treasure in the cold ground seemed almost cruel, but she knelt and placed the box in its new home.

Marie crouched on the opposite side of the hole and grasped Isabelle's hand. "Swear that if I am caught, you will take this money and flee."

She jerked her hand away and shook her head. The idea didn't bear thinking of. "*Non.* You won't be caught. We will get to England together. We must. I won't let the *Révolution* take you from me."

"Anything could happen to me, to us. We've no guarantee of reaching England."

"We've been hiding for nearly a year, and no one has discovered us. 'Tis guarantee enough."

"We've no certainty of earning money for a second ship fare, no promise that we can evade the soldiers and mobs forever. If I am caught, I will be killed."

Isabelle's breath caught. They'd not spoken of this before—one of them dying. Her chest felt as though she were being held underwater, and no matter how hard she fought to draw breath, the substance that invaded her airways grew thick and deadly.

"Izzy, look at me."

She brought her shaky gaze back to Marie's.

"If I'm caught, you take the money and map, and you go. Without looking back, without thinking of me. You flee to England. One of us will survive. We must. Whatever happens, we won't let the mobs destroy the last La Rouchecauld."

She longed to tell Marie not to be daft, yearned to promise they'd both see England's shores. But Marie's eyes, dark and serious, kept her from speaking such things. "And if I am captured, you do the same."

And there, beneath the shade of the oak, they sliced their thumbs and pressed them together in that ancient ritual of binding a promise.

"Can you hear me, girl? Are you awake?"

The deep voice filtered through Isabelle's haze of dreams, reaching, clutching, tugging, until it pulled her up, into the bare room lit with day. She blinked at the farmer who towered over her.

Isabelle licked her lips, dry and parched as sunbaked dirt. "What...what do you want?" She barely recognized the rusted sound of her voice.

"To see if you would awaken." Concern shimmered from his eyes—green eyes, the color of dandelion stems. "You've slept another three days. And when you started thrashing..."

Her eyes drifted closed. The farmer should have let her sleep. At least Marie still lived in her dreams.

Isabelle jerked her eyes back open. Marie. England.

The promise. She had to get up. Had to find her way to the shore. She could die once she reached England, so long as she kept her oath to Marie. So long as the La Rouchecauld name didn't die in the clutches of the *Révolution*.

The man bent low over her, the smells of earth and sun and animals radiating from him. "Can I do something to ease your pain?"

Isabelle propped herself up. Pain seared her ribs, but she nudged her pillow against the headboard until she reclined in a semi-sitting position. "You have been most kind to me, *citoyen*. Please, tell me where I am?"

"About a kilometer east of Abbeville." The man measured his words, speaking slowly.

Abbeville. The name settled into her memory. *Oui,* the town she'd been approaching the night of her attack. She was just east of it—so close to the sea. "How far, then, to Saint-Valery?"

He shifted closer and crossed his arms over his chest. "Why do you ask?"

She swallowed. Was heading to a city on the sea too obvious? Did he know that, once there, she would board a ship? Since the British and French warred over the sea, she couldn't go straight to London, but she could sail there via Sweden or Denmark, the only two neutral countries on the continent. "I've an aunt waiting to receive me."

It wasn't a lie, not really. Tante Cordele still awaited her in London. His gaze held hers. "An aunt. In Saint-Valery-sur-Somme. Convenient."

Her chest tightened. "You don't believe me?" He knew everything. He must. Otherwise, he wouldn't look at her thus.

"Why should I believe a stranger?"

"Because I… Why…it's…" Her throat burned. Certainly, it had more to do with being thirsty than telling an untruth. But what else had she to say? He'd saved her life. He deserved the truth, if only the truth wouldn't get her killed—and him as well. Surely she was protecting him by concealing the truth.

She forced a smile. "I beg you, sir. Simply give me the distance to Saint-Valery-sur-Somme."

"Twenty kilometers."

Hope surged through her. Only a day's walk from Abbeville to the Channel. By this time tomorrow, she would be at the port. She gripped the quilt and looked at the man before her. "I am most grateful for your kindness, but I must away."

"Aye, you must away. But you'll not leave afore you've healed."

Isabelle frowned. True, her head throbbed and her ribs pulsed with pain, but still… "I'm well enough to walk to Saint-Valery, thank you."

"You've not tried standing, yet you can walk to Saint-Valery?"

"Of course." She flung the bedcovers back with her bandaged hand. Pain sparked in her fingers and flashed up her arm. Jerking back, she gasped and stared at her wrapped forearm. She trailed her other hand up the wood of the splint that ran along her injured arm beneath the cloth. Surely something was amiss for her injury to smart like this after two weeks' recovery. "This…it's not healing properly. You must call the physician back. Who tended it?"

His eyes narrowed. "I'm rather handy with setting bones."

"You jest. You could no more set my arm than stitch the queen's drapes."

He leaned close, placing his hands against the bed frame on either side of her so she couldn't move. His eyes bored into her, hard and controlled. "I remind you the queen's been executed."

Isabelle closed her eyes. *The queen's drapes?* What was she saying? The blood in her head thrummed against her temples, but a headache didn't excuse her carelessness. She'd kept her appearance as a peasant for five years, but if she didn't mind her tongue, she'd give herself away before she left this wretched bed.

"Repeat after me." The farmer's breath warmed her cheek. *"Thank you."*

She opened her eyes and swallowed. "Your pardon?" *"Thank you for setting my arm."* He held her there, locked between his arms as he studied her. "Put voice to it, woman."

"If you'll give me some space, *citoyen.* I can hardly think."

He straightened and crossed his arms, but she felt just as smothered as she had when he loomed only inches away.

"I'm waiting."

"I…" She looked at her throbbing arm. She should tell him thank-you. Physician or not, he had saved her, thereby putting himself in more danger than he understood. And at least she didn't have to answer a physician's prying questions about where she'd come from and why she'd been traveling alone. *Oui*, she owed the man before her much more than a thank-you. So why wouldn't the words come? She should be thankful to be alive, to have a second opportunity to reach England and fulfill her promise to Marie.

"Is the word so hard? I'm sure a crooked bone is much worse than dying in the woods." His eyes flashed, a green fire that looked nothing like dandelion stems. "Or do you expect me to apologize for saving your arm?"

Warmth rushed to her cheeks. "*Non*, I've no need of an apology. I just…well, I…" She cradled her throbbing arm against her chest and searched for words.

"Still going to Saint-Valery-sur-Somme, are you?"

"I can walk fine with a broken arm."

He backed to the wall, shifted his weight against it and crossed one foot over the other. "Be gone with you, then. Hurry on, I've animals to attend."

Now? He expected her to rise from the bed this instant? She swallowed. He must, for the man watched her as though she were a court jester or some other form of entertainment. Very well.

She flung the covers off with her good arm and scooted to the edge of the bed. Pain clenched her ribs. Biting her lip, she ignored it and stretched one leg to the floor.

She *would* walk out of his house. She simply had to get off the bed first.

She angled her torso up until she could see her foot. The pounding in her head increased. The room tilted, straightened, then spun. She gasped and fell backward onto the quilt.

The farmer came close and crouched in front of the bed, the aggravation in his eyes giving way to worry. "Don't strain yourself." His voice seemed kind but reluctant. "You'll make things worse. I'm...sorry. I shouldn't goad you. You need to rest. You were near death when I brought you here, and you'll only reinjure yourself by attempting to walk."

She shook her head, tears burning the backs of her eyes. "*Non,* you don't understand. I have to leave now, or I might never get to..." *England.* Had she almost said it? He would know everything then. "Saint-Valery-sur-Somme."

He stood and fisted his hands at his side, the corded muscles along his forearms hard as though they were etched in marble.

This time, she moved one leg, then the other, over the side of the tick. She slowly sat upright. Cradling her set arm against her chest, she let out a breath and leaned forward.

Nothing spun.

She shifted her weight from the bed to her feet and paused. Her head pounded, her arm throbbed, her ribs screamed and her muscles ached. Lifting herself off the bed, she straightened her torso, and smiled smugly.

The farmer's face remained placid, his body still. She stepped forward. The room shifted, then stilled.

She tried another step, and another. She'd keep walking. Right past him. Through the open door, out of the house and down the road until she reached Saint-Valery.

Her next step brought her almost to the door. Shadows speckled the edges of her vision. She moved forward, wobbled, then a knee gave out. Blackness seeped into her view, and she cringed. Her chest and arm would explode with pain when she hit the packed dirt floor. Except she didn't hit the floor. A solid arm braced her back, and another stretched beneath her knees. The man lifted her, cramming her against a chest as hard as the brick walls of the *Château de La Rouchecauld*.

"Of all the mule-headed things…" he muttered. Her sight clearing, she looked up into frustrated, swirling eyes.

"Do you think I've spent more than a fortnight nursing you so you can undo your healing in an hour's time?" He deposited her on the tick, and threw the quilt over her. "Now sleep. The sooner you get your strength, the sooner you can away." He turned and stalked toward the exit.

"Wait. Please, don't leave me here."

She couldn't be sure if he didn't hear her, or simply chose to ignore her. Either way, he slammed the door behind him, leaving her alone in a strange room, with a strange bed inside a cottage full of strange noises. Loneliness filled the space the man vacated, an oppressive weight that settled across her chest. Her body ached, and her mind moved sluggishly. She needed a moment's rest. Then she'd up and begin her journey anew.

Sliding deeper into the bed, she stifled a yawn and looked about her prison. No tapestries or paintings graced the dingy walls, and no mirror hung near the chest of drawers. A pitcher and basin of delicate pink sat atop the polished dresser, their beauty out of place against the bare cottage walls.

The bed frames, too, were masterful. Three ticks—two double and one single—rested on elaborately carved frames. But how could a peasant afford such grand furniture? Such an exquisite pitcher and basin?

Closing her eyes, she sank down, trying to get comfortable on the lumpy straw tick, but her nightdress made her throat itch. Strange, for the fabric of her chemise had never irritated her before. She reached up to scratch her neck, her fingers skimming the material. It felt stiffer than usual. Opening her eyes, she examined the foreign gown. Her heart began to pound against her chest. She'd not brought this on her journey. Where were her clothes? She must have her raiment. Not that she missed the miserably rough garments, but she needed her chemise. Her attackers had stolen the funds in her valise, but they hadn't found the forged citizenship papers and money inside the hidden pocket of her chemise—at least not while she'd been conscious. She'd kept her papers and the exact amount of money needed for fare to England on her person.

Had the farmer discovered them?

She tried to calm her breathing even as a tear trickled down her cheek. Swallowing, she reached up to finger the cross about her neck, but that, too, was gone. Like everything else in her life. She curled into a ball and clutched her hand over her neck—where the cross once hung, where the guillotine had sliced her sister. She pressed her eyes tight against the burning tears until sleep overtook her.

But instead of finding respite in her dreams, the dark face of the soldier who ordered her death in the woods loomed before her.

Chapter Four

"Thank you. *Thank* you. Thank you! Thank *you*." Michel practiced the words. First rolling them over his tongue, then speaking briskly, then whispering.

Petty, mayhap, to get his hackles up over two small words, but how hard could it be for the girl to voice them?

He thrust his pitchfork into some sour straw and tossed another clump of muck into the pile of dirty swine bedding. He'd cleaned this stall every Monday since he could remember, but today the pregnant sow eyed him distrustfully, like he would accost her rather than care for her home.

"Come on, now. Up with you." He tapped the pig with his boot. She snorted, then closed her eyes.

Two stubborn females. Just his luck. "I've no mind to put up with you today. Out with you." He poked her with the handle end of his fork. The swine squealed and rolled over.

Michel sighed and rubbed his temple. First the girl, then the sow, what would come next? Maybe the roof on the stable would collapse, or the dam on the lower field would break. A perfect ending to his day.

Images of the girl flooded his mind anew. The tears that glistened in her eyes, the raise of her chin and set of her shoulders when she told him she had to leave, the pain that lanced her features when she strained her arm. The look of triumph on her face when she left the bed. She was determined, if nothing else. But only a featherbrained child would expect to walk after lying incoherent for over a fortnight. Michel raked his hand through his hair, knocking his hat into the straw.

Hopefully she'd settle in a bit, because she'd be in that bed awhile before she could visit her aunt.

In Saint-Valery-sur-Somme.

His grip on the pitchfork tightened. He wasn't a halfwit. She was headed to England, sure as the sun would set. Not that it was any concern of his.

With nothing left to clean but where the sow lay, he shoved the fork into the straw beside the beast's belly. Squalling and grunting, she rolled to her feet, baring her teeth and stomping the straw as though she would charge.

He growled in frustration. How much could a man endure of a day? Not intending to get bitten, he pushed his pitchfork into the ground near the gate and trudged away from the stable. He should finish mucking the stalls and fix the plow wheel. The stable roof needed patching as well as the roof over the bedchamber. He must get to town and buy that ox. And he had to check the sandbags on the lower field before the rains came and flooded the tiresome parcel of land.

He huffed a breath. The responsibilities of the farm pressed down upon him as they did every spring since his father died and his brother, Jean Paul, left. At any given moment, he had two weeks of work to finish and days to do it.

Yet he stormed past all the places needing his attention and opened the door to his workshop, the small familiar building the same as he had left it yesterday. The scent of lumber, instantly calming, wrapped around him. He inhaled deeply and moved to the center of his workspace, his eyes seeing nothing but the chest of drawers he'd spent the past six months making.

He wiped his hand on a rag and trailed his finger up the side of the piece. The elaborate sculpting on the posts contrasted with the straight lines and gentle curves of the wood, and the design of acorns and oak leaves he'd carved twisted and curled daintily against the deep hue of the walnut. This chest of drawers would match the design on his mother's bed. A bedroom set, of sorts. He need only sculpt along the top edge of the dresser. Another week and it would be finished.

Sooner, if that impatient girl drove him to the shop every day.

He reached for his chisel, squeezed the familiar wooden handle, then rolled his shoulders. Too tense. He let the chisel fall to his workbench. He'd gouge through the middle of an acorn if he carved now.

Two strips of walnut lay on the floor beyond the dresser, a reminder of the wood he'd used to set the girl's arm. A walnut splint. Who had that?

She'd uttered nary a comment about how smooth he'd sanded the wood so no sliver would pierce her porcelain skin.

Maybe he should have left her arm broken.

Guilt swamped him at the thought. He raised his eyes to heaven. "*Oui,* Father, mayhap she doesn't deserve a broken arm. But she could still say thank-you."

He rubbed the back of his neck. He needed to create, to saw, to build. Something—anything. Drying wood rested at the back of his shop, an odd assortment of anything he could collect. He blew out a breath. He'd have to start a new piece. But what?

He didn't need another bed frame. Or another dresser. Mayhap a table and chairs? He didn't need those, either, but perhaps Leopold would sell a dining set in his store.

Michel picked up a single piece of richly burled maple and ran it through his hands as he studied his wood selection. He didn't have enough walnut to work with. He could buy more, if only the farm didn't need an ox. So the table would be oak. He walked to the back, hefted a long plank and brought it to his workbench.

Frustration melted with each push and tug of saw against wood. The tension slipped from his shoulders and neck as he planed the wood with long, smooth motions that shaved the legs into equal widths. Fragrant, curly strips of oak floated down and covered the floor as he toiled. He inhaled the aroma, heard the faint crunch of the shavings underfoot, felt the rough wood beneath his palm.

This was all a man needed to be happy.

Betwixt the rasps of his block planer, footsteps echoed on the stone walkway. *Mère.* With the girl and the sow, he'd forgotten his mother. Surely she hadn't been turning over the garden all this time. He stopped the calming movements and dropped his planer with a *thunk* onto the workbench before heading to the door. He deserved a day in the stocks for forgetting his own mother.

"In here, *Ma Mère.*"

"There you are, Michel."

She wandered over to him, carting a burlap sack behind her.

A lump of fear rose in his throat. "You went to town? You can't up and head to Abbeville. I've told you, there are dangerous men about."

She hauled her sack to the workbench. "I thought you'd be in the stable."

So had he. But that didn't change that she'd left despite his warnings.

He grasped her wrist. "*Ma Mère,* look at me. You cannot go off by yourself. Not into town, not into the woods, not anywhere until we know who hurt the girl."

Eyes vacant and dull as two glass marbles stared back at him. She was having another bad day, which at least explained her wandering off.

"It's Monday. I go to town on Monday. You muck the stalls. Did you get the stalls mucked? It's Monday."

Unable to stop himself, he pulled her to his chest and held her head over his heart, which beat at twice its normal pace. "I've some stalls yet to clean."

She wiggled under his hold. "Have you looked at the bottom field?" Her voice muffled against his chest. "The wheat's not flooded?"

He released her, looked at the woman who'd raised him and tucked a stray tuft of graying hair back into her bun. "It's still Germinal."

Her brow wrinkled in more confusion, and he ran a hand through his hair. What had the revolutionary government been thinking to give France a new calendar with ten days in a week and different names for the months and years? He could barely remember the new names or keep track of the day. Was it any wonder his mother got mixed up?

"April, *Ma Mère*. It's the beginning of April. We've not planted yet, and we've not had much rain."

"Oh."

"It's all right. Everyone gets befuddled at times."

She glanced around the shop, her eyes resting on the freshly cut lumber in front of them. "More wood for the chest of drawers?"

How could she forget the month but remember what piece he worked on? "This is for a table."

"You're starting a new piece?"

"That's what happens when I finish one."

"You've a buyer for the finished one?"

He looked at the dresser. Not even close. "Mayhap."

Hope, like wildflowers blooming in a field, sprang into her eyes.

"And this table, you'll be able to sell that, too?"

"Aye." Right after the bottom field stopped flooding and the animals started mucking their own stalls.

"Dear me, I almost forgot." *Mère* hefted her burlap sack onto the half-planed oak and began unloading her treasures. "Look what the Good Lord supplied us with."

"That wood's half-finished. Could you…"

He clamped his jaw. A kettle with a burned-out bottom, a scrap of lavender ribbon and a torn shoe with what looked like a mouse's nest inside had already thudded onto his lumber.

"Oh, and look at this." Her eyes shimmered as she produced a scraggly mourning bonnet from the bottomless abyss.

"It's got holes." Like most things she brought back from the village.

"I'll make a hat for the girl."

With all she forgot, how did she remember the girl? "You haven't any thread left to mend the bonnet."

"Look what else." She pulled ragged brown trousers from her sack. "Madame Goitier wanted to throw these away. Throw them away! What with Joseph being the last of her brood. Said they didn't fit him anymore. I'll use the thread from these. You don't think she'll mind that the thread doesn't match the bonnet, do you? Black and brown are close enough shades."

Michel swung his eyes to his mother's, waiting until she quieted and returned his look. "She's awake."

"What?" *Mère* patted the side of her head before her hand dove back into the sack.

"The girl. She's awake."

Mère stilled, the broken wooden yoyo in her hand pausing midair, then crashing to the table and scattering into more pieces. "Oh. Can't say I expected her to wake."

Bien sûr que non. Of course not. The girl's fever had broken, her bruises faded, her delirium left and her arm half-healed. Why would *Mère* expect her to awake? "She's astir, all right." And madder than a caged cockerel.

"What's her name?"

Her name? Michel swallowed. People probably called her something besides *girl.* "Didn't ask."

Mère bit her cracked lip. "How's she feeling?"

"Poorly. Can't stand."

"Did she eat much?"

He tunneled a hand through his hair. She'd not eaten anything but spoonfuls of broth for more than two weeks. And he hadn't even asked if she was hungry.

Or thirsty. "I should see how she's faring. Come meet her?"

Mère stepped backward, her treasures forgotten and a shine of fear in her eyes. "I don't know, Michel. She's a stranger."

"She'd like to see the bonnet you're planning." If the girl didn't use the bonnet's ties to strangle him for stranding her in the bedchamber despite her protests.

He took his mother's shoulders and stooped to look her fully in the face. "*Ma Mère,* if anyone asks about her, say she's Corinne's cousin visiting from Paris. You can't say I found her in the woods. Not to anyone. It's important."

Life or death important.

He'd repeated those words every day since bringing the girl home, but as always, Mother's glazed eyes just blinked back at him.

Please, Father, let no one ask.

"Come." He returned his mother's discoveries to the sack and reached for her hand. "She'll want to meet you."

Hopefully. God forgive him for lying if the girl didn't. He grabbed his hat off the peg by the door and led her outside. A thundercloud approached from the west. A quick afternoon storm, more than likely, but the spring rains would come soon. He'd best examine the sandbags in the lower field tomorrow.

He tugged *Mère* along. "The girl'll be happy to…"

The gate to the swine's pen stood wide open. "Wait here."

He left her standing in the yard and trudged toward the empty pen. The lily-livered sow! Getting the mean beast back would take the better part of his afternoon. Nothing seemed amiss with the gate while he mucked the stall. The beast must have been angrier than he thought and barreled through the barrier.

But the gate looked pristine with no visible damage to the door, latch or fence post. Michel rubbed his hand over his jaw. His pitchfork rested beside the post. Surely he hadn't left the gate open. He wasn't that daft.

But he'd been awfully distracted with the girl…

He pressed his eyes shut. He'd no memory of closing it. The girl and sow had troubled him, and he must have stormed to his workshop without latching the gate. He eyed the cloven prints that led toward the bottom field and stream, almost as though the sow made a beeline for his neighbor Bertrand's property.

Thunder rumbled closer. He glanced at the gathering darkness, then back at the hog's tracks. If Gerard Bertrand found her, he'd butcher her and the litter without thought, then lie to the magistrate about taking the sow. Michel walked back to his mother. "Better get on inside. Rain's coming, and the sow got loose. You remember, the one carrying the litter?"

She nodded even though her eyes showed no comprehension.

"You just go in and work on your mending. The girl should be sleeping. Leave her for now, and I'll introduce you when I return."

A bolt of lightning, a *clap* of thunder, and the sky loosed a torrent of fat raindrops. He smashed his hat farther down onto his head and watched *Mère* scurry inside. Then he turned to face the elements alone.

⌐.⌐.⌐.⌐.⌐

Thunk.

Isabelle's eyes flickered open at the muted sound of the outer door closing, followed by soft voices from the other room. The candle still burned on the bedside stand, and the book the farmer's *mère* had given her, *The Tales of Mother Goose,* rested facedown on her stomach. The woman had been kind to her, offering broth and water, giving her a book to read. But Isabelle must have drifted off soon after the woman left. Darkness had fully descended now, shrouding the room in its shadows. How long had she slept?

She shifted slightly, and a flash of movement caught her eye. The man entered, barefoot and soaked. Rainwater dripped from his sleeves and trouser hems onto the floor, making a muddy mess as he headed toward the dresser.

He placed his candle atop the dresser, its light illuminating the side of his chiseled face. She'd not heeded how attractive he was earlier, likely because she'd been too concerned about getting to Saint-Valery and then too angry with the man for insisting she lay abed. But now she couldn't deny his comeliness. Muscles played across his back as he hunched down and rummaged through the third dresser drawer. His chest was so thick it would take three of her to fill it, and his arms so powerful they looked as though they could accomplish any task given them.

He must be so strong from working in the fields. She'd never seen her father's torso this closely—he'd always worn layers upon layers of fabric, and none of them soaked to the skin, like the farmer's—but *Père's* forearms hadn't been nearly so muscular nor his hands as beefy. And none of the courtiers at Versailles nor her former suitors had carried themselves the way this farmer did, with his strong shoulders and solid chest. She'd felt the strength of his arms and torso when he caught her from falling earlier.

Oui, he must be a hard worker, indeed.

He turned his head her direction, and she swiftly shut her eyes. He needn't know she was awake—or ogling him. She was too tired to defend her actions or rationalize her thoughts. She'd no desire to engage in another argument, and she'd little reason to rouse and attempt her journey until she determined a way to earn back the money she lost.

Warmth spread over her body. He stared at her, and she felt it from the tip of her toes up through the roots of her hair. Her eyelids involuntarily fluttered, as though they longed to open and let her eyes meet his dandelion-green gaze, but she forced them shut.

The moment passed, the heat leaving her body and replaced by a cold loneliness. Fabric rustled in the farmer's direction.

She opened her eyes. He stood sideways in the candlelight with fresh clothes piled atop the dresser. He undid the two buttons at his collar, then reached down and pulled the bottom of his shirt up.

She slammed her eyelids shut and turned her head away. She'd no business seeing this man bare of chest, especially not when she needed to focus on getting to England.

Chapter Five

The miserable wall. All it did was sprout holes.

Despite the chill in the air the following morn, a bead of sweat trickled between Michel's shoulder blades. He hefted another sandbag from the wagon onto his shoulder and trudged to the weak spot in the makeshift dam. Miserable wall. Miserable field. Miserable sow. Miserable life.

Twenty meters from where he walked, a stream glittered in the sunlight, and two large ash trees on the bank cast shadows over the water. It probably looked picturesque—to someone who didn't know any better.

Nature's deception at its best. One good rain and that creek would flood its borders—and his field. The ground rose on the other side of the stream, forming a gentle hill and Gerard Bertrand's property. But Bertrand didn't need to dam up his fields.

Nature did that for him.

If ever a field should revert back to forest and wetlands, this cursed lower parcel was it. After a few hours of rain from the day before, the ground transformed into a heap of mud that needed draining, not planting. And the creek had yet to flood, as it did every spring.

And every second summer. And every third fall.

He set the sack into position on the wall and headed back to the horse and wagon for another. The farmwork, day in and day out, would rob a man of his strength. Take and suck and slurp until nothing was left. Then in the end, after the land stripped away a man's muscle and mind and endurance, it took his heart. It had stolen his father's. In this very field. One moment the man had been plowing while Michel built up the dam, and the next moment *Père* fell to the ground behind the plow, his hands clutching his heart, his face a deathly gray. Michel had rushed to his side, just in time to promise *Père* he would take care of his mother and the farm.

His throat burned with the memory. How much of *Père's* death was his fault? He'd been the one to leave the family and go off to Paris with dreams of making furniture. After a year of being denied an apprenticeship by every prominent furniture-maker in Paris, he'd returned home, his savings depleted, his dreams crushed, to find his father nearly dead from taking on the extra work.

He wiped his brow with the back of his sleeve. Pursuing his dream cost *Père's* life. He wouldn't make that mistake again.

The wood might call to him and make him long to be in the shop, letting his hands run over silken lumber, carving that last strip on the dresser, joining the tabletop.

But God had given him this land. And like *Père,* he would take care of it until it killed him.

He should have been the second-born son. God and *Père* both would have been better off giving the land to his brother. Farming flowed through Jean Paul's blood the way woodworking did through his. Jean Paul could get a field to sprout just by looking at it, or so it seemed. The man never scowled when planting time rolled around and wore a grin on his face throughout the long, toilsome days of harvest.

Michel looked out over the fields. Where was his brother? Jean

Paul should have returned by now. *Mère* and the rest of the town thought Jean Paul had been living in Paris these past six years, making furniture for the wealthy. But it wasn't true. The master craftsmen furniture-makers wouldn't let anyone new into their ranks. So when someone asked about his brother, Michel smiled and said Jean Paul was doing well. He wasn't lying so much as he didn't have anything different to tell people. In his letters, Jean Paul appeared to be doing well.

Grunting, Michel lifted another sandbag off his shoulders and swung it into place. It burst, spraying loose sand and dirt over his wall.

He kicked the barrier. The force reverberated up his leg, and sand spurted from another sack. Just what he deserved for giving in to his anger, but he didn't much care. He'd a right to get worked up over the field, didn't he? All it did was drain the life from him.

He snatched the ripped bag and trudged back to the wagon. The mud sucked at his boots, making each step a deliberate battle.

The earth smelled of moist dirt after yesterday's rain. A scent he appreciated—when he hadn't spent three hours traipsing around in search of a pig during the downpour, only to return without her. He glared across the stream to his neighbor's land. The greedy man must have found the beast.

At least the girl had been asleep when he returned last night, so he hadn't needed to deal with her.

At the thump of approaching horse hoofs, he turned toward the rise at the edge of the field. Two horses crested the little hill. The mayor undeniably sat atop the first steed, for no one in town carried as wide a girth as Mayor Victor Narcise. On a mule about half the size of Narcise's horse sat Father Albert. A burning sensation of guilt crept across Michel's chest at the sight of the wiry, sunken former priest. Ordinarily, he'd welcome a visit from the mayor, one of *Père's* closest friends, and the father, his former schoolteacher. But the girl changed things.

Not just things, *everything*.

The mayor, sitting atop his magnificent mount and wheezing heavily from the exertion of reining in the beast, reached Michel several paces ahead of Father Albert. "Your *mère* said that your *père* was down here." They talked with *Mère?* Michel stilled, the hair on the back of his neck rising. What if she'd mentioned the girl? "But since your *père's* dead, I assumed she meant you'd be the one working the field."

No talk of the girl. Michel blew out a shaky breath.

The mayor smoothed a gloved hand over the thinning gray hair that stuck out from beneath his hat. "I thought your *mère* knew—"

"She does. Some days." Michel shifted his weight. He need not discuss *Mère's* condition with the mayor. Half the town already thought she belonged in a lunatic hospital. "When she woke this morn, she remembered *Mon Père* was dead."

Narcise hitched a thumb in the waistband of his breeches and watched him. Beside Narcise, Father Albert nodded, his eyes brimming with compassion. The same compassion he would no doubt have for the girl, despite her sharp tongue. Michel glanced nervously in the direction of the house. He worried not what Father Albert would do if the girl were discovered, but Narcise's reaction would be a different matter.

Michel rubbed the back of his neck. Surely Father Albert had helped aristocrats escape France. Though the good father had lost everything—his church, his rectory, his income—when the Convention declared an end to Christianity last fall, he still went about the countryside helping widows and orphans, much like he'd always done. *Oui,* with Father Albert, Michel need not question whether he'd helped aristocrats, but how many.

Father Albert clutched his bony hands atop his lap. "'Tis a good thing you're doing by looking after your mother, Michel. The Lord shall reward you."

Michel couldn't meet the father's eyes. He'd probably canceled any reward for helping *Mère* after how he'd treated the girl. Father Albert should have been the one to find her. He wouldn't forget to offer food or water, nor demand she say thank-you.

"Sometimes the Lord gives special opportunities to serve Him," Father Albert continued. "Do not consider it a burden, son, but a chance to show God's love."

The blood left Michel's face and pooled in his toes. *Mère.* Father Albert was talking about *Mère.* He couldn't know about the girl.

"Well, Michel." Narcise shifted, the saddle creaking under his weight. "We wanted to let you know Joseph Le Bon's said to be coming this way."

Michel wiped his brow with the back of his hand. The *représentative en mission* from the Convention. Great. He'd attended federalists meetings for more than a year now, and rather than sell his grain at the low price Paris demanded, he'd hid last year's wheat in a lean-to in the woods. Now he could be guillotined for both—not to mention harboring an aristocrat. "When?"

"Don't know." Narcise puffed his chest. "*Citoyen* Le Bon's supposedly had a few gangs of soldiers roaming this part of Picardy for a couple weeks, collecting accusations and ferreting out federalists and royalists."

Was that what happened to the girl? Had soldiers, rather than a gang of robbers, found her? He should've asked. "Not to mention grain hoarders."

"Half the village didn't sell their grain last year," Father Albert said mildly, but then, it wasn't Father Albert's life in question. "No one could afford to with the price controls."

Michel took a step closer, his eyes steady on Narcise's. "The federalist meetings. Are the others…have they… Do we have an understanding?" "No one who attended can afford to talk. That's why we're making these rounds. And I've not heard accusations from outsiders." "Doesn't mean accusers won't come once Le Bon rolls his guillotine into town." "Burn your wheat, Michel," Narcise directed. "Burn it! I'd've been better off selling it last fall." "Is one harvest worth your life? I can't protect you if they search your property and find grain." "You can't protect me, anyway," Michel muttered. "I aim to keep things under control. I won't stand for foolish accusations. I'm still mayor here, and we'll not have any Terror in these parts." "Le Bon's from the Convention. You go blathering about how you have authority as mayor, and yours'll be the first head to roll." "I won't watch my friends die for something they haven't done." "That's the problem, Narcise. As far as the radicals are concerned, everyone in Abbeville's done something." Michel blew out a breath, wiped his sweaty hands on his thighs and resigned himself to what was coming. "I'm here if you need a hand." "We just wanted to warn you, son." Father Albert raised his brow, concern etched across his face. "We can't stop the Terror from coming." Michel slid his eyes shut and pictured Isabelle lying in the woods. "Something tells me the Terror's already come."

⁓.⁓.⁓.⁓.⁓

"Look at this one," Jeanette exclaimed. Yet another child's shirt—or what Isabelle thought was a child's shirt—hung proudly between Jeanette's hands. The garment sported three prominent patches, none of which matched either one another or the color of the shirt.

Isabelle settled back into the pillows of the bed and twisted a lock of hair. The smile plastered on her face turned genuine under the older woman's enthusiasm. "You mended that one, too?"

Jeanette had been showing off the clothes she mended for the children's orphanage since she walked inside a quarter hour ago.

"Fixed the shirt all up, I did. Those orphans need good shirts." Jeanette raised her chin and puffed out her chest despite her short, frail body.

How different Jeanette appeared from her own mother's tall, regal build.

Jeanette absently patted the side of her hair, which was done up in a sloppy knot of sorts. A few strands of graying brown came loose, as though she'd napped and not set her hair to rights.

Mère never had a hair out of place but her maid rushed to fix it. *Mère* never sewed an old garment but embroidered only the most delicate of handkerchiefs. And yet, the lines around Jeanette's and *Mère's* faces when they smiled at her, the concern in their eyes when they suspected something wrong, the gentle touch of their hands against her brow when they checked for fever, couldn't be more similar.

"Michel and Father Albert love my donations. Figure it's the best way for me to give back to the Good Lord. Why, He's given me so much, I can't help but return His goodness."

Given Jeanette so much. Isabelle couldn't help the longing for her mother, or the despair that flickered to life in her belly. From talking to Jeanette, Isabelle knew Michel owned enough land to make a decent living. They had a separate stable for their animals and thus no need to share their living quarters with the smelly beasts as so many farmers did. And they owned beautiful furniture, though she wondered how they obtained it.

A decade ago, she never would have called this small cottage and the surrounding farmland a blessing from God. Now these simple peasants possessed more than she did. She should have been grateful all those years ago, for the *château* and servants, the opulent food and dress, and her family. She lived in luxury while Michel and Jeanette and others like them struggled to get by. And now Jeanette's Good Lord had reversed the situation. He'd stripped away all she held dear and still wouldn't answer her prayers. She'd prayed the night she'd been attacked, and the soldiers still caught her and beat her and left her for dead.

But they hadn't killed her.

Could that have been an answer to her prayer?

Bien sûr que non. What kind of a God let His child suffer all manner of humiliation and deprivation and torture before finally sparing her life? Michel's finding her had been luck more than God. She could surely get to Saint-Valery-sur-Somme without more help from heaven.

"And my Michel's so kind," Jeanette prattled on, still chattering about her sewing for the orphans. "He won't even let me mend his clothes. After they wear through, he says he'd rather I cut them up to make clothing for orphans."

Isabelle couldn't help but arch her brow and smile. No sane person could desire to go out in public wearing garments "mended" in such manner. "How charitable."

"One of his shirts will make two or three for the orphans, he's so large."

Yes. He was large, indeed. She shoved the image of his powerful body from the night before out of her head before it could take root.

Jeanette fiddled with the shirt she held. "Fixing up clothes for the orphans started as a little hobby, it did, while my Charles was still alive. Now that he's gone, it's all I…" Jeanette's shoulders shuddered.

"That is...it makes me feel useful, I suppose."

Isabelle's heart caught. Surely this gentle creature didn't doubt she was helpful. "Oh, Jeanette, you are most invaluable. I'm sure your work is important to the children, and I know how much your benevolence has meant to me." Uncomfortable, she looked down and fidgeted with the handkerchief she'd been embroidering. "The orphans, you know, they've nothing at all. At least I have your kindness, and..."

What had she besides Jeanette's kindness? Certainly not Michel's favor. Or her passage money to England.

Moisture welled in her eyes. Certainly not her parents and brother. Certainly not the God whom she had spent her childhood worshiping, the God who allowed her family to be killed by a mob of peasants. And certainly not Marie, whom she had killed. Isabelle closed her eyes against the onslaught of guilt, but she couldn't stop her hand from trembling or a tear from cresting.

At least she was alive. Why had God thought to spare her life, but not Marie's? Not her family's?

Jeanette moved to sit on the bedside, took Isabelle's hand and patted it. "There, there. We'll take care of you, we will. You needn't cry."

The chamber door opened, snapping Isabelle out of her memories. Before she finished wiping away her tears, Michel entered. When she was crying, of all times. He stood by the door, his green eyes seeming to absorb everything about her and his mother. Isabelle tugged her hand away from Jeanette's soothing pats, cleared the moisture in her eyes with two blinks and raised her chin.

The room that had moments ago been comforting filled with an undeniably masculine presence. Michel's muscles bunched beneath his shirt as he removed his wide-brimmed hat and wiped his forehead.

"*Ma Mère*, I need to speak with the girl. Alone."

The girl. Did he not care to learn her name? She'd learned his through Jeanette last night. And what could he need to speak with her about in private? Her throat felt dry yet again; she reached for her water cup and found it empty.

Jeanette laid a hand on Isabelle's shoulder and turned to Michel as she rose. "Be kind to the poor dear, Michel. Oh, and that crate can be sent to the orphans. I finished the last shirt this morn."

He took his mother's hand and led her to the doorway with gentle, caring motions. The thump of the door closing echoed in the room. He stepped toward the dresser, opened the top drawer, retrieved something and approached her.

Pretending he hadn't stopped beside her, she stared at the beams in the roof, then jolted when his rough hand enveloped hers.

"This is yours. I should have thought to give it back yesterday." He wedged a small pouch of coins into her palm.

Isabelle gaped at the money before meeting his eyes. "I…"

"This, too, belongs to you."

She recognized it the moment the cool weight pressed against the center of her hand. "My pendant…I thought…the others, that is, I thought they…"

"You were wearing it when I found you, but it was bothersome while *Ma Mère* tended your wounds."

Her head fell back against the pillow and she clutched the pendant and money to her chest. England. Marie. She could go. One of the La Rouchecaulds would escape this dreadful *Révolution*.

If she ever got out of this infernal bed.

Michel cleared his throat. "I have your citizenship papers, as well. They're in the dresser when you need them."

A single tear slid down her cheek. Horrors! She brushed it away with her bandaged hand, ignoring the pain her movement caused.

He sat down beside her on the bed. "Isabelle." He whispered her name.

The word sounded beautiful on his tongue, and the intimacy of it had another tear cresting. She furiously swiped at it. She'd rather swallow a toad than cry in his presence.

His hand clasped over the fisted one resting on her chest. A bolt of heat raced up her arm. Did he feel it?

His thumb stroked her knuckles. "Don't cry. Forgive me for not giving them back sooner. I didn't intend to keep anything. But you vexed me so yesterday that I forgot and stormed off."

Tears still brimming, she met his eyes, so warm compared to their coolness yesterday. She couldn't help sinking into the comfort they offered, letting the heat from his touch travel straight to her heart. "I thank you."

A smile twisted the corners of his mouth and crinkled the edges of his eyes. He shifted closer, surveying her features. "Ah, the very words I wished to hear yesterday. Come now…"

He shifted, bringing their lips within centimeters of each other. The breath rushed out of her. He would kiss her in another moment, and she should turn away from it, slap him. But his eyes held her, trapping her in their green depths.

She knew not how long they sat, an instant away from kissing, both afraid to make the contact, both afraid to break it. He lifted his hand and tucked a strand of hair behind her ear, and his fingertip grazed the tender spot behind her earlobe.

She lurched back. The bond that held them shattered. Michel sprang from the bed, shifted his weight awkwardly and looked about the room. "I, uh…"

She kept her face down, staring at the pattern on the old quilt. Why must she be so childish and lurch away? He'd meant nothing by the touch. He was just…what?

Her heart felt ready to hammer through her chest, and heat flooded her cheeks. Surely she did not desire his kiss.

He cleared his throat. "I, um, came to speak with you about your attackers. Was it a gang of thieves, or soldiers? And what do they know of you?"

Isabelle stiffened, her hand tightening around her money and pendant. Had he been kind to her only because he wanted information? She couldn't tell him, not anything. If he knew her father had been a *duc,* he might yet turn her over to the soldiers. And if he allowed her to stay, he'd knowingly put himself and his mother in greater danger. *Non.* Information about her family would only put more people at risk. "You need know nothing of me."

"Joseph Le Bon, the *représentative en mission* from the Convention, will be coming to Abbeville shortly. Now, whence come you?"

The *représentative en mission?* An icy finger of fear wrapped around the base of her spine and worked upward. Though the main guillotine for executions resided in Paris, *représentatives en mission* brought other guillotines with them and their soldiers when they traveled, carrying their own little Terror to other sections of the country. She and Marie had barely maintained their disguise when the Terror came to Arras last fall, but to have it come to Abbeville? Now? "Surely you jest."

"I do not. And 'tis reasonable that I know who's sleeping under my roof and eating my food. So I'll ask again. Whence come you?"

She swallowed. The soldiers in the woods hadn't believed her story, but perchance the farmer would. The tale had fooled people for five years. "From Arras, my father was a cobbler, but when my aunt in Saint-Valery suffered apoplexy, I—"

He gripped her wrist with frightening force, angling himself over her until she'd no choice but to look him in the eye. "You lie. And so easily at that. If your hair were not so obviously black and your eyes brown, you'd state they were red, both of them. Tell me, does it upset your constitution to lie so freely? I thought *mademoiselles* were especially sensitive to such falsehoods."

She pressed her eyes shut, unable to meet his prying gaze. *Non.* She hadn't always lied. She'd been nearly sick the first time she was untruthful about her heritage. But the seamstress, Madame Laurent, would have sent her to the guillotine had she gone to the shop claiming she was the daughter of the Duc de La Rouchecauld.

Had lying become so natural over the past five years she now thought nothing of it?

"I'm risking my neck and my mother's by having you here. I'll not hear any more falsehoods. I'd rather you refuse to answer than tell me an untruth."

Isabelle opened her eyes and bit the side of her lip. She still couldn't tell him who her father was, not even with the *représentative en mission* en route. Perchance Michel was willing to help some unnamed aristocratic girl, but in the eyes of most Frenchmen, helping the daughter of the Duc de La Rouchecauld would test even God's mercies. She blew out a shaky breath. "I promise to speak honestly, but I'll not give you my name nor tell you whence I come. Then if I am discovered, you can deny any knowledge of my heritage."

"We both know that will make little difference."

The truth of Michel's words sliced her. They would all be killed if anyone learned her identity.

Chapter Six

"...They appeared of a sudden, coming out of the forest. I didn't stop to look or count. I simply fled. I knew not whether they were thieves or soldiers, but when they started calling me, telling me stop in the authority of France, I knew who they were and what they would do to me."

Michel scrubbed a hand over his face as Isabelle's words swirled around him. He should have never asked to hear it. Her face shone deathly pale, but her words sounded hard, objective. Like a soldier who recounted someone else's experience, rather than her own. 'Twould be better if she cried, raged, anything to get out what must be burning inside her.

"I should have been more prepared for a chase. I see that now. The handful of other times I happened upon someone in the road, I'd time enough to hide in the forest. But the soldiers, they emerged from the trees, not the road. What could I do but run? The shadows weren't enough to conceal me. And I had my valise. I should have dropped it, left it for them. But...I couldn't."

Her voice hitched, followed by a tremble of the lips and the slightest sheen of anguish in her eyes. "I'd already lost so much."

Her determination nearly broke him. How terrible to be forced from your home, constrained to travel at night with wild animals and thieves abounding, impelled to carry all possessions in a valise.

Michel hunched his shoulders and turned away from her. He wouldn't feel sorry for her. He couldn't.

Fire and damnation. Her kin had starved him, taxed his land, house, harvest and made him pay for use of the mill. *Seigneurs* refused him rights to hunt and fish. Now he sat beside a *seigneur's* daughter, and he was supposed to pity her?

Michel stiffened, only half listening as she continued. "Despite my advanced start, I could feel them gaining. Then my valise caught. I turned to jerk it free, but a soldier had hold of it. When I pulled, the bag ripped, but I continued forward. There was a copse of pine ahead, and if I could get there, I thought to lose myself in their dense branches. But I never…that is to say, I didn't…"

She cleared her throat.

How had the woman courage to continue her story? "One wore an old National Guard coat, and they all had on those hideous tricolor cockades. They wanted to know my name, where I was from and so forth. I told them the same story I told you, but they didn't believe me, either. And when the leader demanded the truth, I refused. They were going to kill me regardless. Why give them the pleasure of knowing whom they'd taken?" He'd not look at the girl. He couldn't or he'd lose every drop of the hatred he harbored for the aristocracy. Tunneling a hand through his hair, he paced, but the room was hardly large enough. Four steps across from the chest of drawers to *Mère's* bed and back again.

He wished he'd never found her. Then there'd be no dilemma, no danger to him and his mother by harboring her. No choice between whether to further aid her escape or kick her out once she regained her strength.

He'd not sneak into the woods again to fish for the rest of his days if he could send her on her way. Rid himself of the burden she'd become.

"The leader, a large man not unlike yourself, had at least enough decency to refuse the others the opportunity to violate me. I suppose I wasn't worth dragging to the nearest guillotine, so they'd kill me there, in the woods. Then I felt a blow to my lower back and..."

He stopped pacing. Isabelle worked her jaw to and fro. Why didn't she let her pain out? She should be in tears after reliving such an ordeal. Her hands trembled in what was surely a bitter fight for control, but her eyes stayed flat.

"...I can't recall anything more."

He raised his eyes to the thatched roof. Through the deaths of his father and Corinne, he'd clung to the fact that God didn't make mistakes. Every morning when he rose to milk the cow and feed the animals, every midday when he planted or weeded or harvested rather than build furniture, he reminded himself God's ways were best.

But the arrival of this...this... He knew not what to call her. He could hardly term her "wench" or "vixen" when she faced the memories of her attack with such strength. He could hardly call her "girl" when she had lived through such pain.

The arrival of this *mademoiselle* had him questioning God's ways. Why would God want him to find her? To care for her? In God's great plan of things, this situation was most illogical. Someone else should have discovered her. Father Albert or...

And therein lay the problem. She'd been lying in *his* woods. So God must have given this responsibility to *him,* must intend for *him* to aid the girl.

But why? Michel's temples pounded. He needed the feel of wood beneath his hands, the relaxing motion of the saw or planer to clear his thoughts, roll away the stress.

"Michel?"

He squeezed his eyes shut, then reluctantly looked at the girl. No—the woman. Her lips moved. They were red, the color of apples in September, not the dull pink they'd been when he found her. And her hair, by heavens, he should have hidden *Mère's* brush. It had been comely enough when dirty and matted in the woods, but brushed and falling freely over her shoulders and the pillows, it looked like a cascade of dark silk. He rubbed his forefinger over the pad of his thumb. Surely her hair wouldn't feel so soft.

And this was not happening! He'd not feel attraction for the girl, or sorrow or pity or anything else. She was his duty, his burden before God. Nothing more.

Isabelle watched him as though she expected an answer of some sort.

He scratched the back of his neck. "Did you ask me something?"

"My injuries. How severe are they? My ribs hurt oftentimes, even when I'm sitting."

"Cracked ribs. At least, I think they're cracked. Either way, there isn't much that can be done for them other than to wrap them and let them heal. I sent not for a doctor because I had no way to explain your wounds without compromising my safety. I set your arm the best I could. I've set bones before, although I've never seen a break as severe as yours. And you had considerable bruising on your back and torso."

Her face bloomed bright red at the inference he'd seen her body, and his ears and neck heated in response.

"But I've not, er, that is... *Ma Mère* would know more about those injuries. I merely helped wrap your ribs and arm. She's tended you since."

"Think you that I can journey to Saint-Valery soon?"

"Doubtful, since you couldn't stand yesterday. And, much as you threaten our safety by being here, I'll not have any part in aiding your escape to England. You can walk to Saint-Valery on your own."

She inhaled sharply. "You knew."

"Aye, I'm not daft. The pendant gave your heritage away when first I found you. What need has an aristocrat to journey to the coast of France other than to board a ship bound for Stockholm or Copenhagen, and then probably to England?"

She cast her eyes about the room as though she had some sudden need to look everywhere but at him. Her gaze settled on the window. "Might I sit outside this afternoon? This room is wearisome. Perchance the fresh air will strengthen me."

He recognized the obvious attempt to divert his attention, but answered her, anyway. "You're too weak. You've naught been awake two days."

Her eyes held mirth. "I've never been one to sit still long."

"I thought that art required of ladies."

"Yes, well, that vice caused my mother and nurse much displeasure at times."

"You? Displeasing?" He tried suppressing a smile, but the corner of his mouth tipped up, anyway. "I can't imagine."

"I'm sure not. Perchance if you help me out of doors, we won't repeat yesterday's heated words."

The hope in her eyes nearly forced his consent, but he'd not risk having her about his lands until he had reasonable explanation for her stay. Although saying she was Corinne's cousin would fool most, he had no reason for her injuries as such. "I think not."

Her gaze fell to the quilt, and she toyed with the handkerchief on her lap. He moved closer. She'd clearly been embroidering the worn hanky. A delicate brown flower stem twisted in the far right corner, waiting for a flower or two to be added. "It's exquisite."

"Thank you. I worked for a seamstress, not sewing so much as embroidering. Custom pieces mainly. Handkerchiefs and pillows and the like."

He narrowed his eyes. "I told you not to lie. I'm risking my life and *Ma Mère's* by having you here, and I expect the truth in return. If you choose to share not your name or whence you come or whither you go, then so be it. But I'll not have you sit in my brother's bed and tell me an untruth."

Her eyes lit, and she fisted her uninjured hand in the quilt.

"How think you that I've survived five years of *Révolution* in this accursed country?" The words exploded from her and left her chest heaving. "Do you think that I merely smile and introduce myself and have money to buy goods? Do you think I snap my fingers and have the world fall at my feet? We were on our way to England five years ago. Five! You desire to know what happened? How I got here? Our servants, who had served my family since before my birth, to whom my father had entrusted the safety of me and my sister, stole our money and deserted us near Arras. We would have died had I not hidden spare funds in my boot and found us shelter. I worked for the money you found on my person. My sister and I spent four and a half years earning the rest of the funds needed to get us to England."

He should believe her. Told himself to believe her. But like Thomas with the wounds in Christ's hands, he couldn't help grabbing the pointer finger of her right hand. She tried to jerk away, but he held fast and felt along the pad, paused when he came to the slim, telltale callus formed from hours of holding a needle. He'd missed the small mark the first time he'd looked at her hands.

She yanked her hand again, and he let it go.

He didn't have the heart to ask what had happened to this sister of hers. "Forgive me."

"That seems to be your favorite saying of late." "Indeed it does."

~.~.~.~.~

Isabelle awoke from her nap to stare at bleak, brown walls. She sighed and rolled to her side, gasping with discomfort. Since she'd awakened yesterday, she'd shifted, lain and sat in every position imaginable and found not a single pose to ease her constant pain.

Her gaze traveled to the window, following the sunlight that spilled in and danced across the bedcovers and floor. Outside, two birds chirped and a cricket sang. A faint moo reached her ears, accompanied by the sound of chickens squabbling. She inhaled and, through the stale air of the room, caught the slightest whiff of spring. Isabelle propped herself into a sitting position. How could a person be expected to heal while trapped in the confines of such a dark and unsightly room?

She closed her eyes and imagined strolling through the woods. The trees would leaf soon, and the dirty patches of snow would have melted by now. Unbidden, memories of a similar walk flooded her. A twig cracked beneath her foot as she stepped, and the four walls of the cottage no longer surrounded her. In her mind, she walked through the forest on a day she remembered far too well. It was Sunday, her day off. Yet no church bells rang from the nearby town of Arras, for France now worshiped the Cult of Reason rather than God.

She grasped the cross hanging about her neck, more from reflex than from a desire to cling to her faith. She wouldn't have gone to church even if she could. She'd given up that empty ritual four and a half years earlier, when she'd learned of her parents and brother being slaughtered. What would she say to God if she entered the doors of a cathedral? Thank You for killing my family and sending my beloved country into upheaval? Two squirrels scurried over a patch of melting snow and a rabbit rustled the brush nearby. Isabelle drew a cleansing breath. She'd not think of her family on such a fine day.

She rubbed a finger over her bottom lip. Léon had kissed her the day before last, and it had been…well…she should say wonderful. Every woman's first kiss should be wonderful. And she was one and twenty now, already more a spinster than a maiden.

Brotherly, though, was a better way to describe the kiss. She'd hoped for a spark. Or a tingle. Yes, a tingle that spread all the way from her fingertips to her toes. Instead, all she felt was patience for Léon.

She hadn't told Marie of the kiss, but she could hear Marie's reprimands even now.

Listen to me, Isabelle. You mustn't encourage that boy so. What if he follows you here? What if he learns who we are?

Nonsense. A harmless shop boy like Léon couldn't cause any trouble.

For as long as they'd been hiding, Isabelle had snubbed any man who dared look at her. She'd grown weary of putting men off while Marie wrote letters to her faithful fiancé in England. What harm would come from accepting a little attention from Léon? He was more friend than suitor. He didn't look at her with a wicked grin but as though the sun rose and set on her face alone. No woman minded such overtures.

A voice. A shout.

The sharp sound resounded through the forest. Isabelle paused, her body tensing as she scanned the trees for anything amiss. Another male voice, coming from the direction of home, echoed through the woods. There shouldn't be men at the cottage. Couldn't be.

Yet even as she denied it, she knew.

She raced expertly around trees and over fallen branches, through dormant underbrush, slushy snow and deepening mud. The commotion grew louder as she neared home and Marie, and before the whitewashed wattle and daub of the cottage came into view, she glimpsed flickers of blue—*soldats'* uniforms.

She stopped and doubled over. Unable to wipe away the indelible images visible through the trees, she wrapped her arms around her stomach. Flashes of white and brown and green mingled with the blue. And the red. The color brought waves of terror to her heart, would haunt her indefinitely. The army may have run out of funds for uniforms, but soldiers, whether paid or volunteer, always wore bloodred liberty caps.

One voice rang above the commotion. "Search the house. Find everything. Daughters of the Duc de La Rouchecauld living under our noses. On their aunt's very estate!"

The words sliced her. She pressed her eyes shut against the burning tears. She should hide. Sprint as far as she could and harbor in the woods until it was over.

But Marie?

Isabelle left her home not an hour ago. Had Marie heard the commotion and escaped into the woods? Isabelle couldn't leave without knowing.

She crept forward, her mind whirling. Running would be a wiser decision—Marie would have implored her to do so—and she would, as soon as she knew Marie was secure. Oh, with all their plans of escape, why had they never decided on a meeting place?

The hideous voices of soldiers bounced off the trees as Isabelle circled through the woods to the east of the cottage. The forest nearly engulfed the house there, and a little thicket lined the edge of the woods. At least the ragged brown cloak she wore would blend with the forest floor. The thicket soon grew too dense to walk, and she inched along the ground, using her hands and elbows to pull herself forward.

Something stung the back of her hand. She jerked it away and stared at the blood tricking from three thorn punctures. With shaky fingers, she pulled out one thorn still stuck in her flesh and slid her hand back beneath the briar bush. Bleeding or not, she had to know about Marie. Her cloak snagged on a branch, then made a ripping sound. A mixture of mud and melting snow dampened her chest and stomach and legs, but she clambered forward.

She barely recognized the yard. Nearly everything from inside the cottage had been dragged out of doors. Piles of food, blankets, the pots from beside the hearth, even their spare clothing and boots littered the ground. A soldier appeared in the doorway holding the quilt that graced her bed.

Hot anger balled in her stomach. The mobs had raided her family's things from Versailles. Killed her parents and likely ransacked the *Château de La Rouchecauld*. And now soldiers took belongings from her cottage. Things she and Marie had worked for. No right of birth had given her that quilt. She had bought the fabric and stitched it.

But it made no difference to the wolves who devoured her possessions.

Some of the men sifted through her belongings, putting items in various wagons. She clamped down the desire to scream. She'd heard stories of how the soldiers stole everything they touched, but she'd not seen it happen until now.

At least she didn't see Marie. Isabelle closed her eyes and let relief sweep through her. *Bien sûr* Marie had run. Now they need only find each other.

"The revolutionary tribunal in Paris will be happy to see you."

The harsh voice jolted Isabelle. A moment later, a short, burly man in a National Guard coat waddled out the door of her house. He dragged Marie behind him, his hand fisted in her straight, ebony hair.

Marie! No! Isabelle tried to scream, but the sound caught in her throat, clogged it. She tore at her collar, her breaths coming shallow and quick as her heart thundered.

She'd run out and save Marie. Tell the soldiers not to put their vile hands on her. But her arms shook, and her body sank into the ground with a weight so heavy she couldn't move. Silent tears streamed down her cheeks. Marie had done nothing. Nothing! Except warn her to be careful. Now Marie would die, like her brother, like her parents, like thousands of other innocents led mercilessly to the guillotine.

The sour stench of death surrounded her, if only in her mind. She could almost hear the roar of the Parisian crowd as they cheered her sister's beheading.

Isabelle swallowed another scream.

If only they could trade places. If only Marie could be free and she the one sentenced to death. She pushed herself up on her arms, but they collapsed weakly beneath her. She needed to launch herself from the ground, to race out and save her sister. She didn't know how to stop the *soldats* from taking Marie, but she had to try something. Anything.

Instead, she crumpled in a fit of weeping. Here she—who boasted great things of their futures, who brought home pay and spoke of England with unerring confidence—lay helpless and in tears at her sister's expense.

"Look harder. They've got to have money somewhere," the lead soldier shouted at his men. "And spread into the woods. There's another one somewhere. Isabelle. Short of stature, dark hair, brown eyes. Find her." He yanked Marie against him, his next words too quiet for Isabelle to hear, and then shoved Marie face first onto the ground. He moved to a young man with an overly familiar profile and muttered something. The young man turned. *Léon.* An iron band clamped around Isabelle's chest, squeezing until she couldn't breathe. A moment later, Léon bent over Marie and tied her hands behind her back.

Isabelle sank her forehead into the mud as a fresh tear trailed down her cheek. How she would change everything, if she could but go back in time. She'd never again look at the traitorous boy with the large gray eyes. Never again smile at him or converse about the weather. She should be angry, filled with rage over Léon's betrayal. Yet, she buried her face deeper into the dirt and sobbed.

She stayed in the bushes until night grew around her. Until the soldiers left their search for her and dragged Marie to a cart, taking her to face the military tribunal and guillotine nearly two hundred kilometers away in Paris. Leaving the ground where Marie had struggled, bare and cold.

What would happen if she never moved? If she just lay there, curled into a ball and vanished? She would not wish to die, for death equaled humiliation and failure. But to vanish, as steam from a boiling kettle? That wasn't shameful or painful. The townsmen and soldiers would be back. All of Arras was probably searching for her, Isabelle Cerise de La Rouchecauld, the missing daughter of the Duc de La Rouchecauld. But how little everything mattered now Marie was gone.

Clawing and scratching, Isabelle dug her way out of the abyss of memories and stared at the bleak, brown walls of the cottage near Abbeville. She pressed a hand to her cheek and found it damp. If only she could wipe away the guilt over Marie's death as easily as she could the tears.

She drew in a deep, liberating breath, but the air inside was stuffy and suffocating. She had to get out. Somewhere she could breathe the open, clear air of spring. She rolled to her side, pain hammering her ribs with the movement. How could she get out of bed in such a condition?

Her gaze traveled to the windows. She couldn't lie here, trapped in this bed. It seemed as though the chamber walls would close in on her if she stayed.

The main door to the house creaked open, then thudded shut. Jeanette or Michel? She listened for Michel's heavy footfalls on the other side of the wall but only heard an off-pitch hum. "Our God, Our Help in Ages Past."

Jeanette. Thank heavens.

Isabelle swallowed, and her eyes slid back to the window.

I think not.

Those had been Michel's only words when she'd asked to sit out of doors. He hadn't given a reason. Surely in such a situation, he would understand her need for some air.

"Jeanette!" Isabelle tried to calm her voice, hated the panic edging her call. "Have you my cloak and a spare blanket?" Isabelle spoke when Jeanette entered the room. "I thought I might sit out of doors for a time. Perchance the fresh air will help the ache in my side."

Jeanette worried her bottom lip. "I don't know. Do you think you're well enough?"

She smiled brightly to cover her fluttering nerves. "I'll be fine. I once knew a physician who said breathing fresh air can help the ailing." The physician had been speaking of consumption, but cracked ribs were nearly as debilitating as consumption. Were they not?

Jeanette shifted her weight from one foot to another, then glanced toward the door and back. "Michel's not here just now to ask."

A sign from God that she was to sit outside a spell. "May I inquire of his whereabouts?"

"He headed to town, methinks...or, no...that's not right. He's planting the bottom field." Jeanette nodded to emphasize her point, then wrinkled her forehead. "Or maybe it's one of the upper fields."

Isabelle displayed the sweetest smile she could manage. "If you could help me from the bed..."

The change in scenery instantly calmed Isabelle. Michel's house rested atop a gentle hill covered with forest to the west and north. A stable and a second outbuilding also sat on the knoll, and at the bottom was a road—presumably the one that led to Saint-Valery-sur-Somme. To the east and south, the land gave way to bare fields. The dirt, dry and uneven, rolled over the not-quite-flat country. The ground to the east dipped down toward a line of trees and a stream or river, perhaps, before it rose to higher ground.

Isabelle sat on her blanket and tried to clear her mind from the memories lurking in its corners. Yet the image of Marie quietly whimpering while Léon tied her dominated Isabelle's mind. She shoved it away, took a breath to calm her quickening heart and bit her bottom lip until she tasted blood. She'd not think on Marie, she couldn't.

She drank in the fresh air and looked east. How much of the land was Michel's? One man couldn't possibly farm everything she saw.

She reached a hand over the edge of the blanket. The nubby grass, just coming to life, prickled her fingers. Whether her eyes lit upon the town and fields surrounding the *Château de La Rouchecauld,* the grandeur of Versailles, the quaint forest skirting the cottage near Arras or Michel's bare and rolling farmland, this was France. Her France. And the countryside was beautiful. England would have views such as this, would it not?

Of course, not where she'd be staying in London. Isabelle ran her tongue over the side of her swollen lip.

She'd simply have to marry a gentleman with a country home.

She dug her fingers deeper into the earth until dirt, French dirt, wedged beneath her fingernails. For how long would she take refuge in England? This wretched *Révolution* had taken her family and lifestyle and fortune, now her country.

Non. She must focus on getting to England, accessing her father's money and marrying a powerful man.

She could loathe the revolutionaries and radicals from the safety of England. And once the *Révolution* ended, she would return to her beloved France and the *Château de La Rouchecauld*.

But not if she married an Englishman.

The air rushed out of her lungs. She couldn't leave her homeland forever.

Isabelle held the threatening tears and lay back on the blanket. She worked the lump in her throat and watched as two birds chased each other across the expanse of sky. *Just a few more minutes of sunlight and leisure, then I'll return to the house…*

"What are you doing?"

Isabelle jolted awake. Shaking off the sleep she must have fallen into, she opened her eyes to the image of an irate Michel.

Chapter Seven

Michel towered over her, so furious and masculine Isabelle's pulse raced. He looked more like a Greek god than a man—a god ready to strike her with lightning from the sky. His lips twisted in a scowl as he crossed his muscular arms over his chest. His massive legs planted themselves before her like pillars, and the collar and front of his shirt were damp with sweat. Clearly he'd been working in the field, those hard muscles creating enough heat to drench his body, despite the air's chill.

She tried to swallow the dryness in her throat. How could a man be so simultaneously handsome and angry? "Tell me, is defying my every word some game to you?" He spat the words.

"I'm sorry. I didn't mean to—"

"No. I'm sure you didn't. You just happened to wake from your nap and found yourself outside without any inkling of how you got here. *Ma Mère* probably carried you to the yard while you slept." Eyes smoldering, he pointed toward the door. "I said to stay indoors. Get inside. *Posthaste*. This is my house, and if you cannot abide by my wishes, leave."

Leave? The insidious wretch. Gooseflesh rose on her arms. As though she had a choice about leaving. "Think you I wish to be here? Trapped in a tiny room with—"

"Enough!" He made a slashing motion with his hand. "I've not time for this. Go inside now." He turned his back and stormed toward the stable.

Well, if he wasn't the most irritating man. She should race after him and give him his due, if only she could walk so quickly. Thought he to treat her thus and then stomp away? She balled her hands into fists. Once she was well, she'd stuff every tyrannical word he'd spoken down his thick, arrogant gullet.

She rose slowly to her feet, but when she stooped to pick up the blanket, her head spun. She leaned against the house and pressed two fingers to each temple, waiting for her mind to clear before inching indoors.

She knew not where to stow the blanket, but since Jeanette wasn't in the main chamber to ask, Isabelle headed toward the bedchamber. The quilt heavy in her arms, she stumbled through the doorway. The room tilted, and she reached to steady herself on the dresser. Except her hand didn't find a solid mass to which she could cling, but bumped the fragile porcelain of the pitcher and basin. The basin slid forward, and a sickening shatter filled the room.

She dropped to the floor, the blanket now balled like a babe against her stomach. Her head cleared the moment she sat. Her fingers skimmed over the scattered pink of the porcelain, the tiny, hand-painted flowers, as she picked up the shards. Such an exquisite set, now utterly destroyed.

She'd not have gone outside had she known this would happen.

Should she offer to replace the porcelain? If those soldiers hadn't stolen her extra money, she'd find a new one, but with barely enough funds to reach England... A shadow loomed over her. She sucked in a breath and turned.

"I'm sorry. It was an accident... I can replace the set, or...I—I can..."

Michel's face, so hard and lifeless, could have been carved from stone. His fisted hands shook, a fierce tension radiating from him as he stood framed in the doorway.

Her throat burned as though the porcelain shards had been crammed down it. "I'll speak with Jeanette, I promise."

The muscle in his jaw ticked. His hands clenched and unclenched. "Get back into your bed, and stay until I tell you otherwise."

His voice, deathly quiet, rained down on her. Dropping the pieces she held into a pile, she scooted backward on the floor until her back bumped the bed. Then she climbed atop, more terrified of the quiet Michel who stood before her than the shouting Michel from outside.

"That pitcher and basin were Corinne's. A wedding present from me. Some things, Isabelle, you can't replace."

~.~.~.~.~

Michel left the house and strode down the road. The girl, the land, the wheat—all weighed like anchors about his neck. He might be chained to the land, he might be forced to burn his wheat, but he didn't have to keep the girl.

He followed the road toward town but veered left into the woods before the stone houses of Abbeville grew close. Footprints marked the well-trodden path through the dense woods that shrouded Father Albert's cottage.

Last fall the beshrewed Convention had declared an end to Christianity and made the Cult of Reason the new French religion. A group of soldiers came and burned the rectory. Though the old cathedral still stood, it stored grain waiting to be shipped to the cities. Father Albert now had few possessions and little income, but the town still sought his spiritual guidance.

Pine trees shrouded out the sun above, and a sapling scraped Michel's shirt as the cottage appeared before him. He knocked impatiently. Moments later the ancient door swung open. "Michel." The old man's eyes lit with delight. "If it isn't my favorite former pupil. Come in, my son."

"I'm not keeping her." He needed to voice the words to someone, anyone, lest he burst.

Father Albert stood in the doorway dressed in a thinning homespun shirt and baggy trousers. His brow furrowed. "Your mother?"

"No. The girl." Michel pushed his way inside, and paced the tiny, one-room dwelling. "You must take her, or I know not what I'll do."

"I see." Although the look on the father's face clearly said he didn't. "Sit down, son. You're making me weary. Would you care for some tea?"

Before Michel could object, Father Albert walked to a sparsely filled shelf, pulled off a tiny, nearly empty sack and dug into it. Tea was a rare commodity for the man these days. The father wouldn't even have a place to live had he not purchased a couple acres of woods several years ago and stored food for the needy in the dilapidated cottage. Now the man used a storage shed for his home. "I don't need tea, Father. *Merci.*"

But Father Albert moved to the hearth, the drink half prepared. Michel bit off an oath as the man fumbled about the fire. He'd not come to take of the father's meager food-and-drink supply. The man probably had tea only because someone had given it to him, either in trade for the odd jobs he did around town or as a gift.

While Father Albert finished, Michel eyed the empty shelves along the wall, shelves that five years ago would have been filled with grain and dried meat for the needy. He'd bring the father a sack of wheat—may as well bring the man several sacks, since he needed to burn the rest.

Father Albert turned from the fire, sent Michel a scowl and headed to the table. "I told you to sit. Now, what's this about a girl?"

Michel lowered his large frame into a crooked chair and eyed the wobbly table. He should probably give Father Albert the dining set he was making, as well.

"You must speak, son. Or I cannot advise you." Michel eyed the old man, his sunken eyes and crinkled skin, his baggy clothes and slender frame, then Michel poured out his story of finding Isabelle. The tension stayed in his shoulders, but some of the anger slid away as he spoke. "So, you see, I cannot keep the girl. She's a burden I can no longer bear." He raked his hand through his hair as he finished.

Father Albert got the tea and poured it into one chipped mug and then a mug without a handle. "She was a burden two weeks ago when you found her, yet you took and nursed her."

"The girl slept for those two weeks. Now she's awake and doesn't listen to a word I say. She watches me with her dark eyes as though she thinks I'll beat her, yet she speaks with the tongue of a hoyden and—"

Father Albert held up his hand, stopping Michel. "Tell me, does this young woman go by the name 'girl'?"

"No...I... Her name's Isabelle."

"Ah, and you call her 'girl'? Or 'Isabelle'?"

Michel rubbed the back of his neck, then slapped his hand down on the table so hard the tea sloshed. "What has her name to do with anything?"

"Your interactions with Isabelle might go smoother if you call her by name."

"She disobeys me. Disobeys me, mind you! After all I've done for her."

Father Albert raised his eyebrows. "I'm certain you're the picture of long-suffering and patience with her."

Michel narrowed his eyes.

"She has reason to be afraid, even bitter, Michel. If she's an aristocrat, she's been hiding somewhere since the *Révolution* started. If she's alone, her immediate family is probably dead."

Michel didn't want to think of Isabelle delirious, writhing in her bed and calling for her deceased family. "To be only a day's walk from the Channel when she's discovered and beaten…she must be a strong one to endure so much." Father Albert leaned forward and touched Michel's hand.

Oh, she was strong. Strong enough to claw through a man's pride and defy a stranger's kindness.

What would the father say if he mentioned the porcelain finish on her skin? Or the smooth line of her neck when she raised that regal chin of hers. The way her lips sometimes trembled when she tried to be brave. Or the awareness in her eyes when he'd brushed hair out of her face and nearly kissed her that morning.

He frowned. What had he been thinking trying to kiss an aristocrat? He hadn't. That was his problem. He could hardly put two thoughts together with all that lush hair only a hand span from his fingers and those full, soft lips—

"Where did you go on me, Michel?"

Michel jumped, his senses returning to the cramped little room. "Ah, it matters not what the girl's afraid of or what she's endured. She's a burden, a cross the Lord has given me that I shall not keep. *Ma Mère* and I could be killed for it."

"Perhaps."

"How can you be so calm?" Michel snapped the words and pushed back from the table. "Tell me that you haven't aided others like Isabelle. The Terror is coming to Abbeville. You could be killed as easily as *Ma Mère* and I. The *représentative en mission* doesn't need proof to have a person guillotined, just an accusation made before a wild crowd is enough."

"Here…" Father Albert rose, shuffled three paces from the table to a tiny writing desk and sorted through a stack of papers. When he found what he looked for, he headed back to the table. "You've not heard the news, then. I've received word from Nantes. The Terror there has decided the guillotine too inefficient a process of execution."

The guillotine inefficient? Michel's stomach churned. He nearly covered his ears like a child to block the coming words.

"They've taken to mass drownings. Putting a barge into the river and forcing people to jump. Father Antoine estimates over three thousand innocent souls have…" Father Albert's eyes filled. He pressed a hand to his chest and blinked the tears away. "Sorry, my son. I seem to tremble every time I read the words."

Michel stood and walked around the table, then laid his hands on Father Albert's shoulders. Three thousand people, regardless of gender or occupation. "God will judge the officials in Nantes."

Father Albert patted Michel's hand. "Yes, He will, Michel, as He will judge all of us by our actions in these troubled times. You see, I could be killed. You could be killed. The soldiers could gather everyone in Abbeville and force us into the Somme River. But that doesn't change your situation. God has given you responsibilities, and until the Lord takes them from you, they are yours to accept."

"*Oui,* but surely the Lord understands—"

"Tell me, when Christ healed, did He believe those who left Him cured and whole had been a burden? Did the Lord turn away anyone, saying He'd rather not bother with healings that day? What if the centurion's request for his child's healing had been met with the Lord turning away?"

Michel turned away and paced before the fire. The child would have died, and so would countless others. Just as Isabelle would have died had he not nursed her.

"Isabelle is not your cross, not your burden, but your opportunity to serve Christ. You alone must decide if you will face your responsibility or turn away. She is your privilege, Michel, not mine." Father Albert waited until Michel met his eyes, eyes full of compassion and understanding for an aristocratic girl he'd never met. "If the Good Lord allows you to face the guillotine, your death won't be because you cared for His own, but because God wanted you home."

Michel stilled. He knew this. So why did hearing the words from the holy man make his blood run cold? He could be killed for reasons besides Isabelle, like his grain hoarding or federalist beliefs. He'd always intended to care for the girl until she was well enough to leave. He rubbed his hands over his face, held his palms against his temples. Why had he been so mad? What prodded him to leave his work on the farm and storm here? "But she broke Corinne's wash pitcher and basin. Because she wouldn't listen. They cost nearly a year's salary…and Corinne loved them."

Pain seared his heart at the memory of Jean Paul's wife, and he spoke too softly. "We could have sold them for medicine, to pay a doctor when she was ill. She wouldn't let us. Had we bartered the pieces, anyway, she might have lived."

"The decision was never yours. Think you to go through life making everyone's choices for them? Carrying everyone else's burdens?" Father Albert took a slow sip of tea and eyed Michel's shoulders and torso. "You're young and strong, but not that strong. Don't allow the deaths of your father and Corinne to haunt you. Rest them at Christ's feet, instead. They went because the Good Lord called them home, not because you or Jean Paul or your mother failed them."

The man didn't understand. *Père* was his fault, and would always be his fault. He had abandoned the farm to pursue an errant dream, and *Père* worked himself to an early grave by caring for the land. Michel sat back at the table. Never again would he leave the farm, not even if the most noted furniture-maker in Paris offered to train him.

"'Tis more that bothers you." Father Albert studied him from across the table.

Michel rolled his shoulders. "Only the girl."

"How old are you, my boy? Seven and twenty? Eight and twenty?"

"Seven and twenty," Michel replied.

"What is it you want? When you grow old as I, and you get to the end of your life, what memories do you wish to look back on? What do you want to have accomplished?"

A bug of irritation crawled between Michel's shoulder blades. "I want to farm. Acquire more land, add to my family's legacy like my father did, and his father before that."

"You speak falsely. I've seen your hand with wood." The man spoke with such earnestness and certainty that Michel steamed.

"I don't want to build furniture." The lie scorched his tongue. "'Tis nothing but a hobby."

"Do you see yourself happy if you stay on the farm?"

"God gave me the farm, much as He gave me the girl. How can you say I have responsibility to the girl and tell me to leave the farm?"

"I'm not telling you to leave, Michel. But you must think, examine. You question your need to help the girl, but don't question why you tie yourself to a piece of land you hate. You're wasting your life."

Michel clenched his teeth. He wasn't leaving. He'd promised *Père*.

"Many men spend their lives farming and find fulfillment therein. Your father was one of them." Father Albert cocked his head. "Your brother is one of them. But not you. That farm will kill you if you let it."

"Aye. The farm already killed *Mon Père*. Why not me, as well?" Father Albert leaned over the table, grasping Michel's hand. "God has placed great talent for woodworking in these hands, my son. That in itself is a responsibility you cannot ignore forever."

Michel tugged his hand away. A responsibility to the farm, to *Mère,* to the girl. He couldn't handle another responsibility. Not even if that responsibility consumed his dreams.

~.~.~.~.~

A speck of orange spread against the black night, growing, consuming, devouring. Michel watched the flames lick higher and higher, stealing their way up the wooden structure of the lean-to and inside.

To his wheat.

He should cry or rage or drink at the futility of his labor, as most men would. Instead, Father Albert's comment lingered in his head. *The farm will kill you if you let it.*

Indeed, his soul was already half-dead. Not because of the wheat, the girl, the farm or even *Père*. No. His soul started dying seven years ago, when the first furniture-maker in Paris slammed his shop door in Michel's face.

He turned his back to the angry flames, now nearly finished devouring a year of his labor. He could be mad. He should be mad. But why rage over a year of his life, when the rest of it mattered so little?

Chapter Eight

Isabelle paced the small area of the bedchamber and glowered at the bed. She'd been trapped on that lumpy tick ten days since waking from her fever. Ten! If ever she escaped from this confinement, she'd be happy to never sleep in a bed again.

She'd embroidered hankies until Jeanette had run out of fabric and thread. She'd counted the beams on the ceiling and stared at the cornucopias carved into the headboard of her bed frame until the image etched itself permanently in her mind. Then she'd named the fruits spilling out and counted the number of grapes. Twice. Three hundred and twenty-six, both times.

Whenever both Michel and Jeanette were out of doors, she walked the small rooms like a caged cat. She'd read through Charles Perrault's *The Tales of Mother Goose* three times. But how often could one read of Sleeping Beauty, Cinderella or Little Red Riding Hood before dying of tedium?

Isabelle huffed and shoved both hands into her hair, fisting the roots. This was pure foolishness. She should be in Saint-Valery-sur-Somme by now. Would have been had Michel not walked into the house four days ago, just as she'd been slipping into her dress. She'd had a time explaining herself to him and thought to wait another day or two before leaving, but the rains came.

She glared at the window and the shutters covering it. Even now she could hear the torrent of rain and wind beyond, and the gale grew stronger with each passing day.

First her injuries. Now the rain. Did all of France conspire against her?

She pressed a hand to her ribs, still tender but no longer searing with pain. Yes, she was well enough to walk to Saint-Valery. If she could ever get out of this cottage.

She turned and paced again, certain her footsteps would leave a rut in the floor. But anything was better than lying in that bed with nothing but dark thoughts to keep her company. She'd done everything she could to keep back the memories of her sister, but the images still crept in, winding and twisting their way through her thoughts, regardless of whether she mended or read or slept.

The door to the front of the house banged shut. Isabelle started, then crossed the room in three steps and dove for her bed. She winced as she landed with too much pressure on her arm but scrambled under the covers and fumbled for *The Tales of Mother Goose*.

She was still settling into the pillows when the bedchamber door whooshed open and Michel walked in.

Her mouth went dry.

His hair fell in wet strands around his face, and his drenched shirt clung to his chest.

He watched her carefully, as though he knew she'd been out of bed. Had she given herself away? She lifted a hand to her cheek. Was her face flushed? Her breathing too hard? Probably, but those reactions had more to do with the outline of Michel's chest beneath his shirt than her being out of bed.

Without a word, he walked to the dresser, opened the third drawer and riffled through the contents. His damp hair curled and clung to his neck. Wetness slicked his face and forearms, while muscles played across his back and shoulders with every subtle movement. Heat rushed to her cheeks.

"Have you need of anything?" Michel shut the drawer.

"Pardon?" Isabelle swallowed noisily and shifted on the tick. He'd no way of knowing her thoughts...or so she hoped.

"Mother will be a while yet in the stable. Have you need of anything while she's out?"

"No...that is, um, well, yes...a glass of water, I suppose."

"Are you sure you're feeling well? You seem flushed." He came toward her.

Was it possible for more heat to surge into her face? He rested a hand on her cheek and his eyes turned soft.

Like they had when he'd nearly kissed her all those days ago.

She jolted. Where had that thought come from?

He moved his hand to her forehead. "You seem a little warm. Mayhap you're catching another fever in your weakened state."

He'd all but ignored her for the past week and a half, only speaking to her when necessary since she broke the pitcher and basin. And now he knew about her weakened state? If he'd bothered to ask, he would know that the pain in her ribs had lessened to a dull ache that came and went. And her arm rarely hurt unless she gripped something too hard—or landed on it when she jumped into bed.

"I'm fine," she snapped, the warmth his touch brought suddenly gone. "And I can get the water on my own. I'm able to leave this bed."

"I'll wager you are," he muttered. But he took her mug and filled it from the ugly clay pitcher resting atop the dresser where the beautiful porcelain once sat.

"Oh, that's fine, serve me, anyway."

"I will. It's my house."

"I'm well enough to leave for England. There's no reason I can't be about the cottage. As soon as the rain stops, I'll be gone from here and finding myself a rich, English husband to care for me rather than the likes of you."

"Is that your plan, Isabelle? To snag a rich Englishman and live an opulent life once again?" His eyes glittered like bright, hard emeralds. "Somehow I thought more of you. I let myself believe a sense of principle lay behind your determination to reach England. And here you only want your life of luxury restored. How daft of me."

The words stung like a slap across the face. He straightened and strode toward the door, the single conversation they'd shared in more than a week turning to ash.

"Michel, don't go. I'm sorry...I was just...upset."

He paused in the doorway.

"I shouldn't have said it...about the husband."

"Answer me this. Is a husband the reason you're going?"

How many times had she wished marriage played no role in her decision? She took a sip of water, though her mouth still felt dry as the dirt on the floor, and met his eyes. "Not the only reason. I've money and an aunt there, as well." *And a promise to keep.* "But yes, marriage is a part."

He looked into the main chamber and then swung his gaze back toward her, as though debating whether to stay or leave. Finally he stepped inside and leaned his back against the wall. "That's not what drives you. Some unnamed husband you might happen to wed isn't the reason you call for England in your dreams."

She squirmed under his steady gaze. Did she call for England in her sleep? She dreamed of England some nights, but surely she didn't voice it. "I told you my family has money there. And perchance you don't believe I've an aunt. But my Tante Cordele awaits me in London. I lie not."

"There's more."

His eyes seemed to burn her, searing through her flesh and into her heart. Her breathing grew quicker, shallower. "There's a promise, a promise I made, and a dream I cherish. I have to reach England."

"Or die trying." He came closer, took her hand.

Hot tears pricked the backs of her eyes. Did he understand the power of a promise such as the one she'd sworn to Marie? The strength of a dream such as the one of finding safety in England? She nodded. *"Oui."*

"I hope you get there, then. English husband or not." She smiled and blinked back the threatening tears.

"Merci."

"With your strong determination, you deserve to reach your goal." His soft eyes roved her face as he dropped her hand and touched a lock of her hair, twining it around his finger and brushing it with his thumb.

Something flashed in her mind, an impression, a shadow that sent fear shuddering through her. She jerked back. "Don't. Don't touch my hair."

He dropped it. "Are you well? Your face is suddenly pale."

"Yes, yes. I'm fine," she gasped. Though she wasn't. The breath had rushed from her lungs and she couldn't manage to get it back.

"Here." He took away two of her pillows, easing her flat onto the bed. "You mustn't be feeling well. 'Tis as I said when I first came in and your face was flushed. You're not resting enough. I know you've been out of your bed."

Warmth stole across her face as she gulped air. "And what have you eaten today? You must eat more if you're to regain your strength. I'll fetch you some stew and bread."

He took long strides into the common chamber, his shirt stretching taut against his wide shoulders. She placed a hand on her cheek. What was wrong with her? He'd done nothing more than touch her hair, and she'd gone half-mad. Even now the feeling of terror lingered. He returned a moment later, carrying a tray filled with food. "'Tis nearly dusk. Eat an early dinner, then read, or mayhap sleep? Some rest will clear your mind."

~.~.~.~.~

Darkness shrouded her. She was cold. So very cold from the night air—and from the terror inside her. She tried to hide her fear as the soldiers surrounded her, but her heart pounded against her chest, sweat slicked her brow and her breathing came in short, uneven gasps.

The leader loomed before her, his strong meaty hands gripped her hair and yanked her head back. Then he sneered, his hand stroking a lock of hair, his fingers twirling it back and forth.

No! Let go of it. Don't touch me, you swine.

Isabelle's own screams woke her from the dream.

Her chest heaved for want of air and her heart pounded hard enough to burst through her rib cage. In the darkness, she tried to scramble from her bed, only to find herself tangled in ropes of quilt. She fought free and clambered to the floor. Panic clutching her chest and throat, she stumbled toward the kitchen.

Her hair must come off. She would rip it from her head if she so needed.

Of a sudden, strong hands gripped her upper arms. She fought against them, straining to see who held her in the blackness yet afraid she would look into the eyes of the soldier.

"Let me go. Let me go. I demand it of you!"

"Get back into bed."

Michel's aggravated voice growled in her ear. She took a shaky breath. At least he wouldn't hurt her.

"A knife. I need a knife." She struggled against him, but his grasp remained firm.

"I'm not giving you a knife." He shook her slightly.

"Now. I have to have one."

"Take hold of yourself. I'll find you one in the morning. If I get you one now, you'd carve me up."

"Not you. Me."

"All right, you'd carve yourself up. I'm not giving you a knife."

"My hair." She raked a hand down a lock, as though it were alive and evil. "I have to get it off."

He huffed and muttered something she cared not to hear. "You want to cut your hair? In the middle of the night? No."

She clawed at him. "He touched it. Oh, goodness, he touched it. It's tainted. I have to cut it."

"It'll wait till morning."

"Who needs you?" She jerked away and stumbled into the common chamber, banging her knee against the doorway. Pain shot through her leg but she kept going. She headed toward the light emanating from the embers in the hearth. Where did Jeanette keep her knife?

The kitchen utensils hung on pegs near the fire. She sent a spoon clattering onto the stones as she grappled for the knife.

She could see the soldier in her mind, stroking his rank hand over her hair. Toying with it as he leered at her. As he gave the order to beat her. How could she live knowing his fingers had been there?

Her good hand clasped the handle of the knife, and she gritted her teeth against the terror lapping at the edges of her mind. Michel's form stood in the doorway to the bedchamber. Let him watch if he so desired. Her bandaged arm trembled as she took a lock of her waist length hair, held it out and hacked.

She offed the part the soldier had touched. Was it enough? Or had his fingers stroked more? She grabbed another handful and sawed until it fell into a pile on the floor. Then she took another lock. Had he handled more without her realizing it? She had to get it off. All off.

Fear ripped through Michel as Isabelle took the knife from the wall. He rushed forward. "Isabelle…"

But she took no notice of him as she grabbed a tress of hair and held it out, raising the knife. The breath he didn't know he'd been holding vented through his taut lips. Just her hair. She'd told him as much in the bedchamber, hadn't she? He drew a calming breath. She could cut her hair, as long as she didn't bring that blade near her porcelain skin.

Or so he told himself. But as he stood there, watching her war with knife and hair, her curtain of black silk falling lock by lock to the floor, his heart grew ill. All that lush, dark hair severed from her head. Didn't the Good Book call a woman's hair her glory? And here she hacked it as though it were the sole cause of all evil in the world.

The whimpers and cries in her sleep were normal, even the occasional thrashing no longer surprised him. But she'd never before awakened in such a panic. Never attempted to harm herself or mar her beauty.

His chest ached as she brought the knife down on yet another lock. The girl had endured much. Her fitful sleeping testified of it, then Father Albert had voiced it. He should have better heeded the warnings.

Rain beat heavily against the thatched roof, and the chamber smelled of bread rising for tomorrow's breakfast. The dying fire silhouetted Isabelle's form, her rounded cheek, her smooth neck, her subtle curves. Michel's eyes drifted down her shadowed body. Her ankles were slim beneath the hem of her nightdress, her bare toes peeking delicately out. How far had those tiny feet walked? What horrors had those feet carried her away from?

And what was wrong with him when the sight of a woman's feet made him want to run his fingers over her toes, massage her feet until he'd rubbed away the pain in her heart?

A small sob escaped Isabelle's throat. Having sawed off a good quarter meter of hair the entire way around her head, she grasped the lock she'd started with, moved her hand another quarter meter higher, and brought up the knife.

His heart slowed. "Isabelle." He went to her, closed his hand over hers on the knife. "That's enough. No more."

Her hand tightened beneath his on the handle. "You'll be sorry for this come morning."

She raised wild eyes to meet his. The dim light didn't hide the fear haunting them, nor the shadows beneath. "Whoever hurt you, he can't do so now. You're safe." She looked down, stared at the heaps of hair littering the floor as though seeing for the first time what she'd done, and released the knife.

He laid it on the table, then fingered the newly blunted edges of her hair. "Your hair's too beautiful to cut like this."

Her lips quivered, and a single tear crested. He wiped the tear from her cheek, and unable to resist, he pulled her against his chest and kissed the top of her head. She felt soft in his arms, as limp as a child's doll. "Isabelle..." If she would only let go of her control. Grieve or rage or cry. Release some of what must be locked inside. But she sniffled and simply stayed huddled against him.

He knew not how long he held her, her head buried in the crook of his shoulder, her freshly cut hair falling in waves over his hands. He tangled his fingers in the irresistibly thick tresses, tugging and tipping her face up to his. Her eyes glowed large and luminous with unshed tears, and her lips stood moist and supple, as though waiting for his to meet them.

He ran his thumb over her bottom lip. It trembled under his touch. What would it feel like to lower his mouth a few centimeters to hers? He swallowed.

She pressed those soft lips together and pushed away from him. "I'm sorry. I meant not to…" She held out her hands and looked down, drawing his gaze to the heaps of hair on the floor. "I'm sorry." Another tear slipped down her cheek. But instead of wiping it, Michel backed slowly away. His body shook as he groped for some semblance of restraint. Another moment with her in this quiet, dark room and he'd kiss her. And once their lips met, well, he'd not likely be able to pull away.

His heart kicked madly against his chest as she stood before him, watching him with haunted eyes. He cleared the lump from his throat. "It'd be best if you went to bed now." He dragged his gaze away from her, stared at the piles of hair cluttering the floor and shifted uncomfortably. "You might not, ah, be so upset after more rest."

She moved back to the bedchamber with a grace that belied her ancient nightdress, held her head with a regal air that bespoke her aristocratic birth.

Michel walked to the opposite corner of the house for a broom and rubbed the back of his neck. He'd nearly kissed her. For the second time. What had he been thinking? She was the daughter of a *seigneur*. It mattered little if she had less to her name than he. Families like hers had abused him and his ancestors for centuries. No aristocrat could be trusted—they only cared for themselves.

He grabbed the broom and returned to the piles of hair. Hair he knew felt soft and rich as velvet. He ran the broom through the mess so quickly his action sent stray wisps floating into the darkness. Muttering, he forced himself to move slower.

Space. He needed to put more space between himself and the girl.

But he daily left the house early and went to bed only after Isabelle was settled for the night. He barely looked at her, didn't take meals with her, and the few times he'd entered the bedchamber during the day, he ignored nearly anything she said. How was he to give her more distance?

.⸾.⸾.⸾.⸾.⸾

Isabelle couldn't get the soldier's face out of her mind as she stood alone in the bedchamber the following morning. She pressed a hand to her stomach and shut her eyelids, trying to clear her head of the attack, but the dark, malicious eyes stared back at her from the gloom of the woods.

She cast her gaze to the window, though it was covered tightly and she couldn't see the woods beyond. Still, was her attacker out there? Stalking her? She could almost feel his presence surrounding her. As though the longer she stayed on Michel's farm, the closer the soldier came to finding her.

And she was being childish.

She clenched her hands. The man from the woods had surely run off the very night he had called for her death, and here she'd hacked off half her hair because of a nightmare.

Michel had said she'd regret it come morning. The very thought he'd been right made her cheeks heat.

She laced the bodice of her dress loosely over her healing ribs. Her hair, now ending just beneath her shoulder blades, felt rough and uneven as it tumbled down her back.

How could she have been frightened enough to cut her hair?

Well, she'd no way of reattaching the lost locks. Best to forget what she'd done. Her hair would grow back, and perhaps she'd have Jeanette trim off the ends today to even out the length.

But that would involve explaining why she cut it in the first place.

She could always ask Michel to trim it.

She stilled, recalling the way his hands twined through her hair last night, how he tipped her face up and looked at her with his quiet, green eyes as though he could read every thought in her head. As though he wanted to make the nightmare she lived better. As though he cared what she had gone through...

But he didn't care about her, did he? *Bien sûr que non*—of course not. She was an aristocrat, and he a peasant. She'd probably imagined the look in his eyes last night.

She tied her bodice, wrapped her fichu around her neck and tucked it into her chemise, then decided to leave her hair be. Things would be simpler that way.

She glanced down at the dull blue dress she wore the night she'd been attacked. The only dress she owned now. After spending more than four weeks wearing nothing but borrowed nightdresses, the familiar fabric flowed like spun gold over her skin.

Isabelle moved toward the closed door that separated the bedchamber from the common chamber. No sense eating in bed after last night.

She entered the room and glimpsed Michel pulling on his boots in the corner. Warmth rushed through her, and her heart quickened. She nearly backed out. By heavens, facing the man would be more difficult than she'd suspected. Would he look at her this morning the way he had last night? A breath away from placing his lips over hers and never letting them go? Did she want him to? She pressed a hand to her heart. Perhaps she *should* breakfast in bed.

And wouldn't that make a fine coward of her? She lifted her chin. Isabelle Cerise de La Rouchecauld was not a coward. A fool, perhaps. But never a coward.

"Oh, hello, dear. Are you well enough to eat with us?" Jeanette set a pot of porridge on the table, then turned toward an open shelf and retrieved a third bowl.

Isabelle headed to the table and sat, careful to keep her eyes on Jeanette and not let her gaze stray to Michel. "Yes, thank you. I'm feeling considerably better. I thought, perchance, I could help with chores around the house today."

Jeanette beamed. "Oh, now, there's no need to strain yourself. Glad to see you up and about, is all."

She straightened her spine. She'd have been up and about sooner had Michel not ordered her to bed and ignored her for more than a week.

Michel's footsteps thudded toward them. Isabelle stared at the elegant tabletop, feeling his presence at the table rather than watching him sit. He gave an awkward blessing, then Jeanette took the porridge and served it. Her eyes on Jeanette, she reached for the bread, but instead of finding the cool plate on which the loaf sat, her hand bumped warm, solid flesh. She and Michel jerked their hands away as though the simple touch stung.

"Serve yourself," Michel said, looking everywhere but at her.

Isabelle glanced at her hand. "*Non,* you."

Michel raked his hand through his hair. "How difficult must you make things, woman? Take the bread."

"Michel," Jeanette admonished. "If you can't find your manners, go eat with the pigs."

But Michel only stared at her, bringing heat to Isabelle's neck as she reached a trembling hand to the dish, took a piece of bread and replaced the plate.

Neither she nor Michel uttered a word for the rest of the meal.

Although the rain streamed heavy outside, Michel headed out of doors immediately after breakfast. Though what work needed doing in this weather, Isabelle couldn't imagine.

"Oh, but I've a surprise for you," Jeanette said the moment Michel left. She scurried to her rocking chair by the fire and returned with a faded black mourning bonnet.

At least, Isabelle thought it was a mourning bonnet—or had been, about a century ago. The ties looked as though a mouse had nibbled on them, and the front brim was bent beyond hope. But the top and side had been mended with brown and gray patches, the brown thread used for the repairs clear against the fabrics.

"Fixed it up, I did. Figured it'd look right pretty on you." Jeanette puffed her chest, a look of unadulterated joy on her face.

"For me? Oh, why...how generous."

"I can see you in it now, with that lovely hair of yours tucked up underneath."

Evidently Jeanette hadn't taken too close a look at her hair. Or the bonnet.

"Why, you'll be the envy of every woman in town." Or the laughingstock. Isabelle bit the side of her lip. "Thank you, Jeanette, but I've no need for a mourning bonnet, benevolent as you are—"

"Don't be foolish, child. I want you to have it." Pride filled Jeanette's eyes. "My Charles, he was always so proud of my mending. Sauntering about town in this or that which I'd fixed up for him." A faraway look spread across Jeanette's face, as though she'd just been transported back to the days when her husband still lived.

"You miss him."

"Aye. Every day. Seems I'm forgetful of most things now. Never had trouble remembering anything while my Charles was alive. Life fit into place back then." The lines of kindness and care etched across the woman's face contorted into a mask of pain. "We were married nigh on twenty-six years before he passed."

"I'm sorry for your loss."

"Nothing for you to be sorry about. The Good Lord takes everyone home at one time or another."

Oui, everyone did die at one time or another. And some before their time. Isabelle rubbed her arms. "Tell me more about your husband?"

Jeanette shuffled to the table and sat. "Well, now, my Charles was kind as can be. Loyal, quiet, the type of man people came to, seeking advice and such. The type of man who worked and laughed and lived as though each day were his last. His heart gave out working the farm, it did. Don't think Michel's ever forgiven himself for that." Her eyes sharpened into focus with the memories.

"Michel?" Isabelle straightened. "Why would his *père's* death be Michel's fault?"

"Well, Michel went to Paris, you see. Wanted to make furniture for the king himself. The whole family saved nigh on two years to send him."

Isabelle nodded. If the furniture in the bedroom was any indication, Michel should have done well in Paris. "What happened?" She clamped her mouth shut the moment the words fell out and glanced at the door. Hopefully the man wouldn't barge in while they spoke of him.

"My Charles took on Michel's chores while he was away, you see. Jean Paul was here, but newly married and a bit distracted from farmwork. And Charles, he wasn't the type to tell a man to leave his wife behind and come out to the field. He simply did what needed doing, 'tis all, and Michel was gone nigh on a year."

Isabelle ran her hand over the tabletop, silky smooth, with cornucopias engraved along the side. Had Michel made the table as well as the bedroom furniture? People in Paris would have paid well for his work. Why hadn't he stayed?

Jeanette fiddled with her hands. "My Charles was worn through by the time Michel returned. Not a week later, Charles's heart gave out working in the field."

Isabelle's stomach churned as Jeanette wiped a tear from the corner of her eye. "Jeanette, do forgive me for asking. I didn't know it would be so painful."

"'Tis all right, dear. Just give me a moment to remember *mon amour.*" Jeanette wiped another tear from her eye. "Charles led a long life, and the Good Lord called his time. My Charles was behind the plow, and Michel was over studying the dam. Michel said he tried talking his *père* out of the plowing, but Charles wanted Michel to have a look at the dam first."

Isabelle's mouth felt dry as breadcrumbs. Michel watched his father die while working? She'd not wish that upon her worst enemy.

"Do you...surely you don't think Michel...I mean..."

Jeanette smiled through her tears, then reached forward and patted Isabelle's hand. "No. I don't blame Michel. Couldn't blame him for it any more than I could the field for needing to be plowed, or Jean Paul for working in the stable instead of the field. Or God for creating the field in the first place.

"Though Michel had a time blaming himself, as I recall. Talking about how Charles would still be alive if he would have forced his *père* away from the plowing, or sent Charles back to the house to rest sooner. Or not have gone to Paris at all."

"Bien sûr." How could Michel not blame himself? She knew how that felt—knew the hours spent regretting every decision she'd made that had ended in Marie's arrest.

"If the Good Lord wanted Charles spared, he'd have been spared. I told Michel I forgave him, anyway. More because he needed to hear the words than anything. And Father Albert, our priest, talked with him some. Seemed to help, but the boy's shackled himself to this farm ever since."

Isabelle swallowed. How terrible for Michel. For Jeanette. For all of them. "Do you regret it? Letting Michel go to Paris?"

Jeanette patted the side of her hair, which loosened more strands rather than tucked the few errant ones away. "I've lived a long time, too long to have regrets. When I get to missing my Charles, I think about the twenty-six wonderful years I had with him, and the two strong boys he gave me."

Isabelle looked at the woman who could barely remember the day or season. She'd had no trouble recalling the man she'd loved for a quarter century, almost as though the simple act of remembering healed her.

Would Charles have forgiven Michel for not plowing? Or loathed Michel going to Paris and leaving him with extra work? Work that ended up killing him?

Her chest weighed so heavy she could hardly breathe. And what about her? How did a person seek forgiveness from someone in the grave? From Marie?

Absently, she pulled the pendant from beneath her dress and ran her finger over the silver warmed by her skin. Jeanette hadn't grown bitter or blamed Michel for her husband's death. Was her situation with Marie as simple as Jeanette's?

Certainly not. Michel's father lived a long life and died in the same manner countless other farmers did, while Isabelle had ignored Marie's warning and led the soldiers to their door.

She tried to suck in a breath, but the air was thick and sticky. In her mind, she could see Marie sitting at a scarred kitchen table, laughing, chattering as she chopped vegetables from the garden for that evening's dinner.

Fighting back a sob, Isabelle pressed her hand to her mouth.

"Are you all right, dear?" Concern filled Jeanette's voice.

Isabelle shook her head and squeezed her eyes shut.

Non. She wasn't all right. She'd never be all right again.

Not even in England.

Chapter Nine

Memories of Marie haunted Isabelle for the rest of the morning. She swept the floor, chopped vegetables and helped Jeanette make bread, though the older woman forgot how many cups of flour she'd added to the dough. Twice.

When her arm and ribs began to ache, she pressed through the pain. Anything to keep her mind off her sister. But nothing worked.

The midday meal came and went, but Michel never arrived to eat. With soup for supper simmering over the fire and bread baking in the hearth, Jeanette settled into her rocker with a thick, black Bible in her hand.

Was the answer to Marie forgiving her hidden somewhere inside the Book on Jeanette's lap? She remembered some of the teachings from her childhood. *Forgive seven times seventy. Forgive those who persecute you. Forgive and you shall be forgiven.* But how could Marie forgive her when Marie was dead because of her actions?

Isabelle blew out a breath and blinked back more tears. She'd do something, anything else, to keep her mind off Marie. But everything inside the little cottage seemed in order. She could go back to bed and read or mend—if only the idea of bed didn't repulse her.

She bit the side of her lip and stared at the covered window, the deluge still raging outside. Where could Michel have gone for so long? Surely he wasn't in the fields. He'd be soaked and chilled by now.

She would simply go out to find him and ask when she could journey to Saint-Valery. She'd keep their interactions distant and proper. No intense looks or bumping hands or almost-kisses. If she was well enough to be about the house, she was well enough to walk twenty kilometers to the Channel. Even with a broken arm. Even in the rain.

If they argued about her leaving and he told her she couldn't go yet—which the stubborn man certainly would—she at least would have something to keep her mind off Marie. "Jeanette, where might Michel be?"

"What was that?" Jeanette looked at Isabelle with glassy eyes.

"Michel. I need to speak with him. Where would he have gone?"

"Why to the fields. Always work to be done on a farm."

"It's raining." Had been for four days.

Jeanette's gaze shifted to the window. "Oh, dear me, I suppose it is. Is it Monday? Have to muck the stalls on Monday."

"Thank you. I'll check there." She searched the pegs by the door for her tattered cloak and some solid boots. She slid her feet into a pair that seemed to be Jeanette's, then looked back at the peaceful woman rocking by the fire.

Traces of beauty lingered in a face faded with time and etched with wrinkles. Perchance one day Isabelle would sit in a rocker by a quiet fire, her mind brimming with memories of the man she loved. She swallowed. "Jeanette, when you married Charles, what color was your wedding dress?"

The woman's creased face brightened. "Light brown. He said I looked right pretty, too. What with my hair and eyes and all."

"I…think it's wonderful that you remember such a special day of your life," she answered softly—whether Jeanette remembered the rain no longer seeming important.

She found a worn, wide-brimmed hat she'd seen Michel wear. It flopped over her head, inundating her with the comforting scents of hay and dirt...and Michel. And her thoughts were straying too far. First the rain, then his hat. Did everything make her think of Michel? How did she even know what the man smelled like? "I'll be back in a few moments," she called, and headed out into the downpour. Wind pushed her sideways before she shut the cottage door. She clasped the brim of her hat so as not to lose it, but rain whipped into her eyes, anyway. Though she could hardly see through the stinging drops, she trudged toward the stable. The moment she pulled open the heavy door, she knew he wasn't inside. The structure missed the unmistakable presence Michel carried with him. She looked for him, anyway, the warmth from the animals surrounding her, the aromas of straw and beasts filling the air. But as she suspected, no clear green eyes smirked at her, no lazy half smile greeted her.

Ignoring the biting rain, she stomped back outside, headed to the smaller building in the yard and heaved the door open. The wind caught it, sending it backward until it slammed against the side of the building's outer wall.

Serenity enveloped her the moment she stepped inside. The smell of varied woods surrounded her, dry and tangy and intoxicating, while heat radiated from a small, open-back stove sitting on the hearth.

Lumber filled the room. Long planks lined the back wall, small scraps scattered over a workbench, sawn pieces piled on the sawdust-covered floor. The makings of an elegant table sat in front of the workbench, but in the center of a large open area rested an exquisite chest of drawers. Michel stood there, eyebrows raised at her, his chisel held against the wood.

The sight of him sent more heat through her than the fire in the

---

stove. A calm expression masked the prominent bones and angular planes of his face. The ends of his brown hair curled against his forehead and neck in a way that made her fingers ache to run through their coiling tips. His broad shoulders spanned wide above the dresser, speaking of his strength forged by days upon days of hard labor. And his eyes glimmered with concern, making her think for half an instant he might care what happened to her.

She'd known he was attractive, handsome even. So why, standing in this little workshop, did one look from him give her trouble breathing?

She forced her breath out. "*Bonjour,* I, um…" The door behind her banged against the side of the building. How could she have forgotten to close it? She sloshed back into the rain and pulled it shut, then turned awkwardly to face Michel. "My apologies."

A glint of amusement crept into his eyes. "Did you need something?"

"*Oui. Non.* That is, uh…" The beauty of the chest of drawers drew her forward.

Elaborate acorns and oak leaves wove their way along the top and down the posts of the dresser, the straight, clean lines of the wood contrasting with the elegant carvings. "It's splendid." All it lacked was some gilding over the exquisite design, then the piece would be fit for Versailles or the *Château de La Rouchecauld.* She reached out to touch an acorn, her wet finger leaving its print on the wood.

"I had no idea."

"I assumed *Ma Mère* told you."

"Yes." But she hadn't known, hadn't understood, the scope of his abilities until she stood here, before a nearly finished masterpiece, with the scent of wood wrapping around her and the sawdust crunching under her feet. She cleared her throat. "You see, I expected—"

"That I couldn't possibly have made the furniture in the house?" Frustration tinged his voice, but he didn't step away from her.

She'd believed Jeanette's story, somewhere inside she'd known the older woman spoke truth. She looked up, and he trapped her in his swirling green eyes. She moistened her lips and stared at his mouth, the firm, serious lips. What would it feel like to press her lips to his? A tingle? A wave of warmth? Nothing?

"Oui." she murmured breathlessly, then took a step back. The furniture. They were talking about furniture. "Why is it that you farm? The sale of this one piece would equal a year's crop or more."

"Can't sell it."

"That's preposterous. Of course you can sell it. Why, I would pay handsomely for the cornucopia bed I've been sleeping on. Others would, as well."

"I wasn't a member of the furniture-makers' guild. I can't sell it."

She wrinkled her forehead. "The guild system was eradicated three years ago. Surely you knew."

His hand tightened on the chisel. He turned away, strode to the workbench and tossed it down. "Think you it's so simple?"

"What's so hard? Put a sign advertising your furniture by the road."

He whirled around. "Is everything always so easy for you? Have you never met a rule or stricture you can't change?" Eyes hot, he threw the rag slung over his shoulder onto the floor. "Three years ago was too late to change anything. I went to Paris before the *Révolution,* showed the workers a small chest and got turned down by every master craftsman I met. Same thing happened to my father. The government limited the number of master craftsmen allowed to practice, and those master craftsmen have handed their furniture-making licenses to their sons for centuries."

She raised her chin. "Nothing's that impossible, especially not with talent such as yours. Half the furniture at Versailles isn't as beautiful as this."

"Doesn't matter."

But it did. It mattered more than he said. She read it in the way he hunched his shoulders, in the frustrated stomping of his boots against the floor, in the tightly coiled muscles along his forearms as he paced from the workbench to the wall and back.

"The farm is my responsibility, not making furniture."

"Don't you have a brother? Where is he? Why can you not give him the farm and live your dream?"

He turned to her. His eyes flat and dead. "What makes you think building furniture is my dream?"

"God wouldn't give you such talent and then tell you to waste it. To hide it in a shed."

She expected him to rage at her. To yell for her to stay out of his business, out of his life. But for a long moment, he didn't speak, or even move save for the muscle working along his jaw.

"I admire that about you. Your determination. Your drive to get to England."

She swallowed. He admired her? Surely not. "Maybe if I'd gone to Paris with such purpose seven years ago, I would have succeeded in making furniture. But I'm here now. God gave me the farm. I'm the oldest son, not Jean Paul. It's my responsibility."

"It doesn't have to be."

"Tell me, Isabelle, what would come of the farm, of *Ma Mère,* if I were not here?" Rain pounded against the roof as he stalked back and forth like a caged tiger. "I'm sure you would postpone your trip to England to care for my mother."

A lump rose in her throat. She stood there watching him, his eyes aflame, his shoulders hard and straight, his chest straining against his shirt, his muscled arms rippling—and she couldn't answer.

"And even if I could leave," he continued, "it would do little good. Mayhap the guild has been officially disbanded, but it still rules Paris. Do you think the men whose families have made furniture for centuries will let a peasant waltz into their domain and sell his work? Without the guild system, the furniture-makers will fight even harder to keep the trade in their families. The merchants would take an ax to my designs before I got them in the door of a shop. They'd beat me for stepping on their territory." He watched her face. "You don't believe me."

"I—"

"A *révolution,* they said. 'Liberty, equality, fraternity.' How much equality has the *Révolution* achieved when after five years of upheaval and killing, I'm still barred from working the job I desire? How much liberty do I have when not only am I forced to work the farm, but I'm forced to accept the price Paris sets on my grain? When I could be killed for saving a woman's life, or for saying the representatives in Paris are bloodhungry leeches or for storing my grain until I can get a better price?"

He raked his fingers through his madly curling hair as his taut shoulders slumped, and his broad chest deflated. "Forgive me. I…I meant not to rail on you. It's best if you return to the house with *Ma Mère.*" He looked toward the door. "Still raining out there. Don't want to catch a chill."

She stepped forward and laid a hand on his forearm. "I'm sorry for you, Michel. I am. This horrid *Révolution* has taken something from everyone. I forget that."

"It wouldn't be so bad if the revolutionaries hadn't promised freedom. Change." His eyes were bleak, his voice raw. "I'm more trapped now than I was under the *Ancien Régime.*"

His gaze drifted to her hand, still resting against his arm. "Isabelle…" His throat worked back and forth as though he couldn't say the words he wished to speak. "*Merci* for understanding." He enveloped her hand with his own, raised it to his mouth and kissed it.

She could see nothing but him, smell or feel nothing but his scent and the brush of his lips against her skin. The press of his hand against hers.

He bent closer, his breath tickling her face as his free hand cupped her cheek. "I know the *Révolution's* been cruel to you. Harder on you than it's been on me. I haven't lost my home, my name, my family."

It was almost as though he knew about Marie. Her chin quivered. He was going to make her cry. Right here. In front of him. She pressed her eyes shut.

Then his lips were on hers, hushing her words.

She should pull back, but his arms slid around her, drawing her against the solidness of his chest. She'd been kissed once, but she'd never before felt so swept away by the patient caress of a man's lips against a woman's, the delightful way his tongue snuck inside her mouth, ran over her teeth, her tongue.

His arms tightened around her. How strong they were, those arms forged into muscle by days spent working under the hot sun. His hands crept up her back, the same hands that could turn a scrap of wood into a masterpiece.

She melted into him and sighed against his mouth, still warm and strong on her own. In his arms she had no worries of being discovered, no fear of being dragged to the guillotine. In his arms, she felt something she hadn't felt in more than five years.

She felt safe.

~.~.~.~.~

Kissing her was like drinking the woman's personality. Explosive. Passionate. Enchanting. As Michel covered Isabelle's mouth with his own, the sensations nearly knocked him backward. Aye, he'd kissed women before, but never like this.

He'd feared it would be this way, not a simple kiss stolen out of flirtation, but a deep, passionate meeting of lips and hearts and minds. Isabelle had been so helpless, so vulnerable, comforting him when he hadn't endured near the trials she had. And then she nearly cried. How could he do anything except kiss her?

Oh, but he could stay like this, steeped in the whirlwind of Isabelle, all afternoon.

And she'd probably slap him for doing so.

He slowed the kiss until he could manage enough self-control to pull back. Then he looked into her face, prepared to be backhanded. But her eyes were closed as though locked in a dream, her face tilted up like she expected, almost wished, for more. Her tiny hand was curled into the front of his shirt like a kitten curved into its mother's belly. A fresh flood of warmth swamped his body.

"Isabelle," he whispered. Her eyes half opened, and for the first time since he met her, he didn't know what to say. He wasn't sorry for the kiss, and he could do little but stare into her heavily lidded eyes, begging for another.

It wasn't wise to kiss her again. Ever. She was an aristocrat—sentenced to death. She was leaving the country—gone as soon as her arm healed. And she'd not even been awake a fortnight—not long enough for him to know whether he could trust her. But drawn by a force he'd no desire to resist, he lowered his head and touched his lips to hers again.

The door to his workshop flew open, bringing with it a burst of rain and frigid wind. Michel spun around to find the mayor stomping his feet in the doorway. His gaze darted to Isabelle's flushed face and heated lips. Hopefully Narcise wouldn't notice the evidence of a freshly kissed woman.

"Michel."

Michel cleared his throat and took several steps away from Isabelle. "Good day, Mayor. Uh, this is Isabelle Chenoir. Corinne's cousin visiting from Paris. Isabelle, this is Victor Narcise, Abbeville's mayor."

Michel braced for questions about when she had arrived, how long she would stay, why her arm was bandaged, why he hadn't informed any townsfolk a guest was coming.

Wheezing almost as loud as the rain hammered, Narcise took his hat off, letting the water slosh into a muddy puddle in front of the door. "Michel, I've need of you, boy. The river's going to flood…"

Michel stilled, the sawdust beneath his feet grinding into the floor. The river? The Somme? Flood? The river was huge. Once it crested its banks, it could easily submerge everything in its wake in several feet of water.

"It'll take the town if we don't stop it." Narcise sucked in a heavy breath. "But you know what to do. You deal with that low field every year."

"The river can't flood." His mind whirled. "We've not had that much rain. Only four days."

"Yes, but it's come down hard and fast. The water's nowhere to go."

Michel hunched his shoulders and paced the open space in front of the dresser. "What's being done?"

"I've got riders out getting the men. I was hoping you could direct me from here."

"Sandbags. How many sandbags do you have?"

Narcise shrugged. "I believe there's a few being stored in the cathedral."

"A few?" The man must be daft to try plugging a river the size of the Somme with a few sandbags. Michel strode to the back of the workshop and flung open the doors of a cabinet. It was stacked top to bottom with empty burlap sacks waiting to be filled with dirt and sewn into sandbags. "Don't just gather the men, gather women and older children, too."

"Now just a minute, Michel. We don't need any women or—"

"They can't lug the sandbags, but they can fill the bags with dirt and sew the tops. Find all the extra burlap and fabric you can manage. We can have a group sewing new sacks inside the church. And food." Michel rubbed the back of his neck. "Divide people into shifts to make sandbags. Some fill, some sew, and others dam the river with them. Rotate them to rest, warm up and eat, then return them to work. We can't have half the town coming down sick. Anyone starts coughing, they're done outside. And Doc Gobbins best be volunteering his services.

"We can use the sandbags I've got here, and there's more in the stable. If we need more, we can send a wagon and take apart the dam on my property." Michel sighed. He'd put hours of work into that field, but what was one man's field compared to a town? With all this rain, the lower field wouldn't drain enough to plant this year, anyway.

He turned back around, his mind humming with the details of damming up the Somme. Isabelle stood where he'd left her against the wall, her face still flushed and lips swollen. He eyed the bandage on her left arm. "You can sew with your right hand?"

She nodded.

If he dragged her into town, the people would ask ceaseless questions. He could leave her here, where only the mayor knew of her.

But the woman could sew. Fast. The stack of embroidered handkerchiefs by her bed attested to her abilities.

"Then get *Ma Mère* and her sewing bag ready while we load up these sacks."

Isabelle with all the townsfolk. He pushed down the swirl of fear in his gut and hoped he was making the right choice.

Chapter Ten

Rain streamed off the brim of the overlarge hat Isabelle wore, while her fingers trembled from fatigue and cold. She ignored the growing ache in her arm and fought to sew the rough burlap of the sandbag closed. Frigid water and mud had long ago seeped into her skirt and boots, soaking her knees and legs as she kneeled on the ground. She tried imagining her wool cloak kept her dry, but rain sneaked through the tears and holes worn through the old material and ran in rivulets down her arms whenever she lifted them to sew.

In the predawn light, she looked out over the muddy road and toward the river. Tall stone houses, three and four stories high, lined the street before giving way to the makeshift dam. Beyond the dam, the river churned and swelled. She had glimpsed it once, when they had first arrived last night.

Working people, veiled in shadows, filled the scene before her. With the energy and enthusiasm of the young, children tirelessly filled bags. Nervous women chattered above the noise of wind and rain as they sewed in pairs, and weary men lugged new sandbags onto their shoulders and trudged to the river. All fought to save their town.

Isabelle hunched her back against the relentless downpour and tied off her thread before moving to the next sack. Flexing her weary shoulders, she shivered. She should head to the cathedral for some warmth and food, but once inside, the strange looks and questions from townsfolk didn't cease.

"You're Corinne's cousin?"

"How long have you lived in Paris?"

"Do you like the province better than the city?"

"What happened to your arm?"

"Michel never mentioned Corinne's cousin coming to visit."

Being inside the cathedral left her tired of talking, miserable from lying and weary of wondering who this Corinne was—besides the former owner of the pitcher and basin she had shattered.

"Got another sandbag," Philippe, the boy she'd been working with, called. He winked and blew her a kiss before scampering over to fill a fresh sack.

He was done already? She was getting further behind—another sign she should go inside and rest. Still, she sent Philippe a weak smile and winked in return. Her years working as a seamstress had taught her to sew quickly, and she could almost keep pace with little Philippe, if only her sore arm would cooperate. Most of the other women worked in pairs to keep up with one child filling the bags.

Not far from her, a familiar silhouette bent down to heave a sack. She paused and watched the strength and confidence in Michel's gait as he headed to the dam. He'd worked straight through the night, organizing the making of sandbags, choosing the best spot for the dam, putting people on shifts to work and rest, and lugging finished sacks. The mayor and other men practically bowed in gratefulness over any direction Michel gave. But in spite of all the shift breaks Michel insisted everyone else take, he'd only rested once during the night.

Not that she'd noticed. She'd barely paid him heed…well, maybe she'd paid a little attention.

She shook her head as she thought back over the hours since they'd left the cottage.

She'd been watching him all night. How ridiculous of her! He was nothing more than a farmer...a farmer who had opened his home and cared for her when he could have left her for dead. A farmer whose very act of kindness could cause his own death. A farmer who exuded strength the way most men wore hats, and had muscles a Greek god would envy.

She stopped her sewing and pressed a hand to her forehead. What was she thinking? Michel was irritating, ruled his home like a tyrant and didn't heed a thing she said.

But then he had such a gentle way with his mother, and an immeasurable skill with wood. And he kissed her with such smoldering intensity her bones turned to melting butter. Her pulse sped at the memory, and she scowled at her sandbag. That was certainly her dilemma—she liked kissing him. And sometimes, in spite of herself, she simply liked *him,* the protection he offered, the sense of safety she felt in his embrace. When had the thorns of irritation she felt toward him turned into tingles of admiration and attraction? Well, she'd not encourage such overtures from him. She'd be leaving as soon as the rain abated.

"This one's done, too." Philippe sent her a saucy grin before running to a new sack.

Shaking her head, Isabelle looked at the newly filled bag. Two behind. She was almost as slow as the townswomen. Though her bandaged arm protested, she pursed her lips and sewed with intensity, finishing her sack before the boy completed another.

Muddy boots appeared before her.

"I told you I didn't want you outside. You'll become ill."

"I'm fine." Isabelle looked up into Michel's face and bit the side of her lip. He should look tired after working all night, but his green eyes were wide and clear, his wet hair curling wildly beneath his hat, his face ruggedly handsome rather than haggard. She pushed out a breath and wiped a strand of sopping hair from her face. She wasn't supposed to care if he was tired.

He squatted beside her, his eyes roving her face and body. A cozy ball of warmth formed in her stomach and spread to her limbs. "You're shivering. If you want to work, sew fresh sacks inside with *Ma Mère*."

She tried to still her cold, trembling body. "There're a hundred women inside willing to sew. No one wants to come out here. Besides, I'm one of the few that can keep up with a child." She'd not tell him she'd been outside for two straight shifts.

"You are the most stubborn woman." He grabbed her hand and tugged. "Either you get up and walk to the cathedral, or I'll carry you there."

She tried to jerk her hand free as he pulled her to her feet. "Let go of me, you arrogant oaf. You've no authority to—"

"Close that mouth of yours, or I'll think of a more pleasant activity for it."

Her cheeks burned at his reference to their kiss. "No, thank you." She attempted to pull her hand away again, but he still held it, covering her frigid fingers with his warm, calloused hand. Her heart quickened. Touching him was a bad idea. She cast him a glance. His strong jaw remained set, his long, stately nose prominent in the shadows of early morning and his gaze focused on the cathedral ahead. He didn't seem at all affected by the feel of her skin against his.

The tall, stone cathedral loomed over the town. With Michel still clutching her hand, Isabelle walked silently toward the massive structure. Built in Gothic style, the cathedral's twin square towers jutted so high the clouds and rain swallowed them before they ended. The twelve apostles, carved into towering stone pillars, looked down as they walked across the cobblestones leading to the entrance. Three sets of ancient wooden doors lined the front. He tugged her toward the middle and largest doors, placed beneath a stone archway and an ornate, star-patterned stained-glass window. He held the door for two women who scurried in front of them, then drew her inside without ceremony.

"Oh, Michel, is that you? Thank you for your hard work."

"Aye, the town wouldn't know what to do, if not for you."

"You're a smart boy, you are. You'd make your father right proud."

"Thank you, ladies. Best get down the hall and sit a spell by the fire." Michel removed Isabelle's cloak and hat as he spoke to the other women. He had hung her garments on hooks before she could think to take them off herself. Then he stripped off his wet outer raiment and steered her down the corridor.

The drafty building did little to warm her. The damp, heavy air, holding the scent of grain, barely stirred as they moved.

"Excuse me." A barrel-chested man brushed Isabelle's shoulder as he lumbered toward the exit.

People of all heights, ages and occupations filled the corridor, some sleeping on the floor, others eating and more sewing. Michel pushed her past a group of young, giggling girls, and they entered a warm, crowded room. The aroma of stew and bread replaced the smell of grain. A huge fire roared at the far end of the room, the space in front of it packed with men sitting on benches and on the floor, clambering to thrust off the chill from outside. Cold and tired, Isabelle could imagine herself lying down by the fire and sleeping for a day. But Michel stood between her and the heat source, as did a hundred or so others.

Two young women hastened to them—or rather to Michel. Both had perfectly coiffed hair and looked as though they hadn't spent a minute working. Isabelle inwardly cringed and reached up to finger the uneven tresses on her own head. The brunette wearing a green skirt took Michel's arm, while the blonde stood back and sent Michel a brilliant smile. No mud splattered the blonde's kidskin boots or her dry dress of delicate pink. Pink during a flood.

Isabelle swallowed. Had she ever been that vain? Probably. In another lifetime. She shoved at her tangled hair. If only she'd brought some pins to put it up.

"Michel. Just look at you, working so hard to save our town," the brunette all but purred. She didn't have a speck of mud on her clothing or boots, either.

The little minxes. As though Michel worked alone to save the town.

"*Oui*, the town would be lost without your guidance."

The blonde moved forward, her pink, plump lips moving delicately as she spoke.

Had Michel ever kissed them? Isabelle's heart gave a single, violent beat.

"Why, you must be exhausted." The blonde slipped her hand into Michel's free one. "Come, we've a spot here by the fire for you."

The two women turned and escorted Michel through the crowd with graceful sways of their hips.

Standing by the doorway, Isabelle glanced around for Jeanette. But Jeanette slept, sandwiched between two other older ladies, with her back propped against the wall and the sack she'd been sewing resting in her lap. Isabelle could find another seat, but that meant ceaseless questions from strangers. She pursed her lips. Maybe she should go back outside, or at least to the corridor.

Throughout the room, a dozen or so fresh women stood out from the muddy, rain-soaked crowd. They carried food and drink to the weary workers and offered hopeful smiles that matched their bright, clean clothing. *Oui*, the group of women must have come to help this morning, since she didn't remember them from last night.

At least they helped in their own dainty ways. Six years ago, she would have assisted in the same way, being too refined and mannered to get wet or dirty but still wanting to do her part. Vain she may have been, but she'd never been indolent.

Michel reappeared before her, the beautiful women no longer trailing him.

He took her elbow and bent his mouth to her ear, his breath causing her skin to tingle. "I thought you were going to rest."

"I was searching for a place to sit." She didn't meet his eyes or tell him how inferior the other women made her feel.

"You'll sit with me."

People crammed into the area by the stove, sitting on both benches and the floor. But they parted for Michel as willingly as the Red Sea for Moses, calling out to him as he passed.

"Appreciate it, Michel."

"What do we do next?"

"You think that dam'll hold?"

Four men jumped off a bench along the wall, each offering his coveted seat to Michel. Isabelle tried to tug her elbow out of his hand as he ushered her to the bench, but lacked the energy to free herself from his sturdy grip. Pulling her down, he settled so closely beside her their shoulders touched. She shifted away, until a wiry, rancid-smelling man sat down on her other side.

The blonde appeared with a single wooden bowl of stew and a hunk of bread. She blinked absently at Isabelle, as though she hadn't even noticed Isabelle before when greeting Michel. And perhaps she hadn't. The room teemed with wet, dirty people who looked the same as Isabelle. Why notice one muddy girl out of the crowd?

"Thank you, Jocelyne," Michel said as he took the bowl from her. "Would you mind bringing me another?"

Jocelyne's amorous blue eyes smiled. "Not at all."

Michel held his bowl out for Isabelle. She looked at the steam rising from the thick stew and then into Michel's face. His eyes held hers just a touch longer than appropriate in a public place. The stew's aroma drifted to her, and her stomach twisted into a knot of hunger. She reached for the bowl, but the moment the heavy dish rested in her hands, pain shot through her healing arm.

"Ah!" She pulled her arm away.

Michel grabbed the tilting bowl before it spilled into her lap, his eyes shooting sparks.

Balancing the bowl between his legs, he reached for her arm. "You've been working too hard. You've hurt yourself." His voice was a low growl. "I told you to rest." She held her throbbing limb away from him and cradled it to her chest. To her mortification, tears filled her eyes. The people surrounding them grew silent and riveted their gazes on Michel and her.

She whispered frantically, "I just want the town to be safe, and my arm didn't hurt overmuch until I held that bowl. The weight of the dish must have caused the pain. That's all it is—I promise."

She must have said something right. Because the hard lines around Michel's mouth and eyes softened.

"You've no need to work yourself to an early grave. The fate of the town doesn't rest solely in your hands."

No. It seemed to rest in his. And he didn't even look tired.

"Here, is the bowl too hot for your lap?" Michel set the bowl on her legs, and Isabelle shook her head. "Then eat, and relax. I don't want you working again today. At all."

Her throat too thick with pain and humiliation to speak, she nodded and took a little bite. The blonde brought two more bowls of victuals for Michel, who wolfed down his food, while Isabelle's eyes drifted closed before she ate half her stew. She leaned against the wall to rest her back and head, and let the warmth from the room seep in. She felt cozy. Wet, but cozy. And safe with Michel next to her. No one had asked a single prying question.

The hum of the townsfolk's chatter lulled her further into her peaceful world. Michel's voice rumbled beside her as he answered someone's question, a deep, comforting sound…

Her pillow shifted, and she jolted upright. Her eyes sprang open and she stared at Michel's shoulder, then up into his amused eyes. She'd fallen asleep on him. Heat flooded her face in one mad rush. The conversation around them quieted and snooping gazes prickled her skin yet again.

"I need to get back outside," he told her as though everyone wasn't listening.

She nodded dumbly.

"Rest." He ran a hand over her muddy, tangled hair, then stood.

A man who had been sprawled on the floor jumped into Michel's spot, and she shivered, the calm of Michel's presence replaced by the cold curiosity of the townsfolk.

Someone called to Michel as he stepped away. He moved from person to person, answering questions, giving commands, comforting the worried. Everyone looked to him. Even the mayor sauntered up, a beaming smile on his face as he slapped Michel on the back. The townspeople put the security of Abbeville into Michel's hands. And having stood cocooned in the refuge of his arms as he kissed her yesterday, she didn't wonder why.

"So, you're Corinne's cousin from Paris?"

Isabelle turned to look at the man with yellow teeth and a stick-thin body, who eyed her suspiciously.

"What's Paris like?"

⌐.⌐.⌐.⌐.⌐

Kissing Isabelle had changed everything.

Michel made himself walk through the cold rain, lugging what was surely his seven thousandth, four hundred and third sandbag. He should be resting by the warmth of the woodstove and eating a third and fourth bowl of stew. But how was he to rest when Isabelle snuggled up to him in sleep? He'd wanted to wrap his arm around her and pull her close, lean down and see if her lips were as irresistible this morning as they had been yesterday.

With half the town watching them.

He shook his head and blew out a breath. Unfortunately, the problem didn't stop with her lips. She sat there beside him, completely exhausted from helping a town full of people who would kill her if they knew her true identity. She had worked alone most the night, doing the work of two women. She was dirty and soaked and mud-caked…

And admirable. She had no obligation to help save the town, yet she worked harder than those who had lived their entire lives in Abbeville.

He heaved his sandbag atop the wall, now almost as tall as he. He'd set the barrier in the midst of the lowest ground by the river and extended it until the ground sloped higher. Still, if the river rose high enough to lap around the dam, they were in trouble. Michel raised his head toward the heavens. The rain appeared to be slowing, but that was probably more hope on his part than reality.

Father, please stop this rain. And give us the strength to work until You do.

Michel turned back toward the village. By now, the sky would have fully lightened behind the clouds, but shadows and rain still shrouded the village.

He trudged to another sandbag, his thoughts swinging back to Isabelle. Like any unmarried man twenty-seven years of age, he'd done his share of stealing kisses. But he'd never stolen one so passionate before. The woman had knocked every sane thought from his head.

At least trying to circumvent a flood made avoiding her easy. Or should have…

He groaned when he caught a flash of brown out of the corner of his eye. He looked back toward the cathedral. She stood there, all right, in that brown cloak tattered beyond even what *Mère* could repair, wearing his huge gray hat that did little to keep her riot of hair dry. He dropped his sandbag where he stood and stalked toward her. How many tongue-lashings did that woman need before she realized he wasn't going to let her work anymore? She'd more than likely rebroken her arm at some point during the night. Was she trying to reinjure her ribs, as well?

He expected her to move toward a pile of open sandbags, but she walked around the side of the building, leaned her back against the wall and tilted her head down so the wide hat she wore nearly disguised her. He didn't need to be any closer to see the weary slump of her shoulders or the slow way she dragged her head up when a man stopped beside her.

Michel recognized the man immediately, Gerard Bertrand, his pig-stealing neighbor. The musty scent of stale clothing mingled with the rain and filled Michel's senses when he was yet several steps away. The man owned more land than anyone else in Abbeville, and yet he didn't bother to wear clean raiment. Granted, Michel didn't smell too fresh after working all night, but Bertrand hadn't been working as much as sitting inside eating. And whether in town on business or supervising his workers in the fields, the man always seemed to stink of unwashed clothes and old sweat.

"I never heard anything from Michel about Corinne's cousin coming for a visit. Seems he would have mentioned something around town sometime back." Bertrand leered at Isabelle as Michel, jaw clenched, walked up behind him.

Isabelle didn't notice his presence. Her lips formed a round O, and she shrugged. "Hadn't Michel said anything? How odd. My visit's been planned for quite some time."

She sounded as though she'd recited the answer so many times she could give it in her sleep. "Jeanette and I've been corresponding about my coming for the better part of a year now. Although Michel's so busy with the farm, I doubt he'd be overly concerned with my presence. He does the work of three men around that place." Her voice sounded as sluggish as her actions looked.

Michel opened his mouth to speak, but Bertrand beat him to it. "Oh, don't I know it. I've been trying to take some of that land off his hands since his *père* died. He's got too much land for one man to work."

Aye, Bertrand had been trying to swindle land out from under his family for as long as Michel remembered. The man had land, all right, half of it cheated from others, and half purchased—probably with forged bills—when the National Assembly had stripped the nobility of their land and sold it. Didn't matter to the Convention that Bertrand paid his farmers less and treated them worse than any *seigneur* in the north of France would have.

Bertrand ran his eyes slowly over Isabelle in a way that made Michel's blood turn to ice. "How much longer you here for, then?"

"Just a few days. It's hard to travel with this rain, or I'd be back in Paris even now."

"You can imagine my surprise when Isabelle showed up at my door," Michel piped up. Both sets of eyes turned to him. Isabelle's slumped posture straightened immediately, most likely in anticipation of an argument. "*Ma Mère* never said a word about Isabelle coming, but I unearthed a whole stack of Isabelle's letters under *Ma Mère's* mattress. Well, it seems everyone's anxious to know our Isabelle, but I'm afraid we must away. Just a few sandbags left for others to fill, and *Ma Mère* needs to go home."

Bertrand tipped his hat, his yellow eyes still studying Isabelle. "We'll watch for you around town, then." The man sauntered off.

Michel shifted closer to Isabelle, his eyes scanning the purple bruises that filled the space beneath her eyes. Fire smoldered in his veins. "Have the townsfolk been like this all night, badgering you with questions?" No one had questioned him about Isabelle. Not once. But people were skittish as a day-old colt around anyone new with talk of the Terror coming. A stranger could easily be spying for the radicals in Paris.

Her chin lifted. "I'm sorry I came outside, but—"

"We're going home. You can barely stay awake standing up. Another couple hours and everything will be finished, anyway."

"I'm not tired."

"No, you've the energy of a court jester." He took hold of her upper arm.

She planted her feet in the muck. "You've worked too hard on the dam to leave before it's finished. I'm fine."

"Stubborn woman." He swooped her up, trying to ignore the lithe feel of her body in his arms as he made long strides toward the wagon.

She fought his hold, a laughable struggle to pit her weary, injured slightness against his strength. "I'm not going anywhere. There're more bags left to sew."

"I've told you you're finished. You've done the work of five women. It's time we're done."

"You've done the work of ten men."

"Aye." He plopped her down on the wagon seat. She sucked in a breath the moment her bottom hit the bench, and he looked down. Cold rainwater pooled on the wood. How daft could he be? He should have thought to wipe the seat with something. He glanced in the back of the wagon, but it lay empty, no old blanket or heavy tarpaulin to soak up the puddled water. "Stay here while I get *Ma Mère*. I'll bring back a blanket for the seat."

She nodded, her quivering lips turning blue.

His mother barely stirred as he lifted her from where she slept inside and carried her outside. He rested her head against Isabelle and tried to sweep the water out of the wagon bed with a broom as best he could. After laying *Mère* in the back, Michel climbed onto the bench. He'd come back later today and check the dam—after he got Isabelle away from the townsfolk.

Sylvie moved slower than her usual plod as she waded through puddles and muck. He shoved his hat down harder on his head to keep the biting rain from his face. Isabelle huddled beside him, suddenly hatless. The girl had used her hat to cover *Mère's* face. His heart gave a long, slow lurch. Isabelle might be a spitfire with him, but she sure was sweet on *Mère*. He'd have never guessed a fancy aristocrat would care so much for a peasant farmer's mother, but Isabelle treated *Mère* with the same love she'd likely show her own mother.

Michel took his hat and plunked it down over her hair. Then he immediately squinted to keep the rain from his eyes.

She shifted, and the hat returned to his head. "You keep it to drive. I don't need to see."

She hunkered down, all but curling up like a baby and slanting her head away from him. She'd be frozen by the time they reached the cottage. He opened his mouth to speak but had nothing to say. So he turned his eyes to the road, and forced them to stay off Isabelle until they were halfway home. She slept by then. The ball she'd been curved into had loosened, and her head lolled at an angle that made him wince.

He ran his eyes over her torn cloak and soaked hair. It wouldn't hurt to wrap his arm around her, hold her, warm her awhile. Heaven knew she needed coddling, though the woman would probably punch him if he told her so.

Giving in, he opened his cloak, pulled her against him and wound his arm around her. She still slept, delicate and soft against his chest. His Sleeping Beauty, who argued with him for sport, and paced the house when told to rest, and kissed him until his heart erupted. The woman could send his blood boiling with a word and melt his bones with a look.

Memories flooded back. The way she appeared while sulking in bed, her expression pouty and her hair splayed over her shoulders and pillow. The gratitude in her face when he'd returned her money and pendant. The tenderness in her tone when she spoke to *Mère*. The determination in her eyes when she mentioned England. The openness in her voice when she asked about his furniture-making.

He pressed his lips together to keep from smiling. Maybe Father Albert had been right about Isabelle being an opportunity rather than a burden.

Last night she'd worked so hard she'd hurt herself and hadn't noticed, sewing sandbags until she could no longer stand upright. And all for a town that distrusted her and would kill her without a thought. She had tenacity, for sure and for certain, and no one could call her a coward.

He froze as a thought struck with the force of a hammer blow to his head.

He was falling in love with her.

Chapter Eleven

The warm memories of Isabelle turned to icicles in Michel's head. Still a kilometer from home, he steered the wagon around a giant, water-filled rut. Mud sucked at the wheels, nearly pulling the wagon into the crevice. His hat offered little protection from the rain pelting his cheeks and chin. He shifted on the wet seat and rolled his aching neck. A stream of water poured down his back from the hat brim, jolting him with the sudden cold.

He blew out a misty breath. Even the weather seemed to conspire against him, showing him what a fine mess he wallowed in, falling in love with someone feisty and full of trouble—the daughter of a *seigneur*. Her people had caused his kinsmen pain and suffering, starvation and death for centuries. How could he love someone whose family had committed such atrocities?

He scrubbed a hand over his chin. He'd no business incriminating Isabelle. She'd been little more than a girl when the *Révolution* started. France's condition had been no fault of hers. Who was he to judge her? He knew her heart—and it held nothing like the calloused indifference of the nobility that had trampled him all his life.

He scowled and flicked the reins, though Sylvie trotted no faster. And what of himself? What if he'd been born into nobility? Would he want to be judged by his father's actions? Surely not. Isabelle hadn't invented the system that took such advantage of the third estate; she'd simply been born into the other side of it.

He dragged his eyes away from the road and watched her sleep, still curled against him. Mayhap he made excuses for her? Trying to justify her situation so he could give into his heart's desires without any guilt.

Maybe he wasn't in love at all. He had feelings, yes. But what man wouldn't have feelings for a woman who looked like Isabelle? And attraction differed from love. Attraction sparked and smoldered for a moment, then left cold ash in its wake. How many times had he watched it happen to his childhood friends?

But love…well, love drove a man to sacrifice, to put others before himself. *Greater love hath no man than this, that a man lay down his life for his friends.*

He slapped the back of his neck. He'd been risking his life since he picked her up in the woods. Surely he hadn't loved her from the first moment he saw her?

No. She'd been a duty then, and his love for God had constrained him to nurse the beautiful, unnamed woman.

But she'd become much more than a burden the Lord had placed in his path. For one thing, the woman could work the backside off a plow horse. Even confined to her bed, she had worked. She sewed an army of hankies for him and *Mère* to sell, helped *Mère* with clothes for the orphans and read through *The Tales of Mother Goose* at least thrice. And look at how hard she'd labored through the night and early morning. Any farmer would want a wife like her.

And why was he thinking about a wife? Since when did he even want one?

Well, mayhap he wanted a wife. But Isabelle? Michel rubbed the back of his neck. The woman loved fiercely and had endless patience with *Mère*. She was courageous and determined and loyal.

Hang it all. He'd been half-lost since the moment she fixed her fiery brown eyes on him and demanded he call a doctor for her arm. He might not love her completely yet. But a few more weeks of being around her, and he'd be as sunk as *Père* had been for *Mère*, as Jean Paul for Corinne. And Isabelle even wanted to be a wife. In England. To another man.

Every muscle of his being stiffened. Coldness filled his body, spreading outward until the tips of his fingers and toes were icy, not from the wind and rain, but from his heart. *England.* How could he forget? Reaching England had been her single goal for as long as he'd known her.

He tried to shift away from Isabelle and lean her against the back of the seat instead of his body, but she only whimpered and burrowed closer. Could he ask her to stay in Abbeville? To marry him? True, no one in town knew who she was, but she risked her life simply by remaining in the country. And Michel had little to offer her but a two-chamber house and hours of ceaseless farmwork. Once she reached her aunt's home in England, she'd be surrounded by all the comfort and luxury he could never give her.

And what were her feelings for him? He hadn't romanced her, and he fought with her more than anything else. Sure, she responded when he kissed her—and had gotten a little jealous of the women inside the church this morn, if he judged correctly—but more than any other female would have? Whatever her feelings, he doubted they ran as deep as his. The woman had enough emotional troubles already. She didn't need to add love to the mix.

Best to keep his distance before he got her more tangled in his life. She would risk too much by remaining in France. And he couldn't leave *Mère* and the farm for England, even if she wanted him to.

He rested his gaze on her again and gripped the reins. He

wouldn't be the first man left with a broken heart in the wake of a woman.

The wagon bumped and jostled.

He jerked his gaze from Isabelle, and he steered Sylvie out of another gaping rut. He deserved as much for staring at a woman instead of the road.

Isabelle moaned slightly and shifted against him, then sat up straight. "What's wrong? Is everything all right? Why'd the wagon buck?"

Sylvie turned off the road and started up the hill to the house. Michel poked his tongue in his cheek and tried not to smile. Her reflexes were only running a full minute behind.

She watched him through bleary eyes. "You didn't doze off, did you? I knew you were too tired to drive."

"*Non.* I didn't doze off."

"*Oui,* you did." Softness edged her voice. "Why, look at you. You can barely hold your head up."

She sounded concerned for him. The edges of his lips curved in a bitter half smile. He pulled the wagon to a stop in front of the house. Concerned or not, she would still leave him for England. "You're not any more alert than I."

He climbed out of the wagon, rounded it and gathered *Mère* in his arms. He expected Isabelle to follow him inside, help remove *Mère's* wet clothing and get her into a dry nightdress, but she never came. He glanced at his dry bed as he pulled covers over *Mère.*

He headed out the door to find Isabelle standing by the wagon watching him. He sighed. Couldn't she see he wanted to sleep? Needed some space from her?

Shoulders slumped, she shifted uneasily on her feet. His eyes roved over her, rumpled and sluggish and muddy from the long night. Had he ever seen anyone more beautiful?

"Do you need help putting Sylvie away?" Her voice sounded sincere, despite her weary posture and tired eyes.

He raised his eyebrows as he neared.

"I just...I wanted to make sure you're all right," she stammered. "That you're not ill or anything. You...you had a long night. Worked so hard, and I..."

She cared. The emotion haunted her face.

She'll walk away from me. Maybe not tomorrow, but soon. He fisted his hands at his sides, suddenly more willing to lug another seven thousand sandbags than confront their feelings for each other.

What would she do if he told her he loved her? Laugh? Impossible. She'd never been cruel. Accept it? Maybe. Stay? *Non.* England meant too much to her.

"Go to bed," he growled.

Hurt flickered in her eyes and held. His throat closed. Didn't she understand his dismissing her now would save her from more pain when she left? He swallowed pathetically and stepped so close she shifted her head backward so she didn't bump his chest, so close he need only lift a hand to tangle it in her hair.

"Isabelle—"

"You arrogant oaf! I'm trying to help." She spoke sharply but moisture glistened in her eyes. She shoved her palm against his chest. "You spent all night traipsing around in the cold and rain. You refused rest, barely ate and now you disdain my politeness. Why! You deserve to catch pneumonia for a month." She all but sobbed the last words.

Being this close to her was a mistake. He couldn't think, could barely breathe. A longing spread through him until his arms ached to hold her and his chest craved the feel of her slender form pressed against him. He clasped her wrist instead. "You don't mean any of that. You're just tired."

She blinked, banishing the unshed tears from her eyes. "Unhand me."

He would, but she was too near. Her cheeks too flushed, her mouth too soft, her eyes too defenseless.

She stopped tugging on her arm, and like a drowning sailor locking his gaze on shore, his eyes fixed on hers. Rain pounded the ground. Wind whipped through trees and tore at their cloaks. Coldness circled them. But neither moved.

His gaze dipped to her mouth, the taste awaiting him there both explosive and sweet. She shifted subtly forward until her breath tickled his lips.

Father, help me! He dropped her wrist as though her skin singed him and took two steps back.

She shivered. "Why?" she asked, looking up at him through innocent, longing-filled eyes. "Why do you keep trying to kiss me?"

"I'm not trying to kiss you. I'm…" What? Trying *not* to kiss her? He looked at her gnarled and filthy hair. Her slender form hidden beneath the ratty brown cloak. Her luminous eyes and mud-smeared face. She should seem filthy and loathsome in her current state. So why did he find her heart-wrenching and irresistible?

I love you. The words rested on his tongue. But speaking them wouldn't change her leaving.

Distance. He took another step back. He needed to put space between them.

Suddenly preferring to sleep with the animals rather than under the same roof as her, he spun away, took Sylvie's reins and tugged the beast and wagon toward shelter, leaving the woman he loved alone in the rain.

~.~.~.~.~

Isabelle's arm throbbed in rhythm with her pounding heart as Michel turned his back. Why was he leaving her? Deserting her? Tears swelled in her throat. She needed to tell him about her father. He'd be safer not knowing who she was, but with the entire town suspicious of her, he at least deserved to know the risk he took in harboring her. *Oui*, she'd expected him to turn away from her, but had assumed it would come *after* he knew she was the daughter of the Duc de La Rouchecauld.

"Michel!" She called above the rain. He didn't answer.

She drew a shuddering breath. He had feelings for her. Why else kiss her? Why else turn away?

And she was being featherbrained. They hadn't even kissed a moment ago. He could walk away from her if he so pleased, for he owned the house and land whereon she stood. And what was a little attraction between them when she was leaving and he had a town full of women happy to serve him?

She headed inside and checked on Jeanette, who slept peacefully. Then she changed into Jeanette's spare gown, sponged the mud from her boots and hung her filthy dress and cloak by the fire to dry. Still, Michel didn't enter.

Wetness saturated the bandage on her arm. The crate under Michel's bed held a fresh wrap, but he'd always changed them. So she climbed into bed, took up Perrault's book and fell asleep before she finished the second sentence.

Isabelle woke to the scent of coffee brewing and meat roasting. Jeanette had left her bed, but Michel's tick lay untouched. She arched her back and stretched, but pain shot down her arm, making her eyes water.

In the main chamber, Jeanette sat at the table, chopping potatoes in her nightclothes. Michel stood by the fire, a chicken roasting over it. He wore dry raiment and held a mug in his hand. His back stretched strong and broad beneath his shirt, and he stood on legs sturdy as pillars while he stared into the flames.

As if sensing her gaze, he turned, and their eyes locked over the rim of his mug.

"I trust you slept well, Isabelle. Would you like some buttermilk?"

She shook her head. "No, I…" What did she say to the man who kissed her until she dissolved in his arms one day, turned his back on her the next, and now pretended nothing transpired?

"It pains me, and the cloths are wet." She dumbly held out her arm. "Perchance you could look at it and wrap it fresh."

He set his buttermilk aside and strode toward her. "I'm sorry. I had forgotten." He took her chin and lifted it. "Why did you not ask earlier?"

Because they'd been too busy not kissing or fighting or whatever happened outside.

Her jaw trembled as he searched her face. Oh, heavens! One almost-kiss and she forgot how to act around him.

His thumb and forefinger still held her chin, forcing her to answer. "I—I called to you, and…you must not have heard me," she whispered weakly.

His face hardened, and his eyes grew distant. "Come. Sit by the fire."

He led her to the hearth and brought an elegantly carved chair from the table. Kneeling, he touched his fingertips to the most sensitive spot on her arm and watched her face.

She tried not to wince. Tried.

Tenderly, with the care of a mother for her ill babe, he untied the thongs that held the cloth and unwrapped it.

Six strips of wood, spaced evenly around her arm, ran from the base of her hand to below her elbow. The long sticks had caused her little discomfort over the past weeks, but then, they appeared as smooth and polished as any of Michel's furniture.

He removed them, and her skin beneath appeared sallow and

translucent, as though she could see through to the bone. It clung to her muscles, which were shriveled compared to those of her right arm. A thumb length from her wrist, the skin had swollen and turned unhealthy shades of purple and black and green.

Michel slipped both hands beneath her injury. "Move your fingers."

She obeyed despite the searing pain.

He laid her arm in her lap. "This may hurt a moment." He worked his fingers upward in tiny strokes, causing her nerves to scream from the gentle pressure. She wanted to pull her arm away, cradle it and tell him to stop. But he moved past the sore area and farther up, his head bent and shoulders slumped over the limb.

Had he been this attentive when he treated her injuries after finding her in the woods? She wished she'd been awake to remember. Wished she could take snippets of his tenderness at this moment and carry them with her to England.

A warm, cozy feeling settled in her stomach. Was this what having a husband would be like? The attention, the comfort, the concern?

She cupped his cheek with her right hand and tilted his face up. His fingers stilled, and his eyes, unguarded and soft, found hers.

She sucked in a breath. Why hadn't he told her how he felt when she tried to ask? And why did his feelings matter so much to her?

She'd be going to England in a few days. Surely she didn't care for him. Did she?

She dropped her hand from his face, the air in her lungs growing so thick she could hardly breathe.

"Tell me of this Corinne." She searched for a distraction. "Was she your wife?"

He resumed work on her arm. "No…*non,* she was Jean Paul's wife. She died of pneumonia six years back. That's when Jean Paul left. Said he couldn't abide staying here without her. There's a one-room cabin where they lived back in the woods a piece. Jean Paul writes once or twice a year, though I know not where he is. I tell *Ma Mère* he's making furniture, which keeps her happy. And Corinne had kin in Paris, which suits your story."

He set her arm in her lap. "I cannot feel a break."

Nothing that needs to be set, anyway. But the pain and swelling make me think you've a slight break where the old crack was. Your bone was healing, but not yet strong. You did too much last night, Isabelle. I'm sorry."

Her mind raced to keep up with his words. "Break? But it can't be broken. It's healing."

He shook his head. "You must have reinjured it. I wish I could do more."

His eyes held so much compassion she turned away, even as tears clogged her throat and filled her eyes. "How long?" she whispered.

"Normally one month plus half or more for a broken forearm. But with yours already being injured, I can't say."

She straightened her back and nodded.

"The doctor might be able to say better. Do you want me to send for him? I've money for one."

The sob she'd squelched burst forth. Covering her mouth, she shook her head.

He clasped her good hand in both of his. "Come, now, Isabelle. It'll heal fine, just bring you a little fresh pain. You'll need to mind it better this time around."

Her head pounded as one tear and then another slipped down her face. Mortified, she struggled for control, but Michel rested a hand on her cheek, used his thumb to wipe the moisture away then feathered a hand through her hair.

"I'm sorry." He brought her head to his chest and cradled it against him. She pressed her eyes shut. She wouldn't cry. Not here, not now, not in Michel's arms. What was a little break in her arm? She was being infantile.

"Michel, what have you done to the girl?" Jeanette left the table and hunched down before her.

She tried to speak, but found her throat thick with unreleased tears.

"Nothing, *Ma Mère*. Her arm's suffered a bit of a break, is all, and just when it was getting better."

"Her arm, you say? Well, the dear girl. Is there anything I can do?" Jeanette absently took Isabelle's injured hand and patted it.

Burning pain surged through her arm. She gasped and jerked her arm away.

"Oh, dear, forgive me. I didn't mean to..." Jeanette looked near tears, as well.

"It's fine... I just..." Isabelle hiccupped.

"I'll hold her a moment longer till she feels a bit better." Michel smiled at his mother. "You get those potatoes on. The chicken smells delicious."

She didn't know how long he held her, how long it took for her breathing to calm and the tears to clear from her eyes and throat. "England." The word grated against her vocal cords. "I can still travel with a broken arm, right?"

Michel's hold turned rigid. He took her shoulders and pushed her back. "Is that what this is about, your need to find a husband?" Had he spewed ice crystals from his mouth, the words couldn't have been any colder.

"*Non...* I..." Why was he mad? Did he think stealing a kiss and comforting her meant she no longer needed to go to England? "I only want..." She sniffled as a new tear trickled down her cheek. "The Terror's coming, and I—I promised Marie and—"

"Could you walk with a broken arm?" Michel crossed his arms.

"You're a foolish and determined one, so I suppose you could if you'd nothing to carry. But a vessel full of sailors is no place for a single woman. Not even one who's healthy and hale. How is it you plan to protect yourself from the men?"

"Protect myself?"

"Do you know what kind of men sail the seas? The rough, unmarried kind that can't get respectable jobs on land. You think they'll leave a fair woman like yourself untouched?"

"You think... Surely no one would... Why, there'll be other passengers. The sailors can't possibly ravage every woman who steps aboard."

"No, just the beautiful, young ones who travel alone, too innocent to conceive of what might happen."

"How dare you!"

"How dare I? How dare I?" He sprang to his feet and stalked back and forth. "Yes, how dare I care that you walk out from under my protection onto a ship full of men who would use you. How dare I warn you your decision's foolish. You're right. How dare I!" His chest heaved from yelling, and he raked a hand through his hair, causing the front to spike.

"I didn't—"

"Yes, that's right. You didn't. What are you thinking even attempting a journey to England by yourself?"

Her body trembled with indignation. He accused her so easily. But he hadn't lost everything he loved. He hadn't been hunted for four and a half years. He hadn't sworn an oath to a dying sister.

She stood, despite her shaking legs and painful arm, and met his gaze with eyes as cold as his were hot. "Has it occurred to you that I hadn't planned to travel alone?" The image of Marie lying in the dirt sprang to her mind.

She shoved it away. "That I'm traveling this way so I can stay alive?"

Her voice quieted even as her resolve strengthened. "Either I'll reach England, or I will die trying to get there."

Chapter Twelve

Michel took his first bite of chicken and nearly spit it out. His eyes watered from the strong salt taste. *Mère* must have forgotten how much she added. Again. He glanced at the hunk of chicken on his plate. How long since he'd eaten plain meat rather than soup or stew? The repugnant taste of his first bite still clung to his mouth. He lifted his mug to his lips and drained half the water. *Mère* looked his way. He tried to smile at her and slowly forked up another bite. "The rain let up a bit ago. I'll head back to town after dinner. Want to make sure the dam looks as it should."

He cut toward the inside of the chicken—maybe that wouldn't be so salty—then ate another forkful.

Mère reached for his hand. "Wonderful. You can take Isabelle, then."

The only palatable piece of meat he'd eaten turned dry on his tongue. Isabelle sat, chin raised, lips stiff as she watched *Mère* with flat eyes. She hadn't said a word to him since their argument an hour earlier. Michel scowled. Try warning a woman she flirted with danger by boarding a ship alone, and she got her hackles up.

"*Ma Mère,* I'm not taking Isabelle."

Mère looked perplexed. "Why, you must. You'd never be able to pick out good fabric for a dress on your own."

"A dress?"

Isabelle set down her fork. "Really, Jeanette, I don't need—"

"Nonsense! Aren't you headed to England, dear?"

"I, um…" Isabelle sent him a pleading look.

He wanted to close his eyes and disappear. Of all the things for *Mère* to hone in on, why did it have to be Isabelle's journey to England? If *Mère* said something to the wrong person, they could all be standing before a military tribunal. "She has family in London, *Ma Mère,* but the trip's a bit of a surprise for her aunt. So it's best not to mention anything, if one of the townsfolk asks."

"The poor thing needs a dress. No. Two dresses. That dress by the fire is ruined. Just look at it."

Michel looked at the ragged dress, then at Isabelle. Her dark hair curled gently against her creamy skin. Her delicate hand clutched her fork until her knuckles whitened. Her eyes remained downcast, but their color and shape had long ago engraved themselves in his mind. And her lips were redder than any woman's had a right to be. If only he didn't know how soft they would feel pressed against his. He swallowed and forced himself to focus on her clothes rather than her face.

It didn't take long to see that his mother was right. Heaven knew the woman needed to wear something other than that confounded nightdress of his mother's. He'd tolerated it while she stayed abed, but she was moving about the house too much to ignore the thin white material now.

"And what better time to make up some clothes than while it's raining," *Mère* prattled on.

He nearly sighed. How *Mère* could think of sewing after spending an entire night fighting with burlap eluded him. But Isabelle did need some dresses. And a cloak. Michel rubbed the back of his neck. The cloak she'd worn last night was threadbare and torn more places than he cared to count. And her boots could be replaced, as well.

Heaven save him, he was just as bad as *Mère*.

~.~.~.~.~

"At least the rain has finally slowed." Isabelle sat beside Michel in the wagon, her back straight as a fence post. She didn't look at him but stared at the passing farm, where two dogs stood in the yard barking. Rain had darkened and soaked the thatched roof of the house, but smoke billowed from the chimney, and light shone from around the window coverings and beneath the door.

"*Oui...*" Michel grinned at her stiffly proper voice, so different from her fiery voice when she argued or her determined voice when she spoke of England. His grin faded and a nerve pulsed in his stomach. Mayhap he knew her voices a little too well.

Space. He was staying away from her.

He kept his eyes on the road. Rain had turned the soaked, rolling fields nearly black. Tufts of thick grass, matted down over the winter months, lined the roadside, and no animals, save the farm dogs, ventured into the drizzle. Ahead of them, the Van Robais Royal Manufacturer, which marked the start of town, loomed dark and large, its red stone face glowering at passersby. The textile factory employed nearly half of Abbeville. Fabric from the factory could be purchased in Abbeville at a pittance of the price people paid in Paris and beyond. "What color fabric do you want for your dresses?"

"I need not fabric. Your mother simply couldn't be persuaded otherwise."

Michel eyed her half-dry, mud-caked dress and cloak. "I'll pay for the material." It was the least he could do considering her arm and all.

She inhaled sharply. "Thank you, no."

He nearly rolled his eyes. "How much money do you have?"

"You should know, since you stole it!"

Her angry voice made him want to grin. He poked his tongue in his cheek instead. "Barely enough to get yourself to England, then. I'll buy the fabric."

"You don't think I'll reach England, remember?" The bitter words rained like daggers from her tongue.

If the woman didn't change moods faster than winds in a gale. "Oh, you'll get there. Just not until your arm's healed and you have some plan other than waltzing alone onto a ship full of scoundrels."

"You've no right to prevent me."

"Aye." Michel pulled Sylvie to a stop in front of the mayor's office. "I'll go check the dam and then speak with Narcise. You wait inside."

He walked around the wagon and fitted his hands around her waist to help her down. Her muscles tightened at his touch. He should have been amused, but his own stomach clutched in response.

Confound it all. He should just swing her into his arms and kiss—

Non! Distance. He was keeping his distance. What was wrong with him? She was leaving and he was having nothing to do with her. He lifted her from the wagon and set her in the mud, then led her to the little chamber outside Narcise's office.

"*Bonjour,* citizen." Michel nodded to Samuel, the wiry clerk at the small pine desk.

"*Bonjour.*" Samuel didn't look up as he dipped his pen and scrawled something across the bottom of the paper he studied.

The mayor's door hung open, but the constable stood just inside, with the two men speaking in hushed tones. "Sit here." Michel pointed Isabelle toward a chair, then turned to Samuel. "Is the work finished on the dam?"

Samuel looked up and wiped his cheek, spreading a glob of ink across his cheekbone to match the one on his forehead. "*Oui.* "

"Any water leaking through?" Samuel shrugged.

"I'll go check it and speak with Narcise when I return." The dam probably didn't need checking. The townsfolk had done fine work once he'd gotten things organized and started. But part of him had to see the finished wall.

"Very well, then." The clerk's eyes narrowed at Isabelle, sitting rigidly in the corner. "What am I to do with the urchin?"

Isabelle huffed. "I beg your pardon, sir, but I am not a child."

"Small enough to be one," Samuel muttered.

"Just keep her out of trouble." Michel tried not to smile.

Samuel scowled. "You take her. She's filthy."

"Then have her sweep," Michel called as he headed out the door. He could well imagine the battle that would follow if Samuel attempted that.

He opted to walk rather than take the wagon. The mud sucked at his boots, but he covered the ground with long strides. A few people milled about in the light rain. After being cooped inside for four days, what was a little mud and drizzle? The front door of the bakery was open, the smell of bread and sugar mingling with the scent of rain. A colorful sign marked the entrance to the candlemakers shop, and it looked as though the butcher's storefront was open, as well.

He turned the corner and stopped. Even from a distance, the barrier he'd designed stood massive before him. Pride surged through his blood. If only he could capture the moment, savor the feeling in some way so it could never grow dim or be forgotten. If only he could show *Père*...

Who knew all those years damming the lower field would result in the giant structure before him? A structure the whole town had built. A structure the whole town would benefit from.

His heart almost exploded with fullness as he neared the dam that ran nearly a kilometer. He stood on his toes to see over the wall, then planted his hands atop the wall and heaved himself up for a better look.

Pride drained from him like water from a tipped bowl.

Dirty, rippled water filled his view. He hardly recognized the landscape, could barely tell where the Somme River normally ran with so many landmarks immersed under its swollen waters.

He glanced down at the base of the wall. Only ankle-deep water there. His eyes ran the length of the wall to where the dam tapered off and the ground rose. The dam would hold—for a time. But men could only do so much to fight nature.

Please, Lord, stop the rain.

Shoulders slumped, he sauntered back to the mayor's office, praying for the town. As he approached, a dirty woman with lush black hair flew out the front door. He might be too far away to see her face, but he'd recognize that hair anywhere.

"Isabelle?" he called, but she disappeared around the building.

A wave of fear crested inside him, and he quickened his pace. Maybe he shouldn't have left her with Samuel. If that skinny little clerk had been cruel...

He slammed the door open and strode toward the mayor's office. Narcise stood in the outer chamber, staring absently.

"What happened to Isabelle?" Michel drew an angry breath.

"I, well...I don't rightly know." As though he had the better part of an hour to answer, Narcise, wheezing heavily, hitched a thumb in the waistband of his breeches and tugged them up over his bulging stomach. "When she learned of the prisoners, she went pale as a ghost. Looked ready to swoon."

Prisoners? The breath whooshed out of his lungs. "What prisoners?"

"Then she hurried out of here like a pack of hounds chased her."

Michel fisted his hands. Some days dragging a stubborn mule up a hill was easier than getting information out of Narcise. "What prisoners?"

"Why Alexandre de Bonnet, the Comte de Montpensier, and his family. We caught them this morning, trying to ford the river in a raft, if you believe it." Narcise waddled over to a chair barely wide enough to hold his girth and eased himself down as though standing a moment longer would suck all energy from him. "We found the *comte* just after you took your mother home this morning, my boy. Nearly called you back for it."

Michel's heart thudded against his rib cage. "The former *comte*."

"What did you say, boy?"

"De Bonnet's not a *comte* anymore..." And now he was championing the aristocracy to the mayor? Had Isabelle changed his opinion of gentry that much?

Narcise furrowed his brow. "What has the *comte's* status to do with anything?"

He needed to get out of here and find Isabelle. Michel took three backward steps toward the door. "Nothing. Where are they?"

Narcise frowned. "Who? Isabelle? I told you—"

"The prisoners!" Michel ground his teeth together to keep from screaming.

"Oh, yes, well, we caught them over by—"

Michel strode over to Narcise, but stopped himself from leaning into the mayor's face. "I care not where you caught them. Where are they now?"

Narcise pulled a handkerchief from his pocket and mopped his brow. "Well, good heavens, boy."

A tic worked in his jaw. He drew in a breath and stepped back.

"They'll not be here long. I'm sending word to Paris. A family that prominent will go to the capital for trial."

"Where...are...you...holding...them?" Michel spoke the words so slowly and clearly he nearly choked on them.

"Oh, well, the constable has them in the jail." Narcise's brow wrinkled. "Where else?"

Michel turned and ran.

Narcise's voice trailed him out the door and into the rain. "You don't think Isabelle went..."

The jail. Of course. He should have headed there straightway. Mud sloshed his boots and trousers as he sprinted through the streets and glanced around buildings for Isabelle. Had she known the Comte de Montpensier and his family? And what did Isabelle plan to do when she reached the jail? The question made his heart beat erratically.

Taking a shortcut, he flew through an alley toward the old stone jail. Emerging onto the jail's street between two shops, he spotted Isabelle not ten meters ahead. Heedless of the light rain, she rushed away from him and toward the stone structure.

Trying to appear calm, Michel stepped around a mother with two small children. Coming up behind Isabelle, he took her by both shoulders and turned her toward him. "What are you doing? Didn't I tell you to stay with the mayor?" He whispered the words, then stopped as he noticed her wild eyes and uneven breathing.

She pulled back.

He tightened his grip.

"I have to go! I have to see them. The soldiers have them!"

At her frantic words, Michel could almost feel silence descend over the street. How daft of him. The townsfolk were already far too interested in Isabelle, and here he confronted her in the middle of town. He glanced around, and as he suspected, all eyes were riveted to them—including Bertrand's. His nosy neighbor stood in the doorway of the butcher's shop. Michel couldn't afford to rouse suspicions, least of all Bertrand's.

He steered Isabelle around the side of the butcher's shop. "Where are you taking me? I have to go!" She nearly shrieked the words.

"Quiet." He shook her shoulders harder than intended. "Take a breath."

She clawed at his hands. "Take a breath? Take a breath! I don't want a breath. I want—"

"Isabelle!" The panic in her voice made him want to gather her close and hold her. Instead, he clenched his jaw and dragged her to the alley behind the building. Pushing her back against the wall, he clamped a hand over her mouth. Her eyes went wide and half-crazed with fear. He placed his forearm across her shoulders, pinning her to the building. Her feet kicked, and her hands scratched, first at the stone behind her, then at his arm.

Michel fastened his eyes to hers and struggled to calm his own breathing. "Settle down, Isabelle. Listen to me."

She shook her head, her distraught hands still searching for a means of escape.

"You're going to hurt your arm."

Her eyes darkened and a low grunt escaped her mouth. Then her foot connected with his shin, and a spark of pain flew up his leg.

He pressed her harder against the wall. "Stop fighting me. I'm stronger than you, and you'll only hurt yourself."

Her hands slowed, and her struggling weakened. "Good, that's it. Just calm down. I won't bring you any harm. I promise. Nod your head if you believe me." She nodded. But he kept her mouth covered.

"All right. Now take a breath." She obeyed.

"We're in the middle of town. You can't make a scene." He glanced around the deserted alley, half thankful for the heavy rains and flood that kept so many indoors. "If I take my hand away, can you tell me why you left the mayor's office?"

She swallowed and nodded again. Still holding her against the wall, he slowly moved his hand. Red splotches lay stark against her creamy skin from the cruel pressure of his fingers. He inwardly winced, but he'd had no choice.

"The de Bonnets. They shouldn't be here. They were to escape to Austria years ago. What are they doing in Picardy? And now the soldiers have Meryl...and Angelique. Dear me! And they probably have Noel and Dominique and Jules. And—"

"This is Abbeville, Isabelle. There are no soldiers yet. Just the constable and townsfolk." And he'd have been one of the townsfolk that captured her friends, had he not left the church early. His stomach churned. "How do you know them?" He was almost afraid to hear her answer.

Her eyes filled with unshed tears. "Oh, goodness! I used to play with Meryl when they came to Versailles. We were the same age. And Jules, he's not more than a babe. How could they take a babe?"

"The babe would be five or six now," he said gently. She looked at him through sad, haunted eyes and clutched his arm until her nails dug through his shirt to his skin.

He swallowed the thickness in his throat. "You have to let me go. I must save them."

"No, Isabelle." The words felt like crushed gravel as they moved over his tongue. "I can't let you do that."

"But I have to!" She tried to shove his arm away. He only leaned more weight against her.

"Don't you understand? I let the soldiers take Marie."

The name caught on a sob and tears slid down her face. "I can't let them take Meryl. I won't!"

She flailed hysterically against his hold.

Tearing his chest open and laying his heart on the ground couldn't be more painful than manhandling her as she struggled. His heart broke for her as she wept, but he had to prevent her from helping her friends.

"You can't save them. You'll only expose yourself."

"It matters not. I have to try."

"*Non.*"

"I won't do it anymore! I can't. What's the point in hiding any longer?" She stopped writhing and slumped forward as weeping overcame her. "I'll never reach England, anyway."

The blood froze in his veins. She couldn't give up. "Isabelle, look at me. Look at me." He cupped her face and raised it, but tears blinded her eyes. "You'll not stop now, you've come too far. You're too strong a girl. Anyone who can hide from soldiers and travel from…from…wherever you came from on her own can surely journey twenty kilometers to the sea. Now stop your foolishness."

"From Arras," she said bleakly. "I came from Arras. But you don't know what happened there."

"Then tell me, but I'll not have you march over to those prisoners and give yourself away." The idea of her being caught made his throat ache.

"Everything's my fault," she went on, apparently oblivious to his own anguish. "I'll not hide anymore. How can I go on living when I killed my sister? I should be the one dead, not she. Oh, Marie! What have I done?"

Marie. The name she'd sobbed over and over in her delirium after he brought her home from the woods.

"You…killed your sister…?" And what had a sister to do with anything? Weren't they talking about the *comte* and England?

"Michel?"

At the sound of the familiar voice, Michel looked over. "Ninette."

The butcher's wife, younger than Michel, stood in the door that opened to the alley. He swallowed and glanced at Isabelle. Sobbing "Marie" over and over, she likely couldn't stand without his arm bracing her against the wall.

He'd wanted her to break. To vent whatever went on inside that head of hers. But not in the middle of the town. Not in a way that made his throat dry and his heart ache. Not in a way that drew undue attention.

"Is everything all right?" Ninette's shrewd eyes roamed Isabelle, still pinned against the wall despite her wailing.

"Ah, well... You've met Isabelle? Corinne's cousin from Paris?" Ninettenodded. "She helped sew sandbags last night. A good sewer, that one is."

"*Oui*. Well, Isabelle just, uh, received some disheartening news...from Paris. It seems her, ah, fiancé...yes, her fiancé left her for another woman." Michel clamped his jaw. A fiancé leaving her? Surely his tongue was as addled as his heart. A man would be daft to walk away from the likes of Isabelle.

Isabelle fisted her hands in the front of his shirt and buried her head against his shoulder.

"Come, now, Isabelle. Everything will turn out." He pulled her against him, absently stroking her hair, and watched Ninette over Isabelle's head.

Ninette folded her arms over her chest. "That's odd. I haven't seen the mail coach yet today. In fact, I haven't seen the mail coach at all since the rain started. And it passes right by the shop."

Heat flooded the back of his neck. He glanced at the sky. How many more lies would protecting Isabelle take? At what point did he stop lying and tell the truth? He sighed. The tangle of deceit he and Isabelle wove grew so thick, someone would surely discern the truth before long.

"Ah, I'd gotten the letter for Isabelle several days ago, stuck it in my pocket and just remembered it here in town." He tasted bile in his throat.

"Uh-huh." leaned her ample figure against the door frame and watched Isabelle sob. Would the woman ever leave?

"Um, Ninette… Isabelle'll be fairly embarrassed once all this settles, what with breaking down in the middle of town. Perhaps you could give us a bit of time. Then I'll get Isabelle home and out of your way."

The woman gave Isabelle one hard look, then turned for the door. "Just keep her back here. Don't want her scaring folks off. Business all but died off with the rain."

"Merci," Michel called as the door closed. "All right, now." He spoke soothingly into Isabelle's hair, traced her ear with a fingertip. "Let's get you home, and you can tell me about Marie."

He tried to lead her away from the wall, but she only dug her feet into the mud and cried harder. He could pick her up and carry her wailing through town to the wagon—and a hundred more people like Ninette would see them.

"I led the soldiers to her," she blurted.

"What?"

"Marie." She sobbed harder.

He sighed. "Calm yourself, love. Calm yourself and tell me."

She fought for control the way a battle-weary soldier fights for his life. Her muscles tensed and her breathing slowed. Her slender body shook with the effort. Finally, she tilted her face to look at him.

"Marie, she had warned me not to let Léon get too close." Her voice croaked the words. "Not to let him follow me, lest he learn who we were."

"Who's Léon?"

"A shop boy. Just a shop boy, but he fancied me. I didn't return his affection, I just…" She lifted her shoulders, let them fall wearily. "I liked the attention. Does that make me terrible, for liking a man's attention?"

"I…" The sorrow in her eyes made his chest ache. "Probably just normal."

She sniffled. "One day, I went for a walk, and when I returned, soldiers were everywhere, in the house, swarming the yard. They had Marie...with Léon."

Her lips trembled and her eyes watered. She'd shatter again in another moment.

He clutched her upper arms. "The man betrayed you. He led the soldiers to you." He spoke the words as flatly and devoid of emotion as he could manage.

"I never told him who we were, never allowed him to walk me home. But he must have followed me and figured everything out." Her eyes pleaded with him.

He rested a hand on her cheek. "I believe you."

"They forced Marie to lie facedown in the dirt." Silent tears slid down her cheeks. "I should have run to her, fought the soldiers, saved her, something. And I didn't. I couldn't move. I, who had been so brave, who had told Marie we'd not be caught, who had made maps and laid plans of escape if we were ever discovered. And I just...hid in the bushes. I couldn't scream, I couldn't cry, I couldn't move. I watched them lead her away and set guards for when I returned to the house. But I never returned. The money was hidden in the woods. At least Marie had thought of that."

"I'm grateful God protected you and you were able to escape."

She shook her head. "Marie should have been the one to escape. Instead, the soldiers took her to the guillotine in Paris."

Paris? Michel stilled. Isabelle had sworn she wasn't royalty. But Marie could have only been a step or two away from royalty to be taken all the way to Paris for execution.

"I almost showed myself to the soldiers, just so I could die with her." Her voice lost its passion, resonating bleakness instead.

Michel shook his head and tucked a strand of hair behind her ear. "That only would have let them win."

"Marie had made me promise. If either of us was killed, the other would go to England. I didn't have to go back to the house for the money or the clothes we'd hidden in the woods. So I ran."

"You're brave and strong. I've never met another woman as strong as you."

She shoved away from him violently and balled her hands. "Don't you understand? I'm the one who deserved to die, not her. You call me brave, when I am a coward, for only a coward could watch her sister be led away to the guillotine while she hid in the bushes!

"And now…" Her voice caught. "Now I must find a husband in England. How can I marry? How can I find a husband? How can anyone love me after what I did to Marie?"

Her words ripped into his heart. Her eyes, hot from anger and soft from tears, had him reaching for her. Here he'd resigned himself not to love this woman, when she needed love more than anything else.

God's love—and his.

Chapter Thirteen

Isabelle's eyes shifted from the page of the open Bible she was attempting to understand to the door as Michel stepped inside. He wore the same tan trousers and undyed shirt she'd seen him in hundreds of times, yet heat crept into her cheeks.

The rocking chair near the fire creaked, and Jeanette looked up from her mending. "Good evening, Michel." It was closer to midday than evening, but Isabelle didn't comment. Michel walked to the table and brushed a hand absently across her shoulders. The familiar touch sent warmth spiraling through her body. He'd been doing small things like that for the past five days. Slight touches, little looks, attentive comments.

And each simple gesture left her yearning for another touch or one more look.

"How's your arm?"

She glanced at her painful limb resting atop the table. She'd been a most obedient patient, yet her arm still ached. Granted, it didn't scream at her anymore, but she nearly slumped her shoulders. How much longer would it take for her arm to mend? "It's...healing, I suppose. Slowly."

Keeping a hand on her shoulder, Michel leaned forward and placed his other hand on the table. The heat from his body, so close but not touching, radiated through her clothing.

"Ah, 1 Corinthians 6." He began massaging her upper back with deep, soothing strokes. "'Neither fornicators, nor idolaters, nor adulterers, nor effeminate, nor abusers of themselves with mankind, nor thieves, nor covetous, nor drunkards, nor revilers, nor extortioners, shall inherit the kingdom of God. And such were some of you: but ye are washed, but ye are sanctified, but ye are justified in the name of the Lord Jesus, and by the Spirit of our God.'"

Isabelle swallowed. He read the very verses she'd been studying. How had he known? She'd started in Matthew and had done little but read the Bible since she broke down crying in the middle of town five days ago. If only she could understand God's love and forgiveness. What did God mean by washed? Sanctified? Justified? She'd prayed a prayer of forgiveness when she was younger. But how could she be any of these things when her actions had killed Marie? God forgave sin, but she couldn't ask God to forgive her when forgiveness wouldn't bring Marie back, could she?

"Did you finish damming up the lower field?" Jeanette asked.

Michel kept his body close but turned his head toward his mother. "The lower field's a loss this year, *Ma Mère*, with all the flooding we got. I was in town, not working the fields. A few buildings had some flooding, but besides that, the town's well. The water's receding, so the worst of it's over."

"You went to town?" Isabelle's mouth went painfully dry. "You didn't tell me."

"No, I—"

"Have soldiers taken the de Bonnets to Paris?" The words burst out, burning her mouth before she could block them.

Michel's circular motions on her shoulder stopped. "Isabelle, don't pain yourself this way. The affair with the de Bonnets matters not."

She pushed her chair back and sprang up. "It matters! You know it does."

Jeanette looked up from her sewing. "What matters, dear?"

Why hadn't she kept her voice down? Her eyes pinned to Michel's, she bit the side of her lip until she tasted blood.

"Isabelle's concerned about a *comte* and his family taken prisoner last week, *Ma Mère*."

Jeanette shook her head. "Oh, now, no need to fret about prisoners. The constable'll keep them locked up tight."

"Yes, locked up tight," she whispered as tears pricked the backs of her eyes.

"Soldiers arrived two days ago and took them to Paris for trial." Michel spoke to her in a low voice. "The *soldats* would have been here sooner, were it not for the flood."

The blow from his quietly spoken words nearly threw her to the floor. She took two steps backward. Shards of hot glass caught in her throat, and her lungs wouldn't draw air. She pressed her eyes shut. She'd known Meryl and her family would be taken to Paris. Had cried herself to sleep because of it. So why did confirmation of the situation hurt so much?

"The de Bonnets will be guillotined. Every one of them," she croaked through the jagged edges lining her throat. "Court jesters would make more honest judges than those on the military tribunal in Paris."

"God is with your friends. He'll give them strength. He won't forsake them in their time of need." Michel moved toward her, reached for her.

She backed away and fisted her hands in her skirt. "No. If you'll just…" Why did his kind words and gesture make her want to cry? "Excuse me."

She whirled and fled into the bedchamber, slamming the door

behind her and curling into a ball atop her tick. The door opened before she could even loose a sob. "Leave me alone. I don't want you, or God, or anyone."

She clutched a pillow to her chest and rolled to face the wall.

Michel's footsteps thudded closer to the bed, but he didn't sit or stroke her hair or offer comfort. His presence filled the room as she struggled to hold her weeping. She'd said to leave! Why wouldn't he let her alone so she could cry? And if he had to be here, why didn't he say something? Then she could yell back and vent the pain eating her heart.

Silence descended like death over the room. She pressed her eyes shut and gulped air, ignoring the way it singed her throat and lungs. "God allowed the mob to kill my parents and little brother." The words wrenched from her heart. "He let the soldiers take Marie. And now Meryl and her family."

"He loves you, Isabelle."

"I said I don't want anything to do with Him!"

"Then why are you reading the Bible every chance you get?"

She tucked the pillow beneath her chin. "To understand Him."

"Understand this, He spared you. He wants you."

"He shouldn't. Not after what I've done." A shudder racked her body. Her chest heaved. But she held the impending flood.

The tick shifted as Michel sat and ran his fingers through her hair, a gentle, patient touch.

"What you did with Marie and Léon was make a mistake. A poor judgment."

"A poor judgment that cost my sister's life. Don't you see?" She rolled to face him, her eyes half-blind by tears. "I should be the one going to Paris, not Meryl."

"Dear Isabelle." He laid a hand on her cheek and brushed away the moisture. "You didn't cause Marie's death, and you couldn't have stopped it. Just as you didn't cause Meryl's capture, nor can you stop her trial and death. You can blame God, but blaming Him will only bring you pain and bitterness. The soldiers killed Marie, and the mob killed your parents. Not you. Not God."

"But God could have stopped them."

"Aye. And that's a fine problem there. But God created men to make choices for themselves. That goes back to Adam and Eve and the Fall."

"But my parents, my brother, Marie, they did nothing wrong. They didn't deserve to die. It's all because of this wretched *Révolution*. God could have stopped that, too." The words spilled out in a torrent that she'd no desire to block.

He sighed. "Your parents were aristocrats, were they not? For how many years has your family been unfairly taxing families like mine? You say they did nothing wrong, but years of abusing the lower class comes at a price. Most Frenchmen need no other reason to kill them."

Isabelle sucked in a breath. "Y-you think…my parents deserved to die? My brother…Marie?"

He touched her chin. "No, I wouldn't say such a thing. But that's how most of France thinks. The *Révolution,* the deaths of your kin and myriad others are a result of sin, Isabelle, not God. First, the sin of the *Ancien Régime* that exploited the poor while the wealthy grew richer. Second, the sin of the men who believe death the only solution for the *Révolution.*

"Neither side is right. Neither side honors God. But the curse of sin affects all creation. Death is the penalty of sin. Until God makes all things new, the curse will keep taking lives."

Isabelle swallowed. "I wish it had been my life taken and not Marie's."

"I see that. But God wills for you to stay alive. Otherwise, the soldiers would have come while you were home with Marie. Or the band of men would have killed you in the woods…or God wouldn't have led me to you."

"You gave me life, when I deserved death." She whispered the words, almost afraid to voice them aloud.

Michel grasped her hand. "I gave you a chance. God gave you life. And we all deserve death for our sins—but Christ's sacrifice offers us forgiveness."

He made it seem so right, so logical for her to be alive while Marie and the rest of her family was dead. "But you've never killed someone."

"Neither have you. You made an error, one with horrifying consequences, *oui*. But one for which God will forgive you."

"What about Marie?" Isabelle used her good arm to push herself up to a sitting position. "Would she forgive me?"

"Would your sister want you to spend the rest of your life bitter and depressed? If she loved you—and it sounds like she did—then she would have forgiven you. *Love* is the same principle that motivates God to forgive us." Michel tucked a strand of hair behind her ear. "And God's waiting to forgive you. All you need do is ask."

An unbearable pressure built in her chest. She blinked fresh tears from her eyes. "It's been so long. I haven't prayed, not really, since my parents…"

She swallowed and peered into Michel's eyes, but he offered no words, simply waited for her to finish. "C-can we pray? I want forgiveness."

~.~.~.~.~

Michel sat in *Mère's* rocker and stretched his aching back. His muscles tightened in complaint. One week of plowing and planting, and he was decrepit as an old man. Unfortunately, he still had two fields left to work. Settling back into the seat, he let his eyes wander over the room. *Mère* by the hearth washing dishes. The door his father had built, the cloak rack Michel made beside it. The table and chairs they had toiled over together.

And Isabelle.

He couldn't keep his gaze away. She moved gracefully around the little kitchen, her dark hair spilling down her neck As though sensing his perusal, she turned and smiled. Her eyes shimmered with softness and happiness, so different from the haunted look they'd carried when he first brought her home. Ever since she'd sought forgiveness, she'd been like a new person. He smiled back and exhaled deeply.

The clank of dishes in the wooden washtub sounded from where *Mère* bent over the tub. Isabelle's soft footsteps patted the earth as she cleared and wiped the table. A feeling of contentment swept over him. He could happily settle his aching body in this rocker every day if surrounded by the two women he loved…

The familiar scent of soap and wildflowers roused him.

"You're tired."

Michel opened his eyes. The table was clean and *Mère* had nearly finished the dishes.

"Did you want to skip studying tonight?" Isabelle moved to the arm of the rocker.

Skip spending time with her? Had she gone daft? "*Non.* I'm a little sore, is all." He eased his body out of the chair and headed toward the family Bible sitting on the mantel.

"A long day plowing?"

She knew what he'd been doing out in the field? Since when did she pay attention to his farmwork? "I've never heard of a short day plowing."

She smiled and bit the side of her lip. Unable to resist touching her, he ran a hand down the side of her arm. Her cheeks turned a delightful shade of red.

He brushed the heated skin with his knuckles. She averted her eyes and flushed even more. Interesting. "I thought mayhap we'd study outside. The evening's a bit cool, but it's nothing our cloaks won't ward off."

Isabelle swallowed noisily and looked away. "I have something to…that is…I thought perchance…well, come in here first."

Her hand trembled slightly as she pulled him toward the bedchamber. She stopped inside the door and released his sleeve. Her throat worked back and forth, and her eyes looked as though they would fill with tears.

He frowned. "Did I do something to upset you?"

She chewed on the side of her thumb and stared at him with tortured eyes "No, I just…" She headed toward her bed, then bent and retrieved something from beneath it.

He stepped closer, bumping her as she stood. "Here." She shoved a small wooden tray into his hands.

Swirls of white and pink and tiny flowers lay before him. Corinne's pitcher and basin. Isabelle had expertly glued dozens of small porcelain pieces to the top of the tray. A lump rose in his throat, and he ran his rough finger over the glossy surface.

He'd been nothing but angry when she broke it. Had gone storming to Father Albert and tried to offload her. And she'd been home, picking up the broken pieces, trying to make things right.

"I—I hope you're not mad. I made it last week but couldn't bring myself to give it to you."

Mad? How could he be?

She wrapped her arms around her waist. "I know you told me to stay abed but—"

"It's beautiful. Thank you." Love for the woman before him speared his heart and spread through his body until his blood ached with it. He set the tray on her bed, freeing his fingers to touch her, to run over the features of her face and lose themselves in her hair. He reached out, but she looked up at him with such uncertainty he let his hand drop.

She wasn't ready for his overtures yet. She still needed to heal.

And she still intended to leave him for England.

Chapter Fourteen

He'd tell her he loved her tonight. He had to. He could hardly wait another moment, let alone another day or week. Saying the words couldn't be that hard. He'd said them hundreds of times before—to *Mère*.

Never to another woman.

Walking behind his ox, Michel pressed the plow blade deeper into the earth. Beneath his feet, the plow cleaved into the soil, turning up dirt that had lain dormant through the winter. His calloused hands stung from gripping the handles of the plow off and on for more than a week. The blister on his left hand had reopened, and blood seeped through the cloth wrapped around it. But he had two fields already plowed and planted. Two more hours, maybe three, and he'd be done with the spring plowing.

Michel tightened his hold, his fingers gripping the wooden handles. What if Isabelle didn't love him? Would he look like a fool to throw his heart at the woman's feet? He was being addlepated. She had to love him. He read it in the way she watched him when they studied together. The way she rushed to serve him supper or offer him a second serving of soup before she took one herself. The way she got tongue-tied when he asked a question, and the manner in which her cheeks flushed when he brushed a tendril of hair from her face or planted a kiss on her forehead.

But loving him back didn't mean she would say it. The woman was a stubborn mule—a lovely one, but a mule nonetheless.

Michel ripped his hat from his head and threw it into the dirt. He needed to tell her how he felt. He'd kept it bottled inside since the flood three weeks now. He'd have spilled everything the night she'd given him the tray, but she had looked so frightened. So uncertain. How much more torture could he put himself through?

A figure carrying a basket emerged over the little rise of earth at the top of the field. His tension drained at the sight of her. He grinned, having no desire to hide his enthusiasm as Isabelle drew closer. Her new red skirt swayed in rhythm with her hips, and the breeze caught her tangle of hair. Had it been seven weeks since he found her in the woods? His Sleeping Beauty. With hair so rich he lost himself in it and skin so soft it felt like silk.

With a snort, the ox reached the edge of the field near the woods. Instead of turning the beast to begin a new furrow, Michel pulled back on the plow and halted him. "Whoa, there."

Isabelle's brown eyes danced in the spring sunlight as she neared.

"And what brings a lovely lady like you to the field today?"

"I thought to catch you for the midday meal so we could eat out here."

"Ah. Any excuse to get yourself out of doors." He ran his eyes down her.

She poked her tongue between her full lips and then smiled shyly. "Well, that, too, but if you don't wish to join me, keep plowing. I'll sit here and watch while I eat the strawberries I brought."

Strawberries. He nearly drooled. "Is *Ma Mère's* strawberry patch yielding already?"

With a toss of her hair, she turned her back to him and walked away, calling over her shoulder, "You'll have to join me to see." She strolled to the ancient oak trees lining the field and bent to unfold a blanket.

He scrubbed his hand over his face. Did she think he'd rather plow than share a meal with her? He walked toward her while she sat and pulled food out of the basket.

"You chose to eat, I see."

"*Oui,* I'll eat with you, but you must do something first." He reached for her hand and tugged her up, drawing her so close their bodies nearly touched.

"A picnic isn't enough? What else...?" He brushed his lips over hers.

"Oh..." She sighed, her muscles going lax under his hands, and rested her cheek against his chest. "That was pleasant."

"Pleasant?" After hardly touching her for three weeks, it was wonderful.

He slid his hands across her slender waist, and took her lips again. Softly, slowly, while sunlight flittered through the leaves overhead and the ox lowed. He left her lips and trailed kisses up her jaw, whispering of promises and dreams and tender love, the kind of love that could last a lifetime. He went back and rubbed his lips over hers until her inhibitions faded and her body melted against him, until her heart lay open, nothing held back, nothing hidden.

Finally, he stepped away.

Color flamed her cheeks, and she stared at the ground. "I, uh..."

He smiled and tilted her chin up. Her eyes, glazed pools of soft brown, stared back at him.

"I love you, Isabelle." The words slipped from his mouth.

Her breath caught, and she went so still he wondered if her heart stopped beating. "But I'm... You're..." She tried halfheartedly to pull away.

He tightened his grip. "Don't tell me I can't love you. I already do. I have for the better part of a month, since you hurt your arm helping with the flood."

"A month?" She shook her head, her eyes rounding and her brow wrinkling in a look of confusion. "No, Michel, we can't—"

"Don't." But it was too late. Something shattered inside him at her protest. He let her go. He hadn't expected her to blurt "I love you, too," but the idea of him loving her didn't need to mortify her. He stalked toward a tree. He'd known this could happen, that she might not want his love. Might not want *him*. Turning, he watched her.

She stood staring at the ground, her arms wrapped about herself in a lonely hug. Even with her face down, he saw the traces of worry in the lines on her face and the way she chewed her bottom lip.

He sighed. Mayhap she wasn't mortified, but worried. A peasant and an aristocrat? He blew out a breath and rubbed the back of his neck. He was probably daft for thinking they could have a life together.

~.~.~.~.~

I love you. The words flashed in Isabelle's mind as she stared at the ground, digging the toe of her shoe into the earth.

He couldn't love her. Didn't he know that? Every day she lingered in Abbeville the danger of being discovered increased. She glanced into the woods. Somewhere out there, men lurked. Maybe not the same men who tried to kill her, but others like them. All of France crawled with men who would guillotine her and feel no remorse for dragging Michel and Jeanette beneath the triangular blade, as well.

She absently rubbed her bandaged arm. It grew stronger with each passing day. How much longer until she would be well enough to leave for England? Two weeks? Three?

She wished not to think of it. She didn't want to go.

Michel offered safety here on his farm, in his arms. But the safety wouldn't last forever. It couldn't.

She shifted her eyes to him, arms crossed, standing by a tree. So strong. So confident. So handsome. And he loved *her*. She didn't deserve his love, not for a second. Just like she didn't deserve God's love. But God loved her, anyway. Forgave her, despite what she'd done to Marie.

Isabelle sank to the ground and buried her face in her hands. Her heart beat wildly inside her chest, calling her the name she deserved. *Trai-tor, trai-tor, trai-tor, traitor.* She loved the man.

What a disaster. She didn't know when she'd fallen in love. Probably during one of those quiet moments when he studied with her and answered her endless questions. Perhaps she hadn't so much fallen in love as grown into it.

But if she surrendered to her feelings, if she let them push her to stay in France, she'd continue to put Michel and Jeanette at risk.

Michel pushed off the tree trunk and walked toward her. She swallowed and raised her chin. He already risked too much by loving her. She could see herself so happy with him, a year from now, a decade, a lifetime. If only she'd been born a peasant. If only there weren't soldiers even now searching for the missing daughter of the Duc de La Rouchecauld.

"I'm sorry for storming off." He squatted down, so close the heat emanating from his body warmed her skin.

She traced her finger idly over the design on the quilt and shook her head. *"Non, je suis désolée."* And she was—so very, very sorry. "You wanted me to say the words back, and I…couldn't say them. Anyone would get mad."

"You didn't need to act so mortified by the idea of me loving you."

Mortified? He was kind and sweet and gentle. How could she be mortified by his love?

"I know you're frightened, *mon amour,* but I want you to be honest with me." He cupped the side of her face. "If you're scared, tell me. Don't hide. If you're ready to say 'I love you' back to me, don't hold off."

"Oh, Michel." All the reasons she had for holding back dissolved inside her. He trapped her in a web of love and care, and she didn't know how to escape. Wasn't sure she wanted to. "What if I'm never ready?"

He slid his hand down to her shoulder and rested his thumb in the delicate spot at the base of her neck. Her heart raced in quick, shallow beats. "You'll be ready. You just need time."

He was too close. With a few words and a touch, he shattered every defense she'd erected. "Michel, stop." Air backed up in her chest. She started to push away, but Michel ran his other hand up her back and fisted it in her hair.

"Stay."

"What?" she asked, half-dazed by his touch.

"In Abbeville. Stay with me."

The air that blocked her chest whooshed from her lungs. A flame of panic started at the base of her spine and licked its way upward.

"Michel, I… You could be killed. I could be killed. The Terror—"

"May never come. It was supposed to be here weeks ago. Everyone in town thinks you're Corinne's cousin, and the townsfolk are now more interested in the butcher's nephew moving here from Nevers than in you."

She tugged her hand away and clutched the fabric of the quilt. How to answer him? With a lie? The truth? "Some days," she whispered, "most days…I want to stay."

"Then do." He took her hand and tangled their fingers together.

"Oh, Michel." He didn't understand the danger she brought him. He couldn't, or he'd never have asked her to stay. And he still didn't know about her family. Her father. She looked into his eyes, so full of love. Would that love be there once he learned who she was?

"There's something I should tell you—"

"Shhh." He pressed a finger to her lips. "Just say yes."

"Yes?"

"About staying."

"But that's what I'm trying to talk about." She looked away, her eyes focusing on the field, the ox, a tree, on anything besides the hopefulness in his eyes.

Her distraction did little good. He waited, rubbing her back and toying with the ends of her hair. "We can talk about you staying all you want. Right after you say yes."

"But you don't understand. I can't stay."

"You can stay tomorrow. Promise me that. We'll take things one day at a time."

"I wasn't going to leave tomorrow."

"Then it will be an easy promise to make."

It should be easy. It meant she gave up nothing. So why did she have such trouble forming the word? She closed her eyes again.

Warm lips touched her forehead, then her temple. "Yes," he whispered, his breath tingling her ear.

"Yes."

"For a week. Stay another week."

A tear slipped down her cheek. She wanted this life so much, this man so much. "Yes."

If only she could hold on to him forever.

⌐.⌐.⌐.⌐.⌐

From the edge of the forest, Isabelle paused and studied Michel's homestead. The well-tended house, stable and workshop sat charmingly amid the provincial landscape.

This home, *his* home, could be hers.

She had watched Michel finish plowing that afternoon. All muscle and grit and sweat. She shouldn't have stayed in the field so long. She'd a hundred things to do back at the house. But foolish as it was, she hadn't wanted to leave his presence.

Now the sky held dark clouds, and the breeze kicked into a wind that brutalized her hair and stung her cheeks. But the weather didn't dull the quaintness of the homestead. To the contrary—the house looked even brighter and more welcoming, a shelter against the rest of the world. If only she could believe that was true, that the house would protect its inhabitants from all harm.

Tears swelled in her throat. Why had God brought her here, to a place and man she had fallen in love with?

She lifted her chin and walked toward the house. If she gave in to the slightest tear, she'd likely end up on the ground weeping for all she could never have.

Did going to England even matter anymore? What if Michel was right and she could stay here without being discovered?

A wild gust of wind pushed her sideways, and something in the woods shifted. She peered into the forest, a chill traveling across her shoulders. What had moved? A tree branch? An animal? A person? She'd seen *something*.

Her palms grew sweaty, and panic clawed at her chest.

Suddenly it was night, and she stood in the little clearing, surrounded by trees. Men laughed at her, but she didn't look at them. She stared at the large man before her, saw the cruel look in his eyes. *Kill her, boys.* "No." She shook her head and drew back, the word little more than a gasp. "Don't. Don't touch me. Let me go. Stop!"

They didn't listen. A blow to her stomach. A kick in the back of her knee. She closed her eyes as tears streamed down her face. And she went down, curled on the ground, and braced for the life-taking beating.

~.~.~.~.~

Michel had just stabled the ox when he heard the scream. His heart galloping, he raced out of the stable, following screams and whimpers over the field and to the edge of the woods. Relief swept through him when he saw her curled on the ground. Alone.

"Isabelle? Isabelle? What's happened? What's wrong?"

He fell to his knees and streaked his hands over her. Searching for where she might be injured and finding nothing, he pressed his palm against her cheek. "Isabelle? Are you all right? Look at me. Talk to me."

She slowly opened her eyes, her face pale. She sucked air like a drowning man taking his final breath and looked around.

"Are you hurt?"

She drew her eyes back to him and shook her head. "No, no. I just…" She shuddered, and a sob overtook her.

He gathered her close and cradled her against his chest. Still she trembled. "I was taking the ox and plow back to the stable when I heard you scream."

"I—it was just a mistake. That's all. I saw something move in the woods, and then I thought…I know it's foolish, but it was like men were there. All over again. They were laughing and kicking and—"

"Shhh." He pressed a finger over her mouth. How many recollections did she have to endure? Wasn't surviving the beating enough? Did the soldiers need to haunt her, as well?

"Say no more. I'm here. Everything shall be well."

She stilled, her body going rigid. "I hope he dies."

Something inside his heart turned cold at the dark look in her eyes. "Who?"

She swallowed. "The leader. The man who ordered me dead."

"You mustn't say such things. You have to forgive him. Just as God forgave you." Guilt struck him as the words fell from his mouth. Hadn't he been slow to forgive Isabelle for the way her class had oppressed him? Didn't he even now harbor bitterness toward the *seigneur* who had taken so much of his profits in "tax"? Seeing that bitterness grip the woman he loved revealed the danger of harboring such feelings. *Father, forgive my bitterness.*

"Forgive him? Never. Do you know what he did? Would have done?" She didn't even look at him, just stared off toward the woods. "I was defenseless, alone. He didn't have proof I was an aristocrat. And he ordered his men to beat me. What kind of man does that?"

"The kind that needs forgiveness." His throat ached, but didn't she understand holding such bitterness inside would destroy her, much as her guilt over Marie nearly had? "God forgave you for your role in Marie's death." Just as God would forgive the aristocrats for their oppression of peasants. "Now you must return that forgiveness."

"It's different." She sat up and pushed away from him, still looking at some distant object rather than him. "No one *deserves* forgiveness." She met Michel's eyes. "Not even God Himself would forgive this man. He looked into my eyes. My eyes! And ordered my life taken without flinching."

How was he to argue with the soldier's cruelty? How was he to make her understand the forgiveness was for her sake more than the soldier's? He said simply, "'Father, forgive them, for they know not what they do.'"

"I can't," she whispered, fresh tears pricking her eyes. "I simply can't. Mayhap one day, but not yet."

Michel reached out and squeezed her hand. "Then I'll pray God changes your heart."

~.~.~.~.~

By the time they reached the house, Jeanette had dinner ready. They'd no sooner sat down and said grace when Michel cleared his throat. "*Ma Mère,* Isabelle might stay with us awhile longer, rather than leaving as soon as her arm's healed."

"Leave?" Jeanette looked up from her plate. "Why would she leave?"

Isabelle curved her lips and reached for Jeanette's hand. "I doubt Michel will let me leave when it's time. He'll probably keep me in a splint until I'm ninety, saying all the while my arm isn't healed."

Michel sent her a cocky grin and leaned back in his chair. "Yes, well, you've no need to return to Paris, since your fiancé left you."

"Oh, and a fine story that was! Now the entire town thinks I've been jilted."

Michel smiled, slow and warm, and his foot brushed hers beneath the table. "That's all right. I'll keep you, anyway."

Heat rushed to her cheeks, and she averted her gaze. Isabelle floated through supper and took twice the normal time to finish her chores. Outside, rain pounded, and wind whipped against the house. Lightning cracked and thunder rumbled—the sounds combining in a terrifying symphony.

Her heart beat cozily in her chest when she sat by the fire and read aloud the tale of "Little Red Riding Hood." Even on this wild night, she couldn't have felt safer with a legion of troops guarding the cottage. Jeanette mended in her rocker, and Michel sculpted something at the table as she read. She could do this every night as Michel's wife, sit by the fire and read to her husband and mother-in-law. Then she'd help Jeanette and perhaps one or two of her own little ones into bed before climbing into bed with...

She shook her head. Where had her thoughts been headed? She hastily stood and took a candle from the mantel. "I'm for bed, though I'll probably read a bit more in the chamber."

"Goodness, but it's grown late. I'll be in as soon as I finish these trousers." Jeanette gave her rocker a subtle push.

Michel left the table and met her at the bedchamber's open door. Since her hands were full of candle and book, she stood helplessly as he ran a finger from her cheek to her jaw and laid a soft kiss on her forehead.

"Good night, love. I'll see you in the morn."

Love. "Michel, I..." Could she say it aloud? How foolish was she to keep her feelings bottled inside? Standing with him, in his house, with the fire casting shadows on his face and causing his tanned skin to glow, everything seemed so easy.

But it wasn't. Another world existed outside Michel's farm, and that world wanted her dead. "I'll see you tomorrow."

She turned, stepped into the chamber and pushed the door shut with her elbow. Her knees loose and liquid, she leaned against the door. She had to leave this place. Either leave or succumb to Michel's feelings. She'd not be able to resist him much longer.

Her fingers trembled as she busied herself with the familiar actions of getting undressed. She had no sooner changed into her nightdress, then the house door banged open. She frowned and moved toward the chamber door to listen.

"Jean Paul!" Michel's voice filtered through the wood. "Welcome home, brother."

Isabelle paused. Michel's brother?

"My son!" Tears choked Jeanette's words.

A frenzied scraping of feet against packed dirt echoed through the room.

"Come, warm yourself by the fire," Michel invited. "What are you doing traveling on a night such as this?"

"We reached town just ahead of the storm." The low voice sent a chill through Isabelle. "I came as soon as I could get away."

"Just a moment. I've someone you must meet."

The door to the bedchamber burst open. Before Isabelle could explain she needed to change back into her dress, Michel grabbed her arm and dragged her into the main chamber. "Brother, this is Isabelle. She's come to stay with us."

A large man stood before the fire. She swallowed, her heart stuttering in fear as she stared into his eyes. Eyes forever embedded in her memory. Eyes that had haunted her for the past two months.

This man, Michel's brother, had ordered her beaten. He had leered at her while pain screamed in her ribs and exploded in her arm. And his cold gaze had been the last thing she saw before her world turned to blackness.

Chapter Fifteen

"You!" Jean Paul jabbed a finger toward Isabelle as though he wielded a sword. His eyes shifted from her to Michel, resting momentarily on Michel's arm around her shoulders. "What is *she* doing here?"

Isabelle shrank back against Michel, the air wrenched from her lungs. Jean Paul wore the same too-small National Guard coat he had in the woods, still frayed and torn. He stood taller than Michel and thicker of chest. His forearms were large as legs of lamb and bulged with blue veins. A mean scar twisted around the far side of his right eyebrow. No, she hadn't mistaken him. This was the man who had wanted her dead. And he didn't even know she was the Duc de La Rouchecauld's daughter.

Michel's arm tightened protectively around her. "Do you know Isabelle?"

"Know her? I left her for dead in the woods. I see you found her, though."

Michel's arm turned heavy as stone around her shoulders. "She was on our property." His voice sounded madder and hotter than Isabelle had ever heard it. "You attempted to kill a woman. Now you're upset because I found her breathing rather than a corpse?"

Jeanette reached for Jean Paul's hand and patted it. "There, now, son. Never mind all that. You're home now. Don't be so angry."

Jean Paul ripped his hand away. "Don't be angry? She killed Corinne, Mother. I'm having my revenge."

"Vengeance belongs to God." Michel's quiet words cut the air. "Not you."

"Corinne?" Jeanette's whisper struck a harder blow to Isabelle's heart than Jean Paul's words. She turned pleading eyes to Isabelle. "You killed Corinne?"

"I…" Isabelle's jaw quivered. She hadn't even known Corinne. How could she have killed the woman?

"Deny it." Jean Paul moved a hand to the hilt of his sword. "Deny you sat in your *château* and took our food and money, so when Corinne fell ill, we couldn't treat her."

"Jean Paul, what lies have you been feeding yourself?" Michel's hand gripped Isabelle's shoulder so hard his nails dug through her nightdress and into her skin. "You can't blame Isabelle for Corinne. Isabelle was just a girl."

"Just a girl." Jean Paul stalked back and forth in front of the fire. "Families like hers took our money, did they not? They ate our grain and meat while we worked and sweated and starved. I can blame her for Corinne, and I will. I'll blame every cursed aristocrat until their blood has drenched the soil of France. I'll cut down every one of her entire class." He pulled his sword from its sheath. "Including her."

Isabelle screamed. *Escape.* She had to get out. Michel gripped her arm and yanked her behind him.

"You'll not touch her."

But weaponless, what could he do against Jean Paul? Standing in front of the table, Jean Paul blocked the front door, but perchance she could reach the window in the bedchamber. She slipped out of Michel's grip and ran through the doorway, slamming the door behind her. She clambered toward the tiny window high above her bed. Was she small enough to even fit?

Only the meager light from the single candle she'd lit earlier guided her as she heaved the shutters open. Rain spilled in, the wind tearing at her face and hair.

Behind her, the chamber door banged open. "Stop, or I'll kill you where you stand."

Her heart pounded against her ribs; her breaths came rapid and shallow. She pressed her hands to the windowsill in an effort to heave herself into the fierce elements, but her broken arm screamed in pain at the sudden pressure.

An arm wrapped around her waist, pulling her down. Two massive hands shoved her toward the floor. She sprawled, face-first, onto the dirt beside her bed.

Michel raced into the room as she curled into a ball, hot tears flooding her eyes. Had this been what God intended? That Michel love her and show her forgiveness so his brother could kill her? She muffled a sob. She deserved to die. She just didn't want to anymore. Michel had changed everything.

"Put that away, brother. You'll not harm her in this house." Michel's voice broke through her agony.

She caught her breath and waited for the life-ending blow to come despite Michel's words. But silence, thick and heavy, filled the room. Something prodded her shoulder. She opened her eyes.

The tip of Jean Paul's sword poked at her. "Get up, wench!"

She scrambled back against the wall.

Jean Paul laughed, a cruel cackle that chilled her blood. "Why, she's nothing more than a frightened kitten now. What did you do to her, Michel? She was rather fierce in the woods."

"I said, leave her be."

Isabelle's eyes rested on Michel's familiar form. She'd never seen him look so threatening. Fists clenched and face hard, he stood in the dimness, just beyond Jean Paul. Wind shook the tiny house. A terrifying rumble of thunder resonated inside the walls.

Jean Paul scoffed at his brother. "Do you know the reward I could have reaped had I dragged her to the military tribunal in Paris rather than left her in the woods? I scorned myself for days after I found out. No, I don't intend to harm her here. We'll do that in Paris."

Jean Paul knew who she was. An iron band tightened around her chest, and she glanced at Michel. How many times had she almost told him of her heritage? Dread crawled into her stomach.

Again, Jean Paul prodded her nightdress with the tip of his sword. "Get up, then. We'll go to the jail this night, and I'll see you reach Paris myself."

"You'll do nothing of the sort." Michel rocked up to the balls of his feet as though ready to pounce if Jean Paul made one wrong move.

Jean Paul whirled on Michel, putting the sword between them. "You dare give me orders?"

Lightning split the sky with a *crack,* as though God Himself added His opinion to the spectacle before her. The room briefly illuminated with the light of day, and Isabelle watched Michel, his knuckles white with strain and his eyes glistening darker than Jean Paul's.

"Put that away." Michel didn't flinch as he stared at Jean Paul. "You'll not use it on me or anyone else in this house."

The silence that filled the room sparked with deadly tension.

Jean Paul stepped closer to Michel, leaving Isabelle forgotten against the wall. She should flee, try again to lift herself out the window, something. But she was too filled with terror for Michel's sake to breathe. Had he intentionally turned Jean Paul's wrath from her to himself? Her body sank into the floor, fear crawling through her as Jean Paul walked nearer the man she loved.

Michel lunged for the sword, but Jean Paul evaded, stepping back at the exact moment Michel's palm would have found the handle.

"You've feelings for her in that muddled brain of yours." Jean Paul sneered.

"Mayhap you didn't hear me. I said, sheath your sword." Michel's low growl sent a chill through Isabelle's racing blood.

"Are you protecting her?" Jean Paul's voice mocked. "You should be killed for trying it, but I can beat you without my sword." Jean Paul dropped his sword back into its scabbard. His fist flew at Michel's face so quickly Isabelle barely had time to scream before the sickening crack of bone meeting bone echoed through the room.

Fright for Michel and rage toward Jean Paul surged through her veins. Intending to help Michel, she started to lift herself from the floor, but Michel drove a fist into his brother's gut.

"Ugh." Jean Paul stumbled backward, and the two men tore at each other in a frenzy of fists and grunts.

Isabelle slumped back to the ground and saw Jeanette standing in the doorway, a look of sorrow on her face as she silently held a candle and stared at her sons. The fighting brothers used every open centimeter of the room while they blocked punches and hurled others. They may have fought for a minute or an hour, she didn't know. Though Jean Paul was bigger, Michel evaded the burly man's moves. Michel's work-toned muscles bulged beneath his shirt as he threw his shoulder into Jean Paul's middle. They landed on the floor near her feet, the ground vibrating with the impact. Heaving and struggling, Michel pinned his brother beneath him.

"You'll leave Isabelle alone." Michel gasped air, his eyes ferocious as they bored into his brother's. "You can leave tomorrow if you wish. But you will tell no one who she is. The entire town knows her as Corinne's cousin from Paris. Do you understand? Think now, Jean Paul. For if you turn her in, you'll be turning in your mother and brother, as well."

Jean Paul spit in Michel's face. "You don't know who she is, do you? Who her father was?"

"No!" Isabelle's heart beat frantically while confusion clouded

Michel's eyes. "I meant to tell you. Truly I did."

Michel flashed her a glance, then glared at Jean Paul. "She's not royalty, so it matters little."

"No, she's not royalty." Jean Paul struggled for breath against his brother's hold. "She's the next family over. A La Rouchecauld. A daughter of the Duc de La Rouchecauld. Not just any *duc*, Michel, a *duc* descended from a man who once ruled France. The House of La Rouchecauld is over a thousand years old. Her family's been stealing from peasants since the time of the Romans!" Jean Paul spoke truth. All of it. Her family was no longer royal, but they held one of the highest positions in France.

Michel stilled, staring into his brother's eyes. With the slow movements of an old man, he shifted off his brother. Jean Paul sprang to his feet while Michel stayed on the floor, every emotion fleeing his face until he turned flat eyes on her. "Is it true? Is this who you are?"

"Michel—"

"Answer," he snapped in a voice so rough she pressed herself against the wall.

"Yes," she whispered.

His shoulders slumped. His face drained of color, and she could almost see his love for her draining away, as well.

Michel rose to his feet, while Isabelle hung her head and her eyes welled with fresh tears.

"And you, little girl, do you know what we'll do to you?" Jean Paul's sneering voice filtered through her haze of sobs, but she didn't look up from her place on the floor. How could she now that she'd lost Michel?

"We'll take you to Paris and put you on trial. The crowd will be wild for the blood of a La Rouchecauld." Jean Paul nudged her with his boot. "How do you think it will feel to stand before a raving crowd, huh? Maybe we won't guillotine you at all. Maybe we'll just fling you into the crowd and let them tear you apart."

She trembled. Everything she'd feared, everything Marie had suffered, would now come to her. *Is this Your way of forgiving me, Father? I was better off without Your love and forgiveness. I was better off left in the woods to die.* She closed her eyes and mewled quietly into her hands.

"I was there when your sister was killed."

Marie. Her head snapped up, and her nails dug violently into the dirt beneath her fingers.

"Ah, that got your attention, now, didn't it? Do you know what we did after we guillotined her? We—"

"No! I'll kill you!" She launched off the floor and flew at him.

He caught her before she even reached him, his grip wrenching her bandaged arm. "Ahhh!" More tears sprang to her eyes.

"Let her go. You're hurting her," Michel growled from the side of the room.

"What? Is it broken from our first meeting?" Jean Paul's voice dripped with sarcasm as he kept his hold steady.

Pain shot up her arm as his fingers dug in to the very spot still tender and swollen from the break. "Please, let go," she whimpered.

But before Jean Paul could release her, Michel lunged from the side and punched Jean Paul in the jaw. Jean Paul's head snapped back, and he flew backward before crashing onto her bed. The frame broke beneath his weight, and the beam that braced the bottom of her tick fell to the ground.

"That's enough from both of you." Michel stood there like an archangel, though he handled no sword, set apart from the two of them by something otherworldly. Isabelle held her breath. He'd just protected her from his brother. Maybe he still loved her. She waited for him to speak the words that would banish Jean Paul from the house and fix this mess. But the words didn't come, and an unbearable silence drenched the room.

"It's late, Jean Paul, and I'm weary." Michel pressed his thumb and forefinger between his eyebrows. "Isabelle shall remain here tonight. You can take her in the morn."

Take her? "Michel?" Isabelle clutched his forearm, but he refused to meet her eyes. He may as well drop the guillotine's blade himself.

"In the morning? Hah! She'll flee this very night. I'll take her now." Jean Paul clambered from the bed.

"I said tomorrow." Michel jerked his arm away from Isabelle's grip.

How could Michel betray her like this? He'd said he loved her. He'd asked her to stay. Did everything change because her father had been a *duc?* Or because she had deceived him? Staring blankly at the wall, she wrapped her arms around her chest and sank to the floor, too empty for even tears.

"Then I'll tie her hands and feet so she can't run." Jean Paul's voice echoed from somewhere above her, but she hardly made sense of the words through the hollowness filling her.

⌐.⌐.⌐.⌐.⌐

Without coat or hat, Michel stalked out of the house and into the storm. He barely felt the rain slice his skin or the water soak his hair. This very moment, his brother stood in the bedchamber with a rope, binding the hands and feet of the woman he loved. A thick, rough rope that Jean Paul would surely tie too tight, and that Isabelle would just as surely struggle against until the rope cut into her porcelain skin and drew blood.

Michel strode through the waterlogged earth and banged into his workshop. Standing in the darkness, he buried his face in his hands. "Father, what have I done? I love her. Don't take her from me. I beg You."

Since the moment he realized she was an aristocrat, he'd known she could be ripped away from him and killed. But how to stop it? He couldn't send her to the guillotine. He clenched his hands into fists. He wanted to marry the woman, to spend his life with her.

It would have been better to be discovered by unnamed faces in the dark than his own brother. How did he choose between them? Brother or love?

He should have taken Isabelle to Saint-Valery-sur-Somme the moment she'd become coherent. Then she'd have been safe. But how could he have turned over a beautiful, injured woman like her to a crew of vile sailors? Instead, he'd woven a terrible web of deceit, saying Isabelle was Corinne's cousin from Paris. Now he was trapped.

Oh, why must two of the people he loved most in the world be pitted against each other?

He closed his eyes, but the look on Isabelle's face when he'd turned away from her flooded his mind. So devastated. So bleak. He'd pledged his love. She had trusted him.

The daughter of a *duc*.

Isabelle spoke of her family longingly enough. The Duc de La Rouchecauld had probably been a kind father. As a *seigneur*, he'd have taxed his peasants to oblivion, denied them use of his land and given them no say in the county's governing. But the whole lot of aristocrats had behaved this way. The lifestyle had been learned from their fathers and their fathers before that. Until the *Révolution*, no peasants had stood up to them, or even asked them to change. Now the mobs of Paris and the guillotine's blade had changed everything, leaving innocents like Isabelle in the path of terror.

Michel fell to his knees in the darkness.

With so much sin and death and hatred to sort through, how could he determine what was right? He hadn't known about Jean Paul. Had he any inkling of Jean Paul's actions these past years,

Michel would have headed across the countryside to find his brother. His brother, who had heard the same Bible truths as he in Father Albert's classroom. His brother, who had sat at the table and listened every night while *Père* read from the Good Book. His brother, who had been achingly in love with his wife and sick over her death.

Jean Paul seemed to have distorted Corinne's death into some personal attack on him from the aristocracy. But how could the man go about the countryside thinking Corinne's death justified taking another life? Corinne would sob if she knew. Hopefully she couldn't look down from heaven and see her husband's actions. "Father." He held back the weeping that burned in his chest. "You gave Isabelle to me, did You not? You showed her to me in the woods, You encouraged me to keep her when I thought to get rid of her, You taught me to love her when I wanted to loathe her. And for what? To have her ripped away from me? I love her too much to let her go. Don't You understand? I love her too much. You promise to work everything out for good to those who love You. Well, I love You. Where's the good in this? What do I do? How do I save her? Guide me, Father."

The words of Psalm 82 seared through his fog of impending tears. *How long will ye judge unjustly, and accept the persons of the wicked? Defend the poor and fatherless: do justice to the afflicted and needy. Deliver the poor and needy: rid them out of the hand of the wicked.*

God was the ultimate judge. Not him, not Jean Paul, not anyone else in France.

He sucked in a breath so deep his lungs nearly burst.

He couldn't allow his love to die at his brother's hands. But how to stop his brother?

Michel stood. He knew what he must do. He would leave the farm. He would take Isabelle to England. *Oui,* she would be safe there.

And what about the farm? *Mère?* The promise he made to *Père?* None of it mattered anymore. It couldn't. Isabelle would die if he didn't take care of her. And Jean Paul, who loved farming, could stay and see to *Mère* and the homestead. Surely God would understand why he left.

Snippets from his conversation with Father Albert rushed back to him.

You must think, examine. You question your need to help the girl, but don't question why you tie yourself to a piece of land you hate. You're wasting your life.

That farm will kill you if you let it.

God has placed great talent for woodworking in these hands, my son. That in itself is a responsibility you cannot ignore forever.

A heavenly comfort flooded him, and peace filled his spirit. He raised his face to heaven. "You're taking the farm away from me. You're giving me Isabelle instead." He knew it now, saw Father Albert's prediction so clearly. God had given him the farm for a time, yes. But God had given him Isabelle now, and his hands—his woodworking tools. God had brought Jean Paul, who loved farming, home at the very time Isabelle needed to leave. He would take Isabelle to England. He would marry her, protect her, honor her.

But first, he had to deal with Jean Paul.

Chapter Sixteen

Isabelle woke in the dark, a suffocating fear in her throat. She tried to scream, but the gag Jean Paul had tied about her mouth muffled the sound. The silhouette of a large man loomed over the bed.

He tore the covers off her. She tried to flail, but her hands were tied so tightly, she only wrenched her arm. A hand slid beneath her knees, another behind her back. Her heart raced at his touch, and she sucked in a breath so quickly she choked.

So he wouldn't wait until morning. He would take her now, against his word to Michel. He lifted her from the bed, moved silently through the room and carried her into the main chamber despite her struggles and moans. His hot breath touched her ear, and a shiver raced down her spine. What would he do to her? He had leered at her in the woods. Trailed his black eyes up and down her body until she'd looked away in shame. He hadn't let his soldiers use her then, but now he was in the privacy of his childhood home. Isabelle jerked her head away from his chest and let tears fill her eyes. "Isabelle, calm yourself. I'll not hurt you."

Michel's voice. Her unwanted tears crested. Michel.

Jean Paul. It made little difference. One had claimed to love her and then abandoned her. The other would imprison her.

Michel carried her toward the dying fire and set her in Jeanette's rocker. He took a knife from his pocket. With the haste of an executioner freeing a corpse from the restraints on a guillotine, he cut the ropes at her feet and arms but stopped before removing her gag. "Be silent now. I gave Jean Paul something to make him sleep. But such brews aren't precise in their effects, and he could still wake. Put on your cloak, boots and hat, and we'll go out to my workshop." Her heart thudded warily against her chest. Go to his workshop for what? So he could cart her to the jail first and reap whatever reward was being offered?

He slid the knife against her cheek, the coolness from the blade seeping through her skin and chilling her heart. He cut the cloth that dug into her mouth. She obeyed his orders and covered herself silently while Michel put on his outer raiment.

Despite her warm new hat, cloak and boots, the intensity of the storm seized her. Thunder rumbled with such strength the earth shook beneath her feet. The rain that caused the flood several weeks ago looked like a spring shower compared to the storm that railed around her this night. The roaring wind tore at her hair with such ferocity she couldn't keep her dark tresses from her face and needed to hold her hat, lest it blow away. Small raindrops pelted her, stinging her hands and face. And lightning slashed the sky, illuminating familiar landmarks in its eerie glow.

She put her head down against the wind and pressed close to Michel's back. He held open the door to the workshop. She stepped into the dim lantern light and shivered, her eyes traveling around the room. No fire had been lit in the stove, but a boy's hat, shirt and trousers—clearly patched by Jeanette for the orphanage—were draped over the chest of drawers. Two traveling bags and a sack sat on the floor beside it.

Michel lifted her hat and unfastened her cloak. "Come, we haven't much time. You must dress."

Eyes hot with anger, she whirled on him. "Why? So you can take me to the jail before Jean Paul wakes?"

Michel took her upper arms and looked at her with calm determination. "No, so I can help you escape."

She tried to jerk away, but his grip only grew firmer. "Help me escape?" She laughed bitterly. "You said Jean Paul could—"

"Shhh." He touched his finger to her lips. "I care not who your father was. I love you, Isabelle."

He still loved her? She froze, too afraid to believe his words. She looked into Michel's eyes, into the warm, tender green she knew so well.

"I'll never stop loving you." Michel's thick, low voice slid like balm over her soul.

Her heart softened, even as she clenched her hands in reluctance. He'd said Jean Paul could have her.

"I can't stop loving you any more than I can stop the rain or the wind or the seasons," Michel continued.

Her anger evaporating with each word he spoke, she pressed her eyes shut.

"God gave you to me to love. I forgot that for a moment tonight, when I learned about your father. But God showed me my folly." He wiped a strand of hair away from her face. "Forgive me?" Moisture welled in his eyes.

His tears undid her. For all the tears she'd shed over the past two months, she'd never seen him near crying.

"Oh, Michel." She cupped his cheek with her hand. Was God working everything out despite what she'd done to Marie? Despite what she'd hidden from Michel? "I wanted to tell you about my parents. I meant to. I just…the words never came. It wasn't you. It was me."

His grip on her arms loosened, and his hands slid up to her

shoulders. He pulled her forward and kissed her brow. "I love you."

She swallowed. "I don't deserve it."

He hushed her with a brush of his lips against hers, then pointed to the dresser. "We haven't the time now. We can discuss this later, after we've gone. Sylvie's in the stable, already hitched to the wagon." His gaze traveled to the clothing lying across the dresser. He spun her toward the raiment. "Change out of that nightdress."

"Into boy's clothes?"

"I'll not have to worry about the sailors if you're dressed like an urchin." He turned to face the wall.

She looked at his back and then at the clothes. Her hands trembled as she took the garments. Surely there was nothing romantic about changing clothes in a fireless room while a man faced the wall. Yet her skin warmed against the chill as she quickly put on the garments.

"Are all these sacks for me?" She looked down at them. "I haven't that many possessions, nor a way to carry so much."

Michel came up behind her. "I'll carry yours and the supplies. The last sack is mine."

She stilled, too afraid to turn and look at him. Too afraid to hope for what he said. "You're going? To Saint-Valery?"

"To England, love."

Her heart quickened in her chest. Did he truly intend to come? To protect her? "Oh, Michel!" Grinning, she whirled toward him.

"I'll marry you there."

Her breath clogged in her throat, shock searing through her joy. "Marry me?" The words felt heavy in her mouth. "I must stay in England. I won't be able to return here." She'd dreamed of marrying him, yes, but every dream about their future had included his farm.

"It's you I want, not this land." He spoke heavily, not with the hope of a newly betrothed man. He didn't reach to take her in his arms or even step nearer her. No embrace or kiss sealed their betrothal. Instead, he walked to the bags on the floor and ran his hand along the smooth top of the dresser, trailing a finger over the completed acorn and leaf carvings.

And she knew. He didn't want to leave. Perchance he would come with her, but his heart would still be here. Michel abruptly pulled away from his masterpiece, his eyes scanning the various pieces of wood at the back of his shed.

She could hardly breathe for the tightening in her chest. His farm. His furniture. His mother. Michel's entire existence revolved around being here. He would leave this land that he loved for her. Not for himself. Not because he *wanted* to go with her, but because he gave himself no choice. He needed to leave everything behind in order to protect her.

She licked her dry lips. And what if the Terror caught her before she reached England? He'd be killed with her. Jean Paul already knew everything. If Michel left this way, would he ever be able to come back? The townsfolk would surely figure something out if he up and disappeared with the girl from Paris.

"Non." The word sounded foreign, as though someone else had uttered it. But Michel couldn't leave. How could she ask him to? It was too great a risk. Too great a sacrifice. Her body went rigid with determination. "You love your mother, this land and this workshop every bit as much as you love me. You don't belong in England. You must stay here." The painful words singed her mouth.

He came toward her then. "Isabelle, you're speaking foolishness. I'm going with you. I'll marry you. I'll protect you."

The statement should have brought her comfort. Instead, she began to tremble. He hadn't denied what she said. And she wouldn't ask him to leave everything he loved except for her.

He touched her shoulder. "Quickly, now. We must away, posthaste."

She shook her head. Too much worked against them. He would give up everything for her, and to what end? The guillotine's blade? "I won't let you come with me." She could barely push the quiet words past her raw throat. The noise from the storm swallowed them the moment they reached the air.

He tucked a strand of hair behind her ear. "Don't be frightened, love. We need each other. We'll be fine in England." He pulled her gently against him and slowly lowered his lips.

She should pull away. What would kissing accomplish now that she must leave him? But his lips on hers dissolved all other thoughts. Her eyes fluttered shut, and she sank into the soft layers of the kiss. For a moment, they were suspended in eternity. There was no rain or wind or chill. No *Révolution,* no Terror. No peasant and aristocrat. Just the kiss and embrace of two people who loved each other. She could stay like this forever, wrapped in Michel's arms, cocooned in his strength and protection, locked in his passion.

But as quickly as the moment came, it went. His arms couldn't shut out the inevitable forever. His lips couldn't make her forget their situation for more than an instant. She pushed away, tears filling her eyes. "Michel, no. Don't do this to yourself."

To me. The words ripped her open, left her empty and shaking. Had she known things would come to this, she never would have kissed him from the start, or reveled in his touch. She wouldn't have smiled at him, made that wretched tray or packed a lunch to share that midday. If only she could undo everything, travel back in time two months and never speak a polite word to the man. Leave his house as soon as she could limp.

Oh, why had she stayed? Why hadn't she stopped her feelings? His?

Michel released her only to snake his hands through her hair and bring her forehead to his chest. "What mean you? Isabelle, you want to be with me. You can't kiss me that way and deny your feelings."

She jerked back so quickly his arms fell to his sides. The distance between them, not even a meter, ran cold and deep as a castle moat. Their social standings, their purposes, their goals, their dreams. Everything inside them warred with each other. Everything outside them ripped them apart. He said he loved her, maybe he did. But for how long? How long would he love her once he was away from his family, his land?

He'd chafe in London without his wood or the subtle hills of the countryside. And what if something happened to him? What if he were caught helping her flee? What if their ship was attacked? What if—even worse—they reached England only to have some accident tear her away? Once he fled with her, Michel would never be able to return home, and if she was lost, he wouldn't even have her love to comfort him. She pressed a hand to her temple. If she pulled him from his family now, she could never forgive herself.

"Let me help you." Michel reached out.

She stepped farther back. Did he not see it? The distance, the space, the insurmountable odds? Did he think he could cover the gulf between them without being sucked down into the dark waters?

"No. You can't come with me." Her chest rose and fell with the pressure building in her heart.

Michel clenched his fists at his sides. His jaw hardened, and anger flashed in his eyes. "You're serious, aren't you? Of all times to be stubborn, Isabelle. We haven't time for it tonight. Do you think I want to leave? That I don't have responsibilities here? I'm doing this for you."

"Yes. You are doing this for me. Not for yourself. You can't leave. It's too great a sacrifice." Her voice rose and frustration swam in her blood. "You'd hate me for taking you away from it. Don't you see? It's like a different world here on your beloved little farm. But once we're in England, do you think our differences will vanish? They will pull us apart. They will keep us apart. I'm French aristocracy. *Aristocracy*, Michel. Any hope we had of staying together shattered tonight when Jean Paul walked through that door."

He stretched his fingers and then reclenched them into hard, tight fists. She almost willed his anger to grow stronger. She could handle his fury, but she had no defense against his tenderness.

"I love you." He growled the words like a threat.

"Then stop. I never asked you to love me." The words came more forcefully than she intended, and with them the old wounds that separated her and Michel when she'd first come reopened.

Pain etched his face.

She longed to reach out, soothe him, apologize. But if she did, would he ever let her go?

"You needed me to love you." He spat the words, raked a hand through his hair and paced the ground before her.

Isabelle forced her hands to stop shaking. Perchance she had needed him. But she couldn't let herself need him now. If she broke the bond between them this night, he and his mother would be safe. She'd watched Jean Paul struggle with Michel earlier, and had seen the soldier's efforts to incapacitate Michel without harming him. Jean Paul would never turn his brother in. And with a head start and the wagon, she could escape the cruel man.

She looked at Michel with flat, emotionless eyes. "You deceived yourself, Michel. I didn't need you. I never needed you." Her heart cried out at the words, but she held his gaze.

He whirled toward her and jabbed a finger at her chest. "You lie! You'd be dead in the woods were it not for me. You want to go by yourself? You have to be so independent?" He threw his hands up in the air. "I should let you go and refuse you when you come crawling back after your little adventure ends in chaos."

He stepped closer, and the angry lines in his face softened. "But I can't." He raised his face to the roof. "Father, help me. I'll not let her go, not like this."

He lowered his gaze back to her, his face strangely calm as though he'd received some soundless answer from heaven. He brushed his knuckles down her cheek.

The simple touch sent waves of longing through her. She swallowed noisily, as though it were her only defense against the love he offered. Why couldn't the man stay angry? How was she to resist him when he treated her thus?

"I love you too much to let you go this way." His voice sounded like crushed gravel. "I won't watch you run to your own death." He released her, headed for the bags and lifted them. "I'll at least take you to Saint-Valery and see you board the ship. Mayhap you'll see the daftness of your decision by then."

"No!" The word came out too forcefully. Her mind scrambled for some way to convince him he must stay.

"Isabelle. Love." He dropped the packs at her feet, pulled her into his arms, lowered his head as if to kiss her again and paused when his lips were just a breath away from hers. "You needn't fret. All shall be well."

She yanked away. "Don't, you'll only make this harder on yourself."

She backed up, picked up the ragged valise that held her belongings and headed to the wall where Michel had hung her cloak and hat. She had to get away. Now. For his own good.

Despite the howling wind and raging thunder, a deathly silence descended in the little room. Keeping her back to him, she put on her outer raiment.

Michel shifted between her and the door. "What are you doing?"

"You wanted to leave, did you not?" She fumbled with the latch on the valise. Opening it, she first checked the pocket. Finding her money and citizenship papers there, she sifted through her clothes. Her fingers touched the coarse fabric of the bonnet Jeanette had remade for her.

And the idea formed.

She looked at him, standing tall and proud between her and the means to escape, watching her as his breath puffed little clouds into the air. *I'm doing this for him. I have to protect him. Even if it means lying.*

"My bonnet, the one your mother gave me, I'm missing it. May I go back inside and fetch it before we away?"

His brow wrinkled, and he scratched the back of his neck. "I cleaned everything out of your drawer. It must be in the valise."

She averted her eyes. "No, it's not here. I'm certain of it. Perchance it fell out somewhere? I'll be but a moment." She slid by him and pulled on the latch to the door.

A large hand closed over hers on the handle, another settled on her shoulder. "No. You'll not go back inside. I won't risk my brother waking. I'll fetch your bonnet."

"Merci." She raised her valise. "I'll take this to the stable and wait for you in the wagon."

"Aye." He threw on his cloak and hat, then held the door for her.

She hastened into the storm and toward the stable. Throwing open the wide doors, she turned and searched the yard for Michel. A slash of lightning exploded across the sky, illuminating his silhouette at the door to the house. She rushed inside, hefted her bag and then herself into the wagon and flicked Sylvie's reins. The aging beast whinnied and stomped her front hoof.

Isabelle glanced through the doors at the raging gale and couldn't blame Sylvie's hesitation. "Come on, Sylvie. Posthaste." She slapped the reins against the stubborn animal's haunches. The horse sauntered to the entrance, then stopped.

Panic clawed at Isabelle's throat. Michel would return any moment. How to get Sylvie out and quick? She climbed out of the wagon and scurried to the sack of oats in the corner. Grabbing two handfuls, she ran back and offered them to Sylvie. The horse inhaled them.

"Come on, girl. Just obey me, and I'll be good to you. I promise."

She smoothed her hands over the horse's nose, then climbed into the wagon and flicked the reins hard. The bit of attention worked. Sylvie lurched out into the storm, automatically heading down the path to the road. Isabelle snapped the reins again, urging the beast forward. The cold rain soaked her, Sylvie and the wagon before they reached the road.

As Sylvie turned onto the route, Isabelle glanced back at the cottage that had enfolded her in its love and safety, but in the darkness, she couldn't make out its form.

She bit her lip. A feeling of emptiness opened like a cavern inside her. She held back a sob and blinked, trying to staunch the tears, but another slipped down her cheek, then another and another. Helpless, she succumbed.

Chapter Seventeen

Empty-handed, Michel stepped back into the rain. He pulled the brim of his hat down and trudged toward his workshop. Of all the frustrating things! The bonnet must be in Isabelle's valise. It couldn't be anywhere else. Her dresser drawer had been empty, and he'd checked the hooks by the door for the bonnet twice. She must have missed it when she looked through her belongings. Though he could hardly blame the frightened woman for wanting to take the bonnet with her. No harm done by looking for it, really. What were a few moments of time compared to Isabelle's peace of mind?

He opened the door to his workshop, picked up his bag and the sack of supplies and looked around one last time. He'd no intention of coming back. Once he and Isabelle were in Saint-Valery, she couldn't prevent him from buying a ticket on the same vessel as she. Still… Though they needed to hurry, he inhaled the tangy scent of mixed woods, glanced at the workbench and walked over to run his hands over the scarred, aged wood. How much he'd learned at *Père's* hand standing in this very spot.

He went to the chest of drawers then, spread his fingers over the walnut and waited until the cool wood warmed under his touch. He'd never become the renowned furniture-maker he'd longed to be, but he enjoyed the hobby. France was changing. Mayhap the future of furniture-making would change with it. Until then, maybe Jean Paul could find a buyer for this piece.

He'd look for work in a furniture-making shop in England. Though he'd no guarantee the English furniture-makers would be any friendlier toward his skills than the Parisians had been, he wouldn't ignore this new chance to pursue his dream.

A clap of thunder snapped him from his reverie. Here he was dawdling in his woodshed while Isabelle waited in the stable and Jean Paul slept just meters away. He strode to the lantern by the door, then paused. He couldn't blow it out, as though canceling the flame would extinguish part of his soul. How could he cast his peaceful world of wood in darkness? Aye, he'd blown out the lantern thousands of times before. But he'd always been coming back to light it again. Not so this time. He sighed, letting his fingers slip from the lantern. It would burn out on its own.

He opened the door and plunged back into the elements. In the wind, the open stable doors banged against the walls like a fierce drummer calling troops to battle. He stepped inside, his eyes straining in the darkness. "Isabelle?" He stopped cold.

Gone. No lightning needed to illuminate the sky to reveal what he knew. A chill that had little to do with the temperature or weather crept up his back and wrapped around his heart.

"No." He whispered the word into the hushed building, willing Isabelle to appear from a dark corner of the stable with some excuse for why Sylvie had run off with the wagon. But nothing changed. The smells of straw and manure and rain mingled around him. The animals stayed bedded down in their stalls. The air surrounding him remained empty and stale.

He trudged back outside and looked down the path that led to the road. No sign of Isabelle or the wagon. He ripped his hat from his head and clenched the brim.

It couldn't be.

She wouldn't have left. She loved him.

Rain soaked his hair, but he hardly noticed. He dropped his head and stared at the mud beneath his feet, where the rain battered away Sylvie's tracks and the wagon ruts, washing away the last traces of the woman he loved.

The storm howled around him, but he heard nothing as loss grew inside him. His chest began to ache, an unbearable pressure building. He ran toward his beloved woodshed and burst inside.

The lantern still burned brightly. The wood still rested along the back. His finished dresser sat in the middle of his workspace, awaiting whatever would become of it. And the table he'd started stood near the workbench, anticipating when his hands would again shape it. His soul had been stripped, but nothing had changed inside his haven.

He gulped air, vainly trying to slow his breathing. He could go after Isabelle. She still couldn't prevent him from following her to Saint-Valery. To England.

But why chase a woman who didn't want him?

He let the bags drop to the floor and yanked off his cloak, throwing it over the unneeded packs. She could have left without deceiving him. Without lying and running away as if *he* was the enemy rather than Jean Paul.

England. The word seared his mind. He nearly hoped she didn't reach her destination. That insidious country had stood like a chasm between them since first they spoke. And now it ripped her away from him. What did England offer that he couldn't?

He hung his head and rubbed his hand across his brow. Her aunt. Rich men to make her a suitable husband. Her father's money. Freedom to be herself, use her family name.

Well, she could have her freedom. She obviously wouldn't be free enough shackled to him.

You deceived yourself, Michel. I didn't need you. I never needed you. Her voice played back in his mind, taunting him. Had he misread the signs? The flush of her cheek when he touched her. The sigh in her breath when he kissed her. The time and effort she'd devoted to piecing back together Corinne's pitcher and basin.

She wouldn't have gone through so much trouble unless she cared for him. Loved him. He stalked across the woodshed to the dresser, grappling for a fragment of rationality through the shards of bitterness pricking his mind.

But as quickly as Isabelle appeared in his life, she walked out of it. That wasn't love. He slammed his hand into the top of the dresser. Mayhap she'd never loved him. If she loved him even a fraction of the way he loved her, she wouldn't have been able to leave.

Didn't she understand all he was willing to give up for her? Didn't she realize he loved her enough to break his promise to his father? To leave the only source of income he had to keep her safe? Didn't she care about the sacrifices he would have made for her?

"What's the point, God?" he shouted at the ceiling. "I trusted You. I loved her for You. And she left me."

He covered his face with his hands. And what was he going to do about Jean Paul? He'd drugged Jean Paul and set Isabelle free. His brother would likely never speak to him again, let alone trust him.

For the first time in his life, Michel wanted to walk away. As Isabelle had. As Jean Paul had six years earlier. To walk out the door of his woodshed and into the storm and never, ever return.

A familiar voice whispered in Michel's head. *Trust God. He works all out for good.*

He crushed the thought. God had gotten him into this mess and stranded him. He raised his fist toward the sky. "If it all works out for good, then give her back. How am I supposed to forget her? Am I to live the rest of my life knowing the woman I love is in the arms of some wealthy Englishman?"

Chest heaving, he took a step back. The dresser he'd taken seven months to complete stood before him. Perfect. Refined. Beautiful. Like Isabelle.

He rammed his fist into the side of his masterpiece. His knuckles screamed with the impact, but he didn't dent the tough wood. He was done begging, both God and her. Why should he seek a woman who spurned him? He'd thought his love for her would be enough to hold them together. It wasn't.

Sorrow filled his chest, but he ignored it. Riding his fury, he grabbed an ax from beside his workbench and heaved it into the top of the dresser. His arms sang with the reverberation, and a gash gaped large and deep in the once-perfect top. Red tinged his vision as he stared at the hole, and one swing suddenly wasn't enough. He needed to ruin it all. Hadn't Isabelle done as much to his heart?

He swung the ax into the top again and then into the sides, hacking and hacking until his eyes blurred with tears and his arms ached. Until not a single finished section of wood remained and his masterpiece lay in splinters at his feet.

His heart felt cold and hard in his chest when he turned and walked toward the door. Broken fragments of wood cracked under his feet, the sound desolate to his ears. He stooped to pick up his cloak, and a single, carved acorn rested at his feet. Something inside shouted that he stomp on it, but he bent and picked it up, his fingers running over the smooth wood. Perfect. Without a scratch.

He glanced back at the ruined dresser. How had the acorn survived the brutal attack? His fingers tightened into a fist around it as he slipped it into his pocket.

A perfect remnant of what had once been.

.˙.˙.˙.˙

"Come on, Sylvie. Come!" Isabelle pulled the reins until her boots slipped on the slick cobblestone of the bridge, but the stubborn beast wouldn't move.

The slow horse had taken her faithfully into Abbeville, but the moment they reached the ancient bridge spanning the Somme River, Sylvie had planted her hooves.

The wind whined an eerie song, and the water rushed and foamed beneath them as though angry with the sky for daring to storm.

Sylvie reared, eyes wild. Isabelle's gloved fingers slipped on the reins, but she grasped them before the horse could bolt.

Her heart lurched into her throat. "Sylvie! No!" Her valise lay in the wagon; if the horse ran off, whatever would she do? Gripping the reins tightly, she blew out a calming breath and patted the horse's neck. The beast whinnied but settled. "Stay. Good girl. Good."

Sylvie stomped her hooves, her nostrils flaring. Isabelle had thought to take Sylvie to Saint-Valery and stable her there. But the stubborn horse only slowed her now. She could walk just as fast as Sylvie and not have the trouble of dragging the frightened beast where she didn't want to go.

She walked the length of the horse, trailing her fingers against Sylvie's wet hair. If she let Sylvie go, would the beast run back home? She bit her lip. She knew so little about horses. They'd had stable hands and coachmen before the *Révolution*. And she and Marie hadn't kept a horse in Arras.

"Steady now." She patted Sylvie's rump in what she hoped was a calming manner. The horse held still. Laying the reins atop the wagon, she climbed up, reached over the seat, grasped her valise and hurried down.

A bolt of lightning slashed across the sky just over the river and a crash of thunder shook the ground. Sylvie whinnied and reared. Isabelle jumped away, letting go of the reins. The horse turned from the bridge, the wagon clattering behind her, and ran back down the road toward home. Isabelle watched her go until the last piece of her life with Michel disappeared into the night. Then she turned her back on Abbeville and started to walk.

~.~.~.~.~

"Where's the girl?" Jean Paul's enraged voice filled the house.

Numb from spent rage and grief, Michel glanced up from where he sat by the fire.

The door to the bedchamber burst open and crashed against the wall. Jean Paul appeared in the doorway wearing only the tan trousers he had slept in. His eyes grazed the room before searing Michel.

Michel stood and drew a breath, his heart thudding slowly. Fury radiated from Jean Paul's every pore. The blue veins in his arms and chest bulged against his taut muscles, his sharp cheekbones and strong jaw made more severe by his anger. He took a step forward, then stumbled. Looking more mad than sane, he scowled, held a hand to his forehead and waited a moment before he hulked toward Michel.

Michel nearly took a step backward. He'd known this moment would come since Isabelle fled six hours earlier. But what to do? Did he even want to defend her?

"I said, where's the girl?" Jean Paul growled through his clenched jaw.

Michel met his brother's gaze evenly.

"She's gone." Jean Paul sprang at him. Michel tried to sidestep, but even in his drugged state, Jean Paul moved quickly enough to slam Michel, back first, into the wall.

Jean Paul's hands shook as he pinned Michel against the hard surface. "Why didn't I wake when she fled? And why are my hands trembling? Why can't I walk straight?"

Michel pressed his lips together, sweat beading on his forehead.

Jean Paul shoved him harder into the wall. "What did you do, drug that tea you gave me last night and help her escape?"

Dear Father! Did so much depend on this moment of truth? "You would have killed her."

"Traitor!" Jean Paul moved a hand to the waistband of his trousers. The moment Jean Paul's arm left Michel's shoulder, he thrust his brother backward. A blade flashed, and an instant later Jean Paul held a knife to Michel's throat.

Hard, lifeless eyes bored into Michel, shooting terror through his body until his heart pumped fear rather than blood. He'd thought himself safe, thought Jean Paul wouldn't truly harm a member of his family.

He'd been wrong.

"Do you know who I work for? Who I came to town with?" Jean Paul leaned so close his breath warmed Michel's face. The furious scar atop Jean Paul's eyebrow seemed to spasm and fist with rage. "Joseph Le Bon. His portable guillotine and military tribunal are in town even now. They began hearing accusations and making arrests last night. I'll take you there and throw you on Le Bon's mercy if you don't speak! Now tell me, where did the girl go?"

Michel's throat felt dry and swollen. He opened his mouth. *Saint-Valery-sur-Somme.* But the words wouldn't come. Isabelle was hurt, traveling in this storm by herself. Had she crossed the Somme River safely? Had she reached the Channel? After all he'd done to save her, from the woods to last night, how could he now give her destination away? Aye, she'd deserted him. But curse it all, he still loved the woman.

He raised his chin.

Jean Paul's Adam's apple worked back and forth and his long, black hair fell wildly about his face. He grabbed Michel's collar, yanked it forward and then slammed Michel's head against the wall. Pain surged through Michel's skull, mingling with the hurt in his heart.

"Tell me where she went, or I'll slit your throat. I swear it!"

Michel held his tongue.

Jean Paul glared at him as though warring with himself: drop his threat or kill his only brother.

The house door opened, bringing in a torrent of wind and rain. *Mère* stepped inside, her wool cape dripping rainwater onto the floor and a basket of eggs in her hand. "Michel, why is Sylvie out of the..." She glanced at her sons and froze. The basket of eggs dropped to the floor with a muted *thwack*.

"Leave!" Jean Paul shouted at *Mère,* his knife scraping Michel's neck.

Michel held his breath against the slicing blade. A trickle of warmth slid down his skin into his collar. He stretched his neck back, further exposing the sensitive skin but shifting away from the knife enough to speak. "We're just having a discussion, *Ma Mère.* 'Tis best you head to the stable for a time."

Mère's hand clenched the door frame. A gust of wind sent an explosion of rain inside, but she kept her eyes riveted on Jean Paul. "Jean Paul, whatever are you doing?"

Jean Paul met Michel's eyes. "No less than Michel deserves."

Michel's mind raced. If he didn't speak against this senseless bloodshed now, then when? "I'll not do anything that results in killing. Either you or Isabelle."

"Then your own blood will be spilled in place of hers."

"Boys, please!" Hands clasped to her heart, *Mère* took a step closer and stopped. Confusion etched her features as she tried to grasp what transpired before her. "Hasn't this *Révolution* taken enough blood already?" The once-cool knife blade had warmed against Michel's skin until he could barely feel it. Any moment could be his last. Just one flick of Jean Paul's wrist…

"There is never enough blood when it's the blood of aristocrats and traitors." Jean Paul's eyes were wild with hatred. "Did you know your precious Father Albert sits in the jail awaiting trial even now?"

The air left Michel's lungs. Father Albert? Had a more righteous man ever walked the ground of France? *"Non."* Tears blurred his vision. Isabelle. Father Albert. Would anyone escape the *Révolution's* Terror? "Not Father Albert. How could you? You loved him. He taught you at his knee!"

"Stop!" *Mère* cried, tears evident in her voice. "Stop this right now. Arresting your teacher? Putting a knife to your brother's throat? There's no cause for such behavior." She rushed to Jean Paul and wrung her hands.

"I didn't turn Father Albert in." Jean Paul's hold wavered, guilt flickering across his face. "Others did. No one is safe, Michel. Tell me where the girl went before others come for your blood."

If the price of living involved turning his back on vulnerable women and generous old men, the Terror could have him. "Why wait for others to come? Just take my life now. Or haven't you the courage to kill me yourself? You'll turn me over to the military tribunal as long as you don't pull the lever on the guillotine? Or hold the blade that slits my throat?"

"It's not like that." The fire left Jean Paul's eyes, and his grip loosened until Michel could have easily pushed his brother off. "I don't want to hurt you."

"Please, Jean Paul." *Mère,* her hair coming out of its knot, placed her hand on Jean Paul's elbow. "Whatever Michel's done, he'll make it right. Sit at the table a spell and talk this out, like I taught you when you were little." *Mère* shook her head. "I never taught you this."

Jean Paul stepped back and dropped the knife. It *thunked* against the dirt floor, a redeeming sound of safety. "I didn't want them to take Father Albert. I don't want them to take you. But if you don't watch yourself, Michel, Le Bon will kill you, and I won't be able to stop him. Now, please, tell me where the girl went. At least protect yourself and *Notre Mère*."

Their mother stood beside them, as though waiting for the hug she'd always demanded when he and Jean Paul were young and fought. Her vacant eyes told Michel she understood nothing of what they discussed, only the danger he'd been in when Jean Paul held the knife.

Michel closed his eyes, his brother's sincere entreaty and *Mère's* expectant gaze harder to resist than the demands Jean Paul had made with the knife to his throat. He'd already taken Isabelle in, nursed her, cared for her, loved her. He'd drugged his own brother and given her a six-hour start. What more could he do to protect her? If she couldn't reach a ship with so much on her side, she'd never survive.

"I can't."

Jean Paul stiffened. "Then you're a fool. Her father was a *duc*. She deserves to die, regardless of your feelings for her. And if I don't search for her, others will. She was walking west when first I found her. Was she headed to the Channel?"

Michel's blood chilled.

Jean Paul smirked. "I see she was." He bent to pick up his knife.

Chapter Eighteen

Isabelle bent her head against the storm. She could smell the tangy mixture of salt and fish and water that indicated the sea. Saint-Valery-sur-Somme couldn't be much farther. Rainwater had seeped into her boots, soaking her stockings and numbing her toes. Her injured arm ached. Her good arm screamed from the weight of her drenched bag, yet she put one foot in front of the other.

Just a little farther. Not more than a kilometer or two. Her eyes, heavy with fatigue, threatened to drift shut. After five years of trying to escape France, she was almost free. So why did her heart sink with every step she took? Why did she feel as though she walked away from her dream rather than toward it?

A fresh gust of wind battered her, working its icy fingers down her back. She shivered against the chill and caught sight of a cottage surrounded by fields. Smoke swirled from the chimney, and light trickled from beneath the covered windows. How pleasant to be curled up by a fire, dry, warm and safe. She took a step toward the little dwelling and then stopped. She didn't want some strange peasant's hospitality, she wanted Michel's.

And Michel wouldn't be the one who opened the door if she knocked.

She swiped at a tear with her bandaged arm and hurried past the cottage, pressing closer to the sea. A fine mess she'd made of things. How had she let her heart become so intertwined with a man she knew she'd leave? She stared at the dreary road stretching endlessly ahead.

I'm going with you. I'll marry you. I'll protect you.

She sniffled. Michel would have been content enough at first, but he'd have grown to despise her. Leaving him was for the best. He would find another to love and marry and carry his children.

Yes, Michel would go on, but could she? A sudden clomping sound.

She whirled, fear stealing her breath. The thud of horses' hooves through the rain? She looked up the road, then down it. Perchance the wind had played a trick on her. Surely no one would ride in this weather. Unless Jean Paul…

No. He hadn't had horses last time. Why would he have them now? Perhaps she didn't move fast with her broken arm, but surely she'd gotten enough of a start to beat the soldiers to the Channel. She glanced toward the sickly gray sky. How long since the sun had risen? She felt as though she'd been walking for hours, but maybe she'd only been traveling for minutes. Had Jean Paul discovered she was gone already?

She shuddered, a reaction having nothing to do with the cold. Her eyes watered from the wind and stinging rain. A large, dark shadow loomed ahead through the veil of rain. Could it be a building? Could the sound have come from there? She hastened toward it, hope surging through her as the ramparts took shape.

Saint-Valery-sur-Somme. Her breathing stopped as she gazed up. Five years of dreams embodied before her as she finally reached the port town. The ancient gate towered before her, its crumbling, moss-covered stone as beautiful as freshly polished gold. She passed under it and into the old walled town built nearly a thousand years earlier.

Her boots squished mud against the uneven cobblestone as she rushed through the town square, past houses of stone and mortar strung together to form defensive walls. The wind whisked away smoke from chimneys and lights burned dimly behind shutters, but no one loitered about the square. And she'd little time for admiration. Her heart beat with a singular purpose: water. She had to reach the sea.

She nearly bumped a woman who rushed into the road before her, then disappeared into a house across the way. Isabelle slowed when she saw the far northern gate. Down the gentle slope lay the sea, the infamous Baie de Somme where William the Conqueror once assembled his grand fleet of ships before attacking England. A thrill shot through her at the remembered lesson taught from her father's knee in their apartment at Versailles. Who knew she would one day see this bay? That she would dream of it for five long years after her father's death? That when she stood beside it, she would be stripped of everything once held dear? That the watery den would be her only hope of refuge?

But today, the water held no hints of grandeur or promises of safety. Covered with white-crested waves, the angry harbor foamed before her. She strained her eyes but couldn't discern the shadow of a sailing vessel. Surely one was there, harboring in northern France's largest port. Numerous vessels would be there, British blockade or not.

Her unease rose with the wild swell of waves. What if no vessels were leaving due to the storm? Her stomach clenched. Certainly something was leaving today. She didn't care what type of vessel she traveled on as long as it carried her to Stockholm and from Stockholm to England.

Hastening toward the shore, she left the walled section of town, then scanned the street and frowned. Where was the shipping office?

She walked along the water, eyeing the shops shut against the storm. An occasional light flickered from the second-story apartments, but nothing on street level seemed open. How early was it? Surely it was late enough for businesses to be open. She hadn't been walking *that* long.

She struggled forward, shoving a snarl of hair up under her cap that the wind had blown free. It would do little good to dress as a boy if her hair hung in curls down her back.

Laughter wafted from somewhere nearby. She passed a man with his hat pulled low against the rain, searched the street for the origin of the laughter and followed the sound. Light streamed from beneath the building's shuttered windows, and two horses stood near the entrance. Taking a nervous breath, she jammed all escaping hair into her hat. *A boy. I'm a boy, not a lady.*

She pulled open the door. With one step inside, she left a world of cold, wet misery and entered a bastion of lightness and joviality. To her left, two large fires snapped and popped, filling the tavern with heat. Isabelle stepped around rough-hewn tables crammed with people wearing work-worn clothes. They lifted spoonfuls of porridge into their mouths while their strong voices and laughter rang through the establishment.

Though the room was built of weathered timber, the dimly lit wood tones didn't dull the atmosphere. The place should have been painted red for all the mirth within its walls.

The smell of eggs and porridge wrapped itself around her and set her stomach to growling. She trudged toward the bar, sloshing dirty puddles on the plank floor with her boots, letting the warmth from the fires seep through her damp clothes. What she wouldn't give to curl up beside the inviting flames and sleep for a day.

The publican, a large man with red cheeks half hidden by a beard, glanced up from filling two mugs. "You're a wet one there, boy."

"*Oui,* it's a terrible storm."

He handed the mugs to a barmaid dressed in a cheerful red skirt and eyed Isabelle.

Heat rushed to her cheeks. She cleared her throat and tried for a deeper voice. "Uh, aye."

The man slid her a glass of ale. She stared into the amber liquid, the stench stinging her nose. She'd had wine numerous times before the *Révolution* started, but this lower-class drink? Her stomach revolted. How did the patrons swallow this stuff, and so early in the morning?

"I'm just, ah, looking for the shipping office."

The man ran his eyes down her. She could feel him staring at the discolored patches on her hat and trousers. She shifted, her heart beating heavily in her chest. She clamped down her desire to press her eyes shut under his scrutiny. Why hadn't she brought her old brown cloak instead of this new one? It would have fit better with her disguise.

The publican laughed, a loud, rolling sound that quieted the nearby tables. "Leaving to try your luck somewhere else, are you? I wouldn't count on it." The man laughed again and pointed over his shoulder. "It's down the road. The little shack attached to the second warehouse. Nothing'll be leaving port in this weather, but you can get a ticket and settle up in the inn."

Nothing leaving? Hope left her in one violent rush, her stomach plummeting along with it. The cursed storm. Why now, of all times, when she was so close to leaving? *"Merci,"* she mumbled.

"Don't be looking so down, there, boy. The storm'll pass. They always do."

Isabelle nodded and fled back into the rain. She fought her way down the street, past two more shops until the quaint buildings of town fell away and she stood before the massive structures undoubtedly used to store imports and exports.

Lantern light flickered through a window on a little addition at the front of the second warehouse. She stepped away from a shop. A gust of wind buffeted her exhausted body, sending her sideways. She bent her head and raced forward, rain pelting the back of her neck.

She shoved through the door and into the quiet warmth. A wiry man with graying hair sat behind a counter. He looked up at her, then gazed back down at the pamphlet he read. Ledgers lined the wall behind him, each meticulously labeled. Imports and exports of various goods: salt fish, timber, textiles, wine.

"I need a ticket to Stockholm." She opened her valise and reached into the inside pocket for her money.

The man raised his dull blue eyes to her. "Nothing leaving for Stockholm till next week."

"But I need to go now."

"Have to be Copenhagen, then."

She slammed some money onto the counter. Did France always have to be warring with England? It was bad enough she had to sail to a neutral county before going to England, now she couldn't even get to the country she wanted.

"Very well, Copenhagen." She couldn't stay here for a week. Perchance she could catch a ship to England from Copenhagen. If not, she could go to Stockholm, then England. Provided she had money enough.

The man blew out a breath, ruffling the tuft of hair hanging over his wide forehead. "Got two of 'em headed for Copenhagen as soon as the storm blows out. You want the one laden with wine or the one carrying textiles? Both got room for passengers."

"I care not, I just want a ticket."

"Aye. Come back after the storm, then."

"After the storm? What good will that do me? I want a ticket now."

The man sighed. "Nothing's coming or going in this weather. The office is closed."

Her hand fisted around her money. "If the office is closed, why are you here?"

The man shifted idly and turned back to his pamphlet. She raised her chin. She knew why he was here, so he could log his hours and get his pay from the government for sitting on a stool reading. She put her hand over the page.

The man nudged the pamphlet away. "Get on with you now. Out."

"As soon as you give me a ticket and have someone row me to the vessel."

"Row you? In this weather?" The man smirked. "You'd be swept out to sea. And I'm not carting down the ledger and getting out the ink and quill to write you a ticket when I can do the same for you and a dozen others once the storm's past. The boat won't leave without you. Got a couple other passengers waiting for the textile vessel. And the crew's not even aboard. Just a few sailors out there to keep the cargo during the storm."

The man's eyes went back to the pamphlet, curse his lazy bones. She opened her mouth, a tongue-lashing waiting to pour out, but a sob caught in her throat instead. She could press the man further, but Jean Paul would come here and inquire at some point. Causing trouble for the clerk would only make her stand out, and might lead to Jean Paul figuring out her disguise.

She took the money off the counter and stepped back. So close to freedom, and still it eluded her like a mirage. She hastened outside before tears came and then stood hopelessly in the rain. Where to go now? She gripped her money. How much would a ticket on a cargo ship even cost? And why hadn't she asked? Had she money for an inn? She swiped a tear with the back of her hand. She didn't even know where an inn was.

The blur of a brown horse barreled down the street toward her. Her heart stopped as she caught a flash of red atop the rider's head. She paused only long enough to see more shadowed horses and riders follow the first, then she ducked around the far side of the building. *Not here. Not now. Please, Lord, don't let it be Jean Paul.* She peeked around the corner. The horses had slowed. One soldier had tied his horse and was pulling open the door to a building. The tavern she had entered? *Please, no.* But she couldn't know for certain from so far away. Two more dismounted and walked along the street, pounding on doors, but the first rider in the blue coat headed straight for the warehouse.

Her heart started an erratic, racing beat. *Run.* Somewhere. Anywhere.

She searched the nearby warehouses and shore for somewhere to hide, but the flat walls of the buildings wouldn't conceal her.

Neigh.

Isabelle jumped. The horse sounded nearly on top of her.

Thump. The shipping office door slamming shut?

She crept to the window and peered in, squinting to see through the murky, rain-smeared glass. Jean Paul strode straight to the clerk and spoke. The clerk said something and pointed to the door. Jean Paul said something more, and the clerk shook his head. Jean Paul whipped his hat off and smacked it against the counter. The clerk scowled and jabbed his finger toward the door. Jean Paul put his hat back on and hastened out.

Sweat beaded along her forehead. Jean Paul hadn't spent more than a minute inside. Surely he couldn't figure out her disguise so quickly, could he? Hopefully he assumed she hadn't made it into town. Gripping her valise, she hurried around the back of the building and plastered her back against the wall.

Sealed barrels of salt fish sat outside, lining the shore several rows deep, probably waiting to be loaded once the sea calmed. A perfect hiding place. She scooted left, toward the opposite end of the building and closer to the barrels. When she reached the northwest corner, she stepped away from the wall.

"Jean Paul!"

Isabelle dropped her bag and froze, blood pumping in her ears.

"Aye, Christophé."

Picking up her bag, she stepped back to the wall. She didn't know how long she stood there, listening to the male voices grow more heated.

"The other soldiers and I want our money."

"You have your share."

"Nay, man, we want more."

Isabelle looked left and then right. Nothing but the storm surrounded her. Should she move back to the other side of the building? She'd be farther from Jean Paul and whoever he spoke with, but also farther from the barrels. And someone could see her from the road. "There is no more. Everything's been divided evenly."

"You lie."

"Get back to your horse. Have you found the girl yet? She's probably escaping as we stand here!" A string of curses filtered through the rain. "I'll not. Leader or no, you'll not cheat us."

"I've not cheated you. I order you to your horse."

Pressure built in Isabelle's chest. Why could she not already have boarded a vessel in peaceful water and sailed away? If Jean Paul and his men didn't find her now, where would she hide to wait out the storm? And would he stay and search the passengers of ships departing after the storm?

"I don't accept orders from a cheat. I'll give you one last chance to redeem yourself."

"There is nothing to redeem save your greed."

"Aye, we'll see about that."

"I'm reporting your insolence to Le Bon. Go to your horse, straightway."

A gunshot pierced the air.

Fear rippled through Isabelle, an icelike cold. She shrank back against the wall, her heart beating so hard someone could surely hear it through the din of the storm.

She expected a shout, a scream. The sound of feet sloshing through mud and voices demanding an account of what transpired. Surely the clerk inside the office would have heard the gunfire.

The wind howled. The thunder rumbled. The sea roared. But no human sounds rang out. Did she dare look? She swallowed. Of course she wouldn't look. If anyone was still there, it would be someone who wanted her dead.

But she could well imagine the murderer running for his horse, and no one discovering the dead body until the storm let up.

Her throat tightened. What if Jean Paul had been shot? She had to know. She'd see whoever it was when she ran to the barrels, anyway.

She inched toward the edge of the building. She could do this. Just a peek. It wouldn't be Jean Paul. Surely not. Jean Paul was such a hothead he'd pull his own pistol first. Besides, wasn't he in charge of the men he traveled with?

And why did she even care whether it was Jean Paul? The man had ordered her beaten to death. But her mind conjured a heartbreaking image of Michel being told his only brother had been murdered.

She took a deep breath and glanced around the side of the building.

A soldier lay on the ground, the blood on his chest matching the shade of his liberty cap, his already pale skin a stark contrast against his blue National Guard coat. She swallowed and stepped closer, but she needn't see his face. Just the size gave him away.

Someone had shot Jean Paul, and no one but her was around to help.

Chapter Nineteen

As though drawn by a force she couldn't repel, Isabelle crept closer to Jean Paul, the mud squishing beneath her feet as she stepped. The blood staining his chest mixed with the rain and trickled to the ground beneath him.

She covered her mouth and stared. Her stomach knotted and uncurled in a sickening sensation, and gooseflesh broke out over her arms.

Should she call for help? Run somewhere and find a doctor? Or was it too late? What if he'd been shot in the heart? She moved to the body, her eyes roving his form for any sign as to where he might be injured, but through the blood, she couldn't tell where the bullet had hit.

A low groan resonated from Jean Paul's throat. Isabelle jumped back, but not before his eyes lolled open. His gaze drifted to hers, as though he knew she was there, watching him die. She waited for the word *help* to roll from his mouth.

Yet he didn't speak. His mouth hardened into the same set line he'd displayed when he told Michel he'd tie her up and take her to Paris in the morning. Hatred still burned in his eyes, even through the sheen of pain. She hadn't understood the vehemence in his stare when he first attacked her in the woods, but she understood the accusation now. *You killed my wife. Now I'll kill you.*

Her heart pumping, she pressed her hands to her ribs and took a step back, bumping into the wall of the warehouse behind her. Fresh fear burst like a devouring fire into her chest. She scanned the narrow, deserted alley between the two warehouses. Were the other soldiers near, waiting to carry her off to Paris and the guillotine?

Jean Paul's eyes drifted shut, and his chest barely rose and fell, his breathing growing shallower.

A shout. A yell. Somewhere in the distance. Had she imagined it?

Cold sweat beaded on her skin, and her breathing came in short gasps. She had to hide. Hopefully the murderer and other soldiers had left town, but if not… Grasping her valise, she ran to the barrels of salt fish.

She tried to slip behind a barrel, but the containers were grouped so close together she couldn't squeeze in. Setting her bag on the ground, she gripped one of the barrels in front with both hands and tried to pull it forward. The barrel lurched a bit, digging deeper into the wet sand as it moved.

She looked back at Jean Paul, still lying in the mud. Surely someone would discover him soon. She had to hurry before the person also spotted her. Grunting, she heaved the barrel a hand-span or so away from the others. Just enough to squeeze her slender body and her bag between the aged wooden drums.

She sank to the ground, rain slashing at her. She squished her hat farther onto her head and pulled the hood of her woolen cloak up over her hat. Through the blur of biting rain, she watched tiny drops bead and roll off the untreated wool of her cloak. Her hands felt like icicles. She pulled her knees to her chest, wrapped her cloak around them, tucked her hands inside the thick folds and huddled into the warmth of the heavy fabric. Safe at last. Who would look for her here?

Jean Paul's men could search all the inns in town, and she was hiding in the middle of the storm. As long as no one came close enough to notice the slightly displaced container, she was safe.

She peeked through the space between the tops of two barrels. Jean Paul still lay sprawled in the mud. Isabelle swallowed and ducked her head. Just because the man wanted her dead didn't mean she needed to watch him bleed to death.

She'd dwell on something else entirely. What would Jeanette be doing today? Mending, probably. Trousers? A hat? And Michel, he'd be in his workshop, likely sanding the table he'd started. She pressed her eyes shut and tried to conjure up an image of Michel smoothing the tabletop, but what if he wasn't sanding? What if he was out searching for her or so upset with her he couldn't bear to work? She shoved that thought away only to have the image of Jean Paul lying in the rain cling to her mind instead.

Did God think she had a heart made of marble that she could watch the brother of the man she loved die? She took a deep breath. Jean Paul had probably killed dozens, maybe hundreds, of others. God was just giving him what he deserved. Besides, someone would surely discover him soon.

She peeked back at Jean Paul, hoping to see a man standing over him, calling for help. But for the lone body on the wet earth, the alley between the warehouses lay deserted. She swallowed.

God, please, I can't watch him die. Send someone to aid him. Quickly. Even if he can't be helped, at least send someone to find the body.

She waited expectantly but no one came. She looked around as best she could through the little space between the barrels while seconds languished into minutes, and still, nobody appeared.

It was just her and Jean Paul. No one came for her—and no one came for him. Though meters stretched between them, she felt as though she stood over him, watching the pool of blood slowly expand on his chest.

~.~.~.~.~

"You're not hungry?"

Michel stirred the squash soup in his wooden bowl and didn't bother to look at *Mère* across the table. *"Non."* How could he eat with Isabelle out there, alone in the storm while Jean Paul searched for her?

"It's your favorite. Just take a bite."

It had been *Père's* favorite, never his. But Michel took a bite, anyway.

"See, I knew you'd like it."

He sent her a halfhearted smile.

Her brow wrinkled as she looked at the chair Isabelle usually occupied. "Wherever is Isabelle, I wonder? It's not like her to miss a meal. Did you tell her supper was ready?"

"She's gone." He could hardly get the words over his tongue. "She's not coming back."

Mère's eyes rounded in alarm, and he nearly sank his head. How many times must he tell his mother Isabelle wasn't here and wouldn't be returning? For just once, he wanted the old *Mère* back. The *Mère* who looked at him with understanding rather than confusion, who remembered he liked venison stew, not squash soup, who let him sit in the rocker and stare at the fire without interrupting his reverie with a hundred questions about Isabelle and Jean Paul. The *Mère* who—

"We should pray for the dear girl, then." *Mère* glanced toward the window. "How terrible to be out in this storm."

He felt it then, a sudden heaviness descending upon the room, pressing against his heart. His own heartache seemed to evaporate under the ominous weight.

Isabelle. No. She'd been captured. How else to explain the darkness in his soul? He had to go to her. It mattered not that she'd left him. Lied to him. He couldn't sit back and eat and wait. Even if she wanted nothing to do with him, even if he was too late to help, even if she escaped and left for Stockholm without him, he needed to make sure she was safe, if not fight for her.

He reached out and grasped both of *Mère's* hands. "Yes, let's pray. And when we're done praying, I'll take you to Narcise's house. You'll pass a night or two there. I've business to attend on the coast."

~.~.~.~.~

Isabelle shrank back against the wet barrel but still couldn't take her eyes from Jean Paul. What if God already sent someone to save him? What if God sent her? No, God. You can't mean for me to save this man. *Have someone else help him.*

Her body trembled with revulsion. But hadn't God done the same for her, hadn't God sent Michel to save her despite her role in Marie's death?

And how hard could it be to call for a doctor? That's all she need do, just find a doctor and then hide until she could leave for Copenhagen. No one need ever know she helped.

She gulped in a breath and stood on shaky legs. She clasped her valise and shimmied her way between the barrels. Once out, she moved swiftly toward Jean Paul. From a distance, Jean Paul's face and hands appeared paler than before, though that hardly seemed possible. What if he was already dead? What if he had died while she waited for someone else to come? Her stomach churned as she broke into a run and sailed several steps past Jean Paul. Fisting her hands, she banged against the small window on the side of the shipping office. "Help! Help!"

She dropped her valise, moved back to Jean Paul and hunkered down. His chest rose and fell slowly, but what had once been a little puddle of blood now drenched the entire side of his National Guard coat.

"Jean Paul. Are you still awake?" She ran her hands over his face. "Open your eyes if you can hear me. Jean Paul."

No response.

Wearing a thick, hooded cloak, the clerk appeared from around the front of the building and sauntered toward them.

"Hurry, quick! Go for the doctor. He's been shot!"

The clerk stared back at her, his eyes blank. "You want a doctor? You better have money. Doctor won't treat anyone without payment first."

Money? Since Jean Paul had stolen her extra funds, she hardly had enough to get to England. Her hands raced through the pockets of his coat and trousers. Nothing. Whoever shot him must have robbed him, as well.

She swallowed thickly. At least Jean Paul had already lost consciousness and wouldn't feel more pain.

She couldn't give up England. For Michel, maybe.

But not for Jean Paul. How could she?

The clerk cleared his throat. "So do you want a doctor or not?" He crossed his arms, his foot tapping against the mud. "Me? I'd leave him lay."

Isabelle bit her lip. She'd tried to help. Wasn't that enough?

But a man shouldn't die for something as trivial as lack of money. Not even Jean Paul.

Tears sprang to her eyes and streaked down her face, mixing with the rain in an endless stream she'd no desire to stop. *Father, no. You can't ask this of me. It's too much. He hates me.*

Couldn't someone else appear? Someone with money who could see to Jean Paul while she hid?

But no wealthy gentleman appeared in the alley or fell from heaven or arose from the sea.

Rain streamed in sheets around them, welting the ground, mixing with the blood gurgling from Jean Paul's chest and splattering the hem of her trousers with mud. The wind grew eerily still, as though heaven itself held its breath and waited for her decision. England or Jean Paul?

She put her hand to Jean Paul's forehead. The strong nose and prominent chin similar to Michel's. Oh, why couldn't she look into Jean Paul's face without seeing traces of Michel? Without thinking of Jeanette and how she'd already lost her husband? Isabelle clutched her hands to her chest. Perchance she could ignore God, brush off His urgings and proddings. But how could she turn her back on Michel's brother when Michel had risked his very life to save her and then sheltered her?

She glanced up and nodded toward the clerk. "Go." The word felt like sawdust in her mouth.

The clerk didn't move.

"Run!" she screamed. "And if you don't hurry, his death will be on your hands!"

The man hastened away. Isabelle took Jean Paul's wrist. But where to find his pulse? She felt nothing but the slick rain on his skin. She stared at Jean Paul's blood-soaked jacket, then scrambled toward her valise, unlatched it and grabbed the skirt on top. Stop the bleeding. Wasn't that the first thing she should do? She wadded up the garment and pressed it to his chest.

~.~.~.~.~

"Sorry, *citoyen*, but I've not seen anyone by that description." The innkeeper spoke above the clamor of a room stuffed with patrons eating and drinking.

"Are you certain?" Standing near the entrance to the kitchen, Michel hunched his shoulders under his rain-slicked cloak and rubbed his tired eyes.

The innkeeper, a portly man with a bushy beard, scratched the top of his balding head. "Well, there was a woman with wavy black hair who rented a room, but she's married. Came in with her husband who'd been shot earlier today. Poor man's body was covered in blood. Doubt he'll live to see the morrow, but if you'd like to speak to the wife, I can ask her to come down."

"*Non, 'tis* not the woman I seek." His chest felt hollow inside. His search for Isabelle was turning out futile. He probably shouldn't be checking the inns. They were the first place soldiers would search, and thus the last place she would hide. But with the rain still pounding and the wind still screaming outside, he didn't know where else to look.

"You seem in need of a good meal and a warm bed, yourself." The man turned back toward the kitchen. "Marcel, fix me up a bowl of stew and biscuits."

The thought of food churned his stomach. The owners at the first three inns he'd visited offered him similar fare. But how could he eat when Jean Paul might already have Isabelle in his clutches? "There's no need. I must away, posthaste. But tell me this, have you seen *soldats* about?"

"*Oui.* They barged in here a few hours ago, looked around and left." The man's eyes darkened. "Why? They looking for you?"

"*Non.*"

Carrying a wooden bowl, a plump woman with auburn hair twisted back into a bun emerged from the kitchen, probably the Marcel to whom the innkeeper had just spoken. She waddled to the other man and shoved the bowl toward Michel. "This for you?"

His stomach twisted and roiled as he stared at the meat and

vegetables in their thick, disgusting sauce. He should be famished. He'd eaten nothing since those two bites of *Mère's* soup at lunch.

But he shook his head, afraid he would gag if he tried to speak, and turned for the door. Food, rest—everything could wait until he'd found Isabelle and either seen her safe, or died protecting her.

Chapter Twenty

Isabelle watched the bed opposite hers in the tiny, dingy room. Jean Paul's rhythmic breathing filled the space between the ancient stone walls, while sunlight streamed through the room's single window. From somewhere on the square below, children shouted, women chattered and horses clomped. But she couldn't take her eyes from the bed where Jean Paul lay.

He'd wake eventually. The bullet had missed his heart and lungs, entering just right of his left shoulder. He fought not against internal damage, but loss of blood and possible infection. At first, the doctor thought Jean Paul had lost so much blood he wouldn't live. Since she had already paid for a room at the inn and Jean Paul needed a nurse, she claimed to be his wife so she could tend him until he died.

But Jean Paul hadn't died that first night. Or the next night, or the next. For four days, she cared for the man who wanted her dead. And each day his breathing grew deeper and his pulse stronger.

A chill raced down her spine. Those dark eyes couldn't open and find her here. What if he tried to kill her again? Each moment she lingered brought her closer to the inevitable.

She stood and walked across the room, her footsteps echoing on the floor as she headed to the rickety chest of drawers. She opened the top drawer and grasped her dwindling bundle of money.

Perchance she could find him a nurse. Someone on the street who needed employment. She'd pay for a week's worth of care. If Jean Paul needed nursing after that, he could pay for it himself. That way she'd have enough money to go…

Where? She didn't have enough to go to Stockholm, and she could hardly abandon Jean Paul in Saint-Valery and head back to Michel. What would she say to him? "I saved your brother's life, then became frightened he might still try to kill me, so I left him half-dead in Saint-Valery"?

As though Michel would be willing to listen to her after how she'd tricked him.

She clutched her money to her chest and reviewed the words they'd exchanged in his workshop.

You deceived yourself, Michel. I didn't need you. I never needed you.

I should let you go and refuse you when you come crawling back after your little adventure ends in chaos.

She slumped forward until her head touched the dresser. Oh, Michel. Would she forever be so independent and stubborn? If only she had listened to him that night, had let him come with her. He would know what to do for Jean Paul.

How to protect her.

"What are you doing here?"

Isabelle stilled. The bedcover rustled behind her. Though the voice was groggy, she couldn't mistake it.

Her stomach churned, and her heart beat like the slow, heavy rhythm of a funeral dirge.

"Well? Answer my question, wench."

"I…gathering some things." She could barely get the words past her thick throat.

"Get out." His voice, hardly more than a rasp, held a razor's edge.

I was there when your sister was killed. Do you know what we did after we guillotined her?

Fury swept through her. She put her money back in the drawer, then slammed it shut and whirled around to face him.

Vehemence burned so hotly in his eyes she nearly staggered back. Instead, she raised her chin. *"Non."*

"I said, *Get out!"*

"I paid for this room. *You* leave." The instant she spoke, she regretted her words. A spark of fear ignited inside her. Had he the strength to get out of that bed?

Thankfully, he didn't try. "You think nursing me will save your neck?" Jean Paul growled. "You're wrong. I'll laugh as I watch you die."

"Why do you hate me? I love your family. I saved you, though only heaven knows why. You would have bled to death in the storm. Do you realize that? You want to know why I'm here rather than on a ship to Copenhagen or Stockholm or New York? Because I spent my money saving your vile, filthy life. You'd be dead if not for me."

"I still hate you, I'll always hate you. And you know why."

"Why? Because your wife died, like you told Michel? I didn't kill your wife. That's preposterous. I didn't even know her."

Jean Paul's hands fisted in the quilt. "She starved to death, because of aristocrats like you."

"Ugh." Had a more insufferable man ever been born? She fought between the urge to pull her hair out and the desire to clamp her hands around Jean Paul's neck and squeeze. "She died of pneumonia."

"She caught pneumonia, but that didn't take her. It was—"

"Stop." She'd no desire to hear of the circumstances that had prompted Jean Paul to leave his family and kill innocents in the name of the *Révolution*. That had caused him to cheer when Marie was executed or that made him drive her from Michel's arms.

Jean Paul hardened his jaw. "A little uncomfortable to speak of, is it? We followed the doctor's instructions with Corinne and gave her the medicine."

Isabelle worried the folds of her skirt, wishing she could shut out the story.

"She started to get better, but she was thin. We had barely any food. We'd sold half our chickens. The hail the summer before took our harvest and destroyed our garden save a few root vegetables. And the price of flour was rising."

His brow wrinkled, and fresh pain and bitterness swept his features. "I gave her my food and went without. So did Michel and *Ma Mère*. But Corinne didn't...she couldn't..."

A tear swelled in the corner of his eye. Jean Paul used his good arm to push himself farther up on the bed, his face whitening under the strain. "I went to Seigneur Montrose and asked for grain. He had a whole barn filled with wheat from the harvest two years earlier. And more chickens than he could count, and hogs and cows. And..."

The scar beside his eyebrow bunched into an angry fist as his muscles tensed. "The *seigneur* laughed. Asked if I knew how much a sack of grain was worth because of the famine. I told him half the grain in the barn wasn't his, anyway. He hadn't worked for it. He'd stolen it from peasants and called it his land duty." Jean Paul's hands shook. "The *seigneur* had me thrown out."

Isabelle wrung her hands. She could well speculate as to what happened next.

"Two mornings later, I woke, and Corinne was dead. Seigneur Montrose had laughed at me, and Corinne starved to death. Practically on his doorstep."

"I—I'm sorry." Her words sounded weak.

"Sorry? You say Corinne's death wasn't your fault? What about your *père*, the Duc de La Rouchecauld?" Jean Paul seared her with his smoldering gaze. "Did he throw open his barns and storehouses that winter so the peasants living on and working his land didn't starve? Did he pay for a doctor when a widow fell sick or take grain to a starving child?"

Isabelle took a step backward. "*Mon Père?* I don't know."

"You lie. You were how old, fourteen, fifteen during the famine of '89?" The smoldering fire in his eye burst into a blaze.

"Sixteen."

"You'd remember."

She stared into his blind hatred, and heaven help her, a tear streaked down her face. She deserved it, she supposed. This man's wrath, the hatred of the entire French working class. "We—" she cleared her throat "—we were at Versailles during that time. At court."

He laughed, the cruelest, most bone-chilling sound she had ever heard. "Ah, so you were playing games and entertaining the king. How many peasants working for your father do you suppose died during that famine, while you were away?"

Bile rose in her stomach. Why was he saying such things? She'd no control of her father's affairs. "I—I don't know. No one, I think."

But she felt the guilt somewhere deep inside, as the bile surged to her throat. Had she even bothered to ask her father what he was doing about the famine? She knew about it, *oui,* but only as a subject of conversation within the palace walls. While others were dying, her family and friends lived in opulence, feasted even, during their last days at Versailles…until a mob of women demanding bread drove them from the grand palace.

"You only hope no one died." Jean Paul sneered, disgust covering his face. "You think you deserve my gratitude because you saved me? You were playing while my wife starved. Where were your grand gestures then? Even now, you're not here because of me. You'd have let me die if not for my brother, *oui?*" His eyes narrowed. "Get out of this room. If I ever see you again, I'll kill you."

Her chest tight, she fled out of the room, through the corridor and down the stairs. She barely reached the door before the bile building inside her swelled to her mouth and she retched.

Sunshine filtered down on her, a haunting contrast to the misery in her soul. She jumped out of the way as a horse-drawn wagon filled with a family rolled by. To her left three boys chased a ball. Past the boys, two men with red faces looked to be in a heated debate. The town square teemed with people coming and going, women with children in tow, men with purposeful strides, even a meandering dog.

Air. She needed air. And space. But the busyness of the town pressed upon her, the walls of the medieval village closing in. She raced toward the northern gate and the bay, gulping breaths but never seeming to fill her lungs.

How dare Jean Paul refuse her help? She had saved him. Paid for a doctor and room at the inn. Given up England for him. What did he think? That without funds she could just board a ship to Copenhagen or Stockholm or some other such city?

She wanted to say his actions didn't matter, that his words didn't hurt, that he could rot in that lumpy inn bed for all she cared. But if it didn't matter, why did her heart feel as though it had shattered?

A tear rolled down her cheek as her feet tapped against the weathered cobblestones. She could feel people's eyes boring into her back. What a fright she must look. A woman with a basket of eggs sauntered into the street in front of her, forcing her to move to the other side of the road.

She swiped at the tear. So what if she'd saved Jean Paul because of Michel? Did her reason make that much difference? She'd still saved him, and he was alive today because of her. Didn't that mean something? Anything? She reached the harbor and sank down in the sand.

Jean Paul had haunted her dreams for months, ever since that first attack in the woods. And four days ago, when she had stood over his lifeless body with the opportunity to either save him or walk away, she had saved him.

Still he hated her, blamed her for a death over which she'd had no control.

Michel had said she needed to forgive her attacker, just as God had forgiven her. Isabelle stiffened as she recalled the words. Had he spoken them only five days ago? It seemed the whole world had changed since then. She'd told Michel no. Perhaps God had forgiven her for a mistake. But Jean Paul's actions against her had been calculated, deliberate. Even now, after saving his life, he still wanted her dead.

She stared out into the harbor. A vessel laden with exports looked ready to disembark and fishing boats dotted the bay. One small craft edged toward the open sea, free to sail or float wherever it willed, despite the threat of British warships lurking in the waters beyond. Yet she was stuck in France, with nothing but a handful of coins and a few dying dreams to sustain her.

No... She didn't even have her money. She'd left that and her belongings in the inn with Jean Paul.

Her hands dug into the sand and fisted around the tiny granules. "Wasn't saving him enough, Father? You would require forgiveness from me now? I can't forgive him. He tried to kill me. Would have killed me if Michel hadn't found me." How much more could she endure?

But God had forgiven her despite what she did to Marie.

"I can't, Father. I just can't. I'm not as strong as Michel. Oh, God, how do I even start to forgive him?" *Father, forgive them; for they know not what they do.* God asked no more of her than He asked of His own Son.

Did she want to face her life racked with bitterness toward Jean Paul? Her bitterness over Marie's death had nearly destroyed her.

So, what were her choices? She could walk away this instant and leave Jean Paul. The man wasn't likely to forgive her anytime soon.

Though if she left, she didn't know what she would do, nor where she would go. She would find work somewhere, perchance. Until she earned enough money for passage—and how many more years would that take?

Or she could forgive Jean Paul.

The revolutionaries in Paris spouted nobility as the only cause for the *Révolution,* and people like Jean Paul believed it. Who was really to blame for the attack on her? Jean Paul, or the commander who sent Jean Paul to patrol northern France, or the *seigneur* who had laughed when Jean Paul wanted food for his wife, or God for allowing it all to happen?

But Michel had told her that even though sin motivated the actions of men, forgiveness came from God. She fell forward, her forehead touching the sand. "I forgive him." Sobs tore from her chest until it ached. "God, I forgive Jean Paul for trying to kill me, for wanting me dead even now. Forgive me for waiting so long to do so."

⁓.⁓.⁓.⁓.⁓

"I told you before. Three times before. I haven't seen a girl like you describe, and the boy that came in during the storm hasn't been back for his ticket."

"You're wrong." Michel ground his teeth as he stared at the wiry clerk in the shipping office. He'd visited the man for the past four days, and every day the man gave the same answer. No one matching either Isabelle's description or disguise had purchased passage. "Nothing would have stopped this person from boarding one of your ships."

"You're daft, *citoyen.*"

"Could she have snuck onto a boat without you knowing?"

The man smirked. "A wench sneaking onto a boat without the sailors noticing? Not likely."

Something hot clenched in his gut. "What if the sailors didn't tell you?"

The man's eyes went cold, flat. "A single woman sneaks aboard a ship, I'm going to hear about it. Though I can't comprehend why any woman would do such a thing. The sailors would use her up faster than—"

Michel growled and slapped his hands on the desk.

The man nearly toppled off his stool. "Uh, that is, I don't think the sailors would be all that kind to a lone wench who snuck aboard."

Michel rubbed the back of his neck. He'd spent the past four days scouring every passenger who waited to board a disembarking ship and had given Isabelle's description to anyone who would listen.

But the answer was always the same. No one had seen her.

He spent his nights visiting the eating establishments and inns in Saint-Valery, but the answers he found in those places depressed him as much as the shipping clerk's.

Jean Paul couldn't have caught Isabelle. News of a *duc's* daughter being captured would spread through this port town in an instant, and no one had seen soldiers since the day of the storm.

"You're welcome to go out and ask the sailors if they saw her," the clerk added.

Michel sunk his teeth into his tongue and beat back his urge to strangle the wiry man. He didn't have time to speak to passengers today or talk to innkeepers, sailors and publicans yet again. He had to go home. He'd told Narcise he'd be gone one night, maybe two, and he'd been gone four.

He slapped a fistful of coins on the counter. "I have to leave today. Here's money. If you find the girl I seek, send information to my farm near Abbeville, and I'll pay you more." Which would, in effect, deplete the vast majority of money he managed to save since taking over the farm.

But he'd give away the farm itself to have Isabelle back. To take her in his arms and taste those full, lush lips and look into those deep brown eyes once more.

The clerk's eyes lit with greed. "Where'd you say your farm was?" After giving the man directions, he pushed his way outside and glanced out over the bay, as though simply looking that direction would make her appear. Where was she now?

Had she escaped him as well as the soldiers? Was she on her way to Stockholm even now, dreaming of the day she landed in London? Was she happy?

He lifted his face to the sky. *Father, keep her safe.*

He couldn't return to the farm without her. How could he bear to look at the bed whereon she slept or her spot at the dinner table? How could he forget the way her eyes danced in the sunlight, the way her chin quivered when she tried to be strong...or the way she felt in his arms?

Pain gripped his chest as he turned his back toward the bay and started the long walk home.

⌐.⌐.⌐.⌐.⌐

Isabelle brushed the sand from her hands and skirt as she stared at the closed door of Jean Paul's room. She'd no concept of how long she'd lain on the beach making her peace with God, but as soon as she arose, she headed straight here. She grasped the door handle, slowly lifted the latch and pushed the door open.

Jean Paul lay on his bed sleeping peacefully. She walked to him and laid a hand on his arm, warm and strong. His eyes sprang open.

"I'm sorry your wife died without help from the *seigneur*. And I'm sorry my family lived lavishly at the expense of people such as you. Please forgive me."

He jerked his arm away. Wincing in pain, he covered his shoulder with his other hand and propped himself up against some pillows. "Aye, I'll forgive you—when I see your head roll."

But his cruel words no longer made her skin crawl; his hatred no longer brought fear. "Know this, then—I forgive you."

Fury radiated from him like heat from a fire. He spit at her feet. "I don't want your forgiveness. You deserve to die."

"I forgive you, anyway." The simple, quiet words filled the room with a power more explosive than Jean Paul's hatred. "What you do with it is your choice."

Jean Paul glared. "Maybe you didn't understand when I said I'd kill you if you ever came back."

She ran her eyes over his injured body. Such a strong specimen of manhood. He should be home, helping Michel on the farm. Instead, he'd allowed years of bitterness to feast on his heart until his magnificent body became a shell for the soul dying inside. "You won't kill me."

"No? Ha! You're a fool." He licked his cracked lips but refused to meet her eyes. "What is it you want? Money for nursing me?"

"I want you to accept my forgiveness."

His face paled, and his breathing grew strained.

"Where are my clothes? I've money in my coat. I'll pay for the room, and you can leave."

"All you have to say, Jean Paul, is 'I accept your forgiveness.'"

He shivered as his name left her lips. "My money, wench!" He reached out and fisted his hand in her skirt, pulling her closer.

"You've no money. Whoever shot you stole it. And I'm not leaving until we resolve whatever's between us."

"Christophé." He shut his eyes and whispered, "The traitor."

She wasn't about to be distracted. "You could also try, 'I shouldn't have attempted to kill you.' Or, 'thank you for saving my life.' Any such statement will do."

He cracked an eyelid, his chest heaving laboriously for the little energy he'd exerted. "Why?" Jean Paul's voice rusted.

"Because you shouldn't judge me by my parents' actions. Did you know they're dead? A mob attacked them as they were trying to reach our *château,* and they were slaughtered along with my little brother. Does that bring you comfort?"

"No." His eyelids drooped. "I understand you want an apology. But why are you rescuing me, forgiving me—" he forced his eyes open "—after I tried to kill you?"

Her throat felt swollen. "Because it's what God wants. It's no less than He did for me."

Jean Paul turned his head away and stared out the window. She wanted to stomp her feet and shout and scream. *You can't ignore me. I won't go away.*

Instead, she raised her chin. He was bound to a bed, and she could wait just as long as he.

Chapter Twenty-One

A draft greeted Isabelle as she walked through the door with Jean Paul's lunch tray. She shivered and glared at the man, who had apparently opened the window to the cold drizzle outside, and who even now stared out it as though it was perfectly sane to keep a window open while it rained. He'd been awake for a week, and though he hadn't tried to hurt her, the brute still hadn't acknowledged her forgiveness.

He was growing stronger by the day. Out of bed and walking around the room now. But a healthy body did little good when one's heart was sick. Much as she wanted to square off and then leave him to his own devices, he might never change if she left now. If she walked out of the inn this day, nothing prevented him from running back to the army and cutting down the next woman he found walking through the woods.

She set the tray on the dresser and moved to shut the window at the foot of his bed.

"Leave it open." Jean Paul spoke without looking at her.

She crossed her arms and stared at him. Such an angry, brooding man. She never knew what to expect. "The quilt is getting wet."

"She was like this."

Isabelle frowned. "Who? What?"

"The rain." He closed his eyes and inhaled, as though the scent of rain could bring him peace. "Corinne was like the spring rain." His opened eyes glazed with both love and pain. "The kind that tinges everything in its path with gentleness, that gives life and color to everything it touches."

The rain. How could such a hateful man say such sweet things of his late wife?

She ran her gaze over Jean Paul's face—his strong nose, his thin dark eyebrows, the hard planes of his cheeks, the square set of his jaw and the scar twisting around the far end of his right eyebrow. Despite his faults, this man had loved his wife.

What would it be like to have such a consuming love for someone...or did she already know?

Could she love Michel as Jean Paul had loved Corinne? Wholly. Entirely. Exhaustingly? Would Michel take her back after how she left? Or had she given up the only chance she'd have at real love?

"You're thinking of him, again."

Isabelle sucked in a sharp breath. Her eyes snapped to Jean Paul's, which stared mildly back at her. Had her thoughts been that obvious? "I know not what you speak of."

"You're lying, woman." He scowled. "Don't play coy. Michel loves you, and you know it."

She turned away. *Non,* she didn't know Michel loved her anymore. Two weeks ago, she wouldn't have doubted his love, but Michel couldn't possibly feel the same after she lied to him and ran away. "You're mistaken."

"I held a knife to his throat, and he still wouldn't tell me where you were."

Her heart stopped, and her mouth turned sour. She whirled around. "A knife! How dare you?"

Jean Paul moved his legs over the edge of the bed and sat. "Don't get uppity with me. I didn't draw blood. Well, mayhap a drop or two, but nothing serious."

"That makes it better." She balled her hands into fists and stalked toward the door. "A knife on your only brother. And France thinks nobility needs to be guillotined."

He chuckled, the lightest sound she'd ever heard from the man.

Rage surged through her blood. "I see you feel the same way."

"What?" She paused at the door and turned back, prepared to tell Jean Paul to find another nurse and his own way back to his family. She was leaving.

"You love him, too."

"Don't you dare. Don't you even think of telling me how I feel about your brother. You know nothing of our relationship. Nothing of what it cost me to leave him. Of what it cost me to stay here and care for a man who still wishes me dead."

"I don't wish you dead any longer." His words, so quiet in relation to her outburst, held the power of a raging sea behind them.

Her jaw dropped slightly. "What mean you?"

"I shouldn't have tried killing you." He rubbed his fingers across his brow. "Though you may well be the only aristocrat in France worthy of life."

She moved closer to him, failing to comprehend the full meaning of his words. "I—"

"And I wasn't in Paris when your sister was killed. I've been in north France all this time. I just said it to get you riled that night."

She opened her mouth, but no words came. "Probably should have told you that bit about your sister sooner, huh?"

"Why the change?" She could barely move the words over the lump in her throat.

"I didn't think you meant it—about really forgiving me." He looked out the window, then back. "But you stayed. I figured you would leave me and go back to my brother."

"I thought about leaving, but then it seemed my forgiveness would have just been with my mouth and not from my heart."

"You saved me because of Michel, didn't you?"

She nodded. Her throat felt too swollen to function, and tears gathered behind her eyes.

"Never thought I'd see the day I'd want my brother to marry the daughter of a *duc*."

Marry? Surely Jean Paul hadn't said the word.

He eyed her, as though observing her posture and stricken face for the first time during their conversation. "You're going back to him, aren't you?"

She shook her head. "You don't understand how I left. I betrayed him." Her heart ripped afresh as she forced the truthful words over her tongue. "I lied to him. And he said…he wouldn't take me back."

"My brother'll do right by you. We'll head back together, in a couple days. When I'm strong enough to walk that far." Jean Paul spoke as though going back to Michel was the easiest decision in the world, as though Michel would want her back.

"You weren't listening. I said—"

"I heard you."

She twisted her hands together. Could she face Michel again? A shiver slid down her spine. Could she live with herself if she didn't try to make things right? She owed him an apology, at the least. Even if he sent her away afterward.

Jean Paul hefted himself from the bed and walked to the dresser. "Three days, mayhap four, and I can walk the distance."

She peered into his concerned eyes and swallowed. "Very well."

"Good, then." He settled his hat atop his head. "I'm going out for a bit."

Her face drained. "Out? You can't go out. You're not well."

He didn't even glance in her direction as he shuffled to the door and pulled on his tattered National Guard coat. "Think you that I can walk to Abbeville several days hence, but I can't stroll around the town square this afternoon?"

"It's raining."

He pulled open the door. "I've a hat and coat." She snatched up her cloak. "I'll accompany you."

He turned and watched her, his eyes softening into more of a gray than black. "You stay and rest." He smiled, the half curve of his lips so similar to Michel's that her heart ached.

She turned away.

Jean Paul let himself out, and numb with fresh thoughts of her love, she moved to her tick...and prayed Michel would take her back.

She awoke to the echo of boots striding down the corridor. Stretching, she sat up and glanced around the empty room. How long had she slept? The boot steps slowed near her room. Jean Paul must be returning even now. She stood as the door creaked open, and a tall figure loomed in the doorway.

She paused. The chamber tilted and couldn't seem to right itself, time freezing as she stared into a pair of warm, dandelion-green eyes.

"Michel." Half-afraid he would disappear, she flew toward him at the same moment he raced to her. They met in the middle of the room. His tall, muscled body enfolded her in its strength, his arms wrapping around her with such force she could hardly breathe. "Michel, oh, Michel. Is it you? I can't believe you're here, that you came...after how I—"

He hushed her with his mouth, a warm, passionate meeting of lips and hearts and souls. Moisture from his rain-damp garments seeped into her clothes, but caught in his arms, the wetness brought no chill to her skin. His hands stroked down her back, up her arms, around her neck as his mouth lingered over hers.

Tears streaked down her cheeks, their saltiness mingling with the frenetic kiss. His lips roamed her face and captured the tiny beads of sorrow and joy even as his hands slid into her hair and held her head. The kisses ceased and he rested his forehead against hers. "Isabelle." No word had ever sounded sweeter.

~.~.~.~.~

A shadow, a wraith, a mirage. Though Michel held her soft, lithe form in his arms, ran his hands over her, he couldn't believe he'd found her. He'd searched for her once, only to come away desolate. But now...

She sighed, drawing him closer and linking her arms about his neck, but he shifted her back, pressing her shoulders away. His eyes roved over every detail of her face and body. Not a bruise or scratch marred her porcelain skin. Somehow, through all the days she'd been gone, she'd managed to stay safe. "I love you."

Her breath caught, hope filling her eyes while a single tear trailed down her cheek. Gray light from the windows fell across her riotous hair, highlighting the glossy mixture of russet and black. Her throat worked, a back and forth movement of her creamy skin and smooth, long neck.

"I love you, too."

The quiet words filled his heart, trickled through his blood, swelled through his muscles until he nearly exploded with joy. He crushed her against himself. How long had he waited for that simple pledge? How many nights had he dreamed of finding her and hearing her say those precious words? "I knew. The day of our picnic, I knew you loved me."

He expected a smile, a slow curve of those full red lips. Instead, she buried her head in his chest and clutched the folds of his shirt. "I deceived you, then left you. I'm so sorry."

He took her chin and tilted it up, then cupped her cheek. "I already forgave you, *mon amour*."

"But that night in your woodshed, you said you wouldn't take me back after—"

"Shhh." He held his finger to her lips. "Don't remind me of my cruel words. You're safe. That's all that matters. Jean Paul told me as much, but I couldn't believe him until I saw you myself."

"Jean Paul?" She gripped his shirt even tighter. "He found you?"

"*Oui,* in the town square. I'd been searching for a soldier who could tell me what became of my brother. And when I looked out the window of the inn, there he was."

"I don't understand. Why would you even be in Saint-Valery?"

"To search for you, my love."

Despair clouded her eyes. "But I left you."

"I couldn't sit home while my brother chased the woman I love." He swallowed, the grief over believing her lost still churning in his gut. He rested his forehead against hers and slid his hands around the back of her neck. "I came, and I searched. I watched ship passengers, spoke to innkeepers and talked with the shipping clerk. No one had seen a single woman who matched your description."

"You didn't give up…*merci*."

He closed his eyes against the face that shimmered with longing for him. "*Non.* I did." He forced his eyes open. "I had to go back to *Ma Mère,* and after four days of searching, I assumed you were…"

"You returned." Her whisper barely carried above the rain. "For me."

"I had to. I couldn't think of you here, alone and scared, hunted by soldiers."

She ran her hands up his arms and cradled his cheeks. "You've grown thin."

"With you gone, I didn't have much desire to eat."

She ran her thumb beneath his eyes, where he knew purple smudges lingered on his skin. "Or sleep."

"I only wanted to find you."

Her hands slid across his back, then pulled him into a fierce embrace.

He nuzzled his face in her hair, sinking into the feeling of those slender arms wrapped around him, of the woman he loved burrowed into his chest. "Marry me, Isabelle. Be my wife, spend your life with me."

Tears glistened in her deep brown eyes, despite the smile that curved her lips. "Yes."

He lowered his mouth to hers. He'd missed the taste of her lips, the scent of her hair, the feel of her skin beneath his palms. So he kissed her again, slow and long this time as the sweetness of his beloved filled his senses.

Isabelle had doubted he'd ever hold her again, yet here she stood, cocooned in his arms, swamped once more by the sensation of his lips against her own. She clutched his forearms and slid deeper into the kiss.

"I see you've made amends with your woman, brother."

Warmth stealing across her face, she jerked away, turned to face Jean Paul and Jeanette, and curled her hands in her skirt.

"Isabelle." Jeanette rushed forward and held her in a tight hug.

Michel glared at his brother. "Mayhap you and *Notre Mère* should walk down to the beach. I wasn't quite finished with my lady."

"Ha. You best marry her first. Shall I fetch the magistrate?"

Nerves swept through her. Surely Michel didn't mean to marry her so quickly, did he? Her entire body heated at the thought.

"Michel said you were in Spain, Isabelle...no, Austria. No..." Jeanette scratched her head.

"England," she whispered. "I would have been in England. But I won't be going now. We'll all return to Abbeville come morning."

Michel scowled. "*Non.* I'm still taking you to England."

He spoke with such authority she nearly believed him.

"You can't, Michel. I've hardly any money left. Your brother…" Passing Jean Paul, she moved toward the rickety dresser where she stored her money. "The doctor's fees were rather high, and then I paid for this room and…" She handed him the small fistful of coins. "It's not enough for even one fare, much less two."

Tenderness filled his eyes. "You sacrificed your trip to save my brother?"

Something welled in her throat until she couldn't answer.

He pulled her against him. "We'll still away to England." His voice was low and rusty. "I've money enough to get the both of us there, though we won't have extra once we arrive."

"You've the farm to run. I won't ask you to leave. I could never do that. I'm coming home with you. Back to Abbeville. Jean Paul and I were headed there in a few days as it was. Just ask him."

He ran his knuckles down the side of her cheek. The look in his eyes caused her breath to stop and her blood to hum. "You were coming back. To me? On your own?"

"*Bien sûr.* Of course I was. I told you, Michel. I love you. *Je t'aime.* I want to be with you, on the farm you promised your *père* to care for."

"*Non.*"

"*Non?* How can you refuse me this? You asked me to stay."

"Before I truly realized the danger to you, as your father's daughter. I won't have you tarry in France when doing so could result in your death. What if a townsman learns of your heritage?"

She opened her mouth to protest, but Michel had already moved toward his brother.

"Jean Paul, I promised *Notre Père* I would manage the farm and care for *Notre Mère*. But God has given me another responsibility now, to my future wife. Will you see to *Notre Mère* and tend the farm in my stead? *Notre Mère's* missed you greatly."

Jeanette offered a shaky smile and a quick bob of her head.

Jean Paul's black eyes lightened. "I would be honored."

Michel placed a hand on his shoulder. "The land should have been yours to begin with. You're the farmer, not I."

"Aye."

"Mayhap if *Notre Père* had given you the farm, you wouldn't have left after Corinne's death."

Jean Paul hung his head. "I needed to go. Doesn't mean I should have fallen in with the mobs, but I had to leave. Here." He sat on the bed and tugged off his boot. He spent a moment fumbling with something inside, then pulled out a small bag and dumped the contents into his hand.

Isabelle gasped. The man held probably fifteen gold *Louis d'or* coins.

"You take this." Jean Paul handed the money to Michel. "It's more than enough to get you and your woman to England. It's—" he glanced at Isabelle "—the least I can do."

"There, now, that's the way brothers should treat each other," Jeanette piped up.

"But I searched your pockets, even your boots." Isabelle rushed to Jean Paul's side. "You didn't have any money."

His smiled thinly. "I always keep money hidden in the sole. Never know what can happen when you're a *soldat*."

Michel turned to her. "So, we away to England."

She stilled, sudden doubts rushing up to cloud her mind. Would their ship out of France be safe, or would a British warship find it? Once in London, how would she ever find Tante Cordele? And without the farm, how would Michel earn a living?

"Isabelle?" Michel pressed his hand to her cheek. "You'll be safer there."

She covered his hand with her own and slid her eyes closed. The warmth of his hand, the brush of his hardened calluses against her soft cheek, the gentleness of his touch, the silent sanctuary he offered. She belonged with this man, wherever he led her.

She trailed the tip of her thumb up his own able fingers.

And she knew how Michel would provide for them.

He would make furniture.

England wasn't only her dream, it was his.

He bent, his lips hovering over her ear and his breath fluttering her hair. "Come live with me in England, *mon amour.*"

She nuzzled her head against Michel's shoulder. The fibers of his rough linen shirt grated against her cheek, and she inhaled the familiar, rain-tinged scents of straw and earth and Michel. The pain of the past weeks fell away as she stood in the arms of this man who loved her despite her faults, as she stood in the shadow of a God who forgave her despite her wrongdoings.

"Yes," she whispered in response.

She looked up into green eyes bright with dreams and realized she didn't need England to feel safe.

She only needed Michel.

Epilogue

Isabelle stood on the deck of the timber-laden vessel they had boarded in Stockholm and peered through the drizzling mist. Waves lapped gently at the ship's hull, the wind off the ocean barely strong enough to tangle her hair, let alone move a ship. Her eyes strained to see through the dense clouds hovering over the sea. A chill slithered down her spine. She hadn't brought her cloak to the deck, so she wrapped her arms around herself, her gaze riveted in the direction the sailor had pointed some time ago.

Why was it taking so long?

"I wondered where you escaped to."

She smiled at the sound of her husband's voice but didn't turn. He came up behind her and stroked his hands down her arms. A shudder traveled through her, the type that had nothing to do with the cold and everything to do with this man's touch.

"You're chilled. Come, let's go belowdecks where you'll be warmer."

She shook her head. "Not until I see it."

"There's nothing to see yet. We're not scheduled to arrive in London until this evening."

"But the sailor said we could see England soon."

She felt more than heard Michel's sigh. Nevertheless his arms wrapped around her, and his chin rested atop her head.

"Merci," she whispered as she leaned back into his warmth and let his body heat surround her.

She slipped her hand into her pocket and ran her fingers over the smooth, wooden acorn. Michel had told her the story of destroying the dresser and had given her this one remaining piece when they married before leaving France.

Rising up from the mist before them, a shadow loomed. Small at first, the blob of dark gray grew on the horizon.

"England," she whispered.

The ship edged closer to the land, and the mist lightened, turning from a leaden gray to nearly white as the sun infiltrated the gloom. The ocean breeze caressed her hair, the salty sea stung her nose and her husband's arms tightened around her. She turned her face to the sky, letting the light's hazy rays touch her cheeks and streak her hair. And knew the sun would break through the clouds.

Soon. So very soon.

~.~.~.~.~

A Note from Naomi

Aren't you glad that Isabell and Michel were able to find a way to be together in the end? I don't know about you, but I'm so happy that Isabelle was finally able to arrive in England with the man she loves. But what will happen to Jean Paul? Having Isabelle save his life is sure to change him for the better, but he's faced so many hardships and struggles. Will he be able to leave the past behind him and start new? Perhaps with the love of a good woman by his side? Michel and Isabelle have learned that God's love can overcome the deepest of hurts, but is that a truth Jean Paul is willing to embrace? Can a man with a bitter past like his find redemption?

Grab your copy of *The Widow's Secret* and discover just how deep God's forgiveness goes.

(Want a sneak peek first? Turn the page to start reading.)

Prologue

Brigitte Dubois wrapped her arms about herself and trudged down the deserted street, darkness swallowing her every step. Night air toyed with the strands of hair hanging from beneath her mobcap, while mist from the sea nipped relentlessly at her ankles and a chill slithered up her spine.

It mattered not that it was summer, warm enough to sleep without a fire in the hearth, warm enough to draw beads of perspiration on her forehead, warm enough to attend her rendezvous with a shawl rather than a cloak. The cold came from inside, deep and frigid, a fear so terrifying she could hardly stay ahead of it. So her feet stumbled forward, over the cracked and chipping cobblestones, past the rows of houses shuttered tight against the darkness.

One night. One meeting. Then she could go home, gather her children and leave this wretched city.

Or so she hoped.

The breeze from the Channel swirled around her, ripe with the salty tang of sea and fish, while the clack of her wooden shoes against the street created the only sound in the deserted city besides the rhythmic lap of waves against the shore. The warehouse loomed before her at the end of the road, dark and menacing and ominously larger with each step she took toward its rusty iron doors.

Another shudder raced through her. Would this place become her tomb on this muggy summer night? No, she'd not think such things. She had a house to return to, children to feed and a babe to tend. Alphonse wasn't going to kill her, not tonight. Her children were too important.

Which was why she had to get them away.

She slowed as she neared the warehouse, raising her hand to knock upon the small side door. But just as her knuckles would have met the cold iron, it swung inward. "You're here." A guard hulked in the doorway, his voice loud against the empty street and tall stone houses.

"As I was told to be." She straightened her back, but not because she wanted to. No. Her shoulders ached to slump and her feet longed to slink into the shadows hovering beside the building, to creep back to her children and her house and the safety those four square walls offered.

But safety was a mere illusion. No one was ever truly safe from Alphonse Dubois.

"Come in." The planes and edges of the guard's face glinted hard in the dim light radiating from inside. He was huge, taller than her by nearly half a mètre and powerful enough to fell her with the club hanging at his side. Her eyes drifted down to the massive hand gripping the door, and she took a step back.

"That's the wrong direction, wench. And Alphonse doesn't like to wait." The guard's knuckles bulged around his club.

"Of course." She spoke easily, as though her body wasn't trembling. As though her lungs didn't refuse to draw breath at the idea of stepping over the threshold.

"I said move." The man yanked her inside.

The door slammed behind her, its bang resonating through the packed warehouse. Gone was the grimy smell of coal smoke and familiar taste of the sea that permeated the streets of Calais. Aromas sweet like chocolate, tangy like salt and smooth like tobacco wrapped themselves around her. Crates towered high, leaving only a narrow pathway through which to walk. Labels marked the sides of each and every box: silk from Lyons, and lace from Alençon and Arras, Dieppe and Le Puy. Tea from India, cocoa and cigars from the Caribbean. Sea salt from the Île de Ré, and more barrels of brandy than one could imagine. All sat stacked one atop the other in endless columns.

The contents of the single warehouse were worth a fortune in any land. But with France and England at war, Alphonse would reap even greater sums for his illegal French goods once his men smuggled them onto the English market. The trade materials like tea and chocolate and cigars would arrive on British shores under cover of darkness and away from the greedy eyes of the king's excise agents, bringing yet more profit to the smuggler.

And Alphonse had warehouses like this scattered through half of northern France.

"This way." A hot hand clamped around the back of her neck and shoved her forward, weaving her in an interminable maze toward the center of the warehouse.

When the crates finally stopped, she stood in a small open area in the middle of the warehouse.

With Alphonse Dubois looking on, seated dead in the center of his smuggling empire.

Heir to a seigneury by birth, he wielded more power now than an inheritance ever would have given him. All of Calais knew his story, though she knew it better than most. He was a firstborn son who hadn't been content to accept the lands handed down for centuries, nor had he wanted to make do with his family's dwindling coffers.

So rather than sitting in his chateau and watching as it crumbled about him while he ran through his precious few ancestral funds, he'd gone off and gotten himself rich.

Illegally.

Now Alphonse had as much money as England's king himself—and just as much power in a town such as Calais. "Brigitte." The thin blade of his voice sliced through the air. "How pleasant to see you."

As though he'd given her a choice, as though earlier this afternoon he hadn't sent two of his henchmen to her house and summoned her while her children watched.

He studied her through eyes yellow with age, that putrid amber and the pale pink tint to his lips the only colors in a face otherwise gray as stone. "Sit."

It had come to this then, time for him to issue orders and her to defy him. Did he see the way her hands trembled? The fear that threatened to burst from her chest in a sob?

"I prefer to stand, mer—"

The guard shoved her forward, and she nearly toppled into the table. "A defiant one, she is. You can see it in her eyes." He planted both hands on her shoulders, forcing her down until she crumpled into the chair.

Alphonse's pink-tinged lips curved into a cruel smile. "You're dismissed, Gerard."

The guard moved back against the crates to stand beside another man, equally as muscular and thick of chest, and carrying another large club.

Alphonse took a sip of steaming liquid from a mug beside his hand, then reached for a sweet biscuit sitting on the table. He wore gray as always, the color matching his silver-tinted hair and aging skin. The monotonous color palate created an image more akin to a corpse then a living, breathing man.

"I hear you plan to leave Calais." He'd found out.

She clutched her shawl against the base of her throat.

"Foolish woman." His eyes hardened into two frigid stones. "Did you think I'd let you steal my grandchildren away in the night?"

She hadn't a choice. He'd suck her children into the smuggling business if she didn't leave. Julien and Laurent were safe in the navy for now, but what of Danielle and Serge at home? How young did boys start running messages for Alphonse? Seven? Eight? Could Alphonse take Serge even now? And as for Danielle...

Brigitte swallowed, the type of work available to a girl in this industry too unbearable to imagine.

"No one leaves my employ without permission," he snapped.

"I'm not in your employ and never have been."

Something calculating and methodical moved behind his eyes. "No, you're family."

She cringed at the word. "My husband's dead. That eliminates any connection between you and I."

"It would, had I not five grandchildren whom you keep from me."

"With Henri dead, the children belong to me, and I'll not allow you to employ them in your wretched schemes. I'm not my husband."

"No, you most certainly are not." Alphonse ran his eyes slowly down her, his gazing lingering until revulsion flooded her body. "You claim you want to leave Calais, and let's say, just for the moment, that you have the money and means to do so. What do you intend to do? Where do you intend to go?"

To Reims. To my family.

She'd never be free of him if she said such things. He'd track her down and find her, taking her two oldest sons when they came home from the navy. Or he'd tell her she'd need to house his men and store his goods when one of his minions was in the area.

"Did you know, Brigitte, I have a rather marvelous memory?" He watched her through those hard, death-colored eyes. "It helps when one runs a business such as this."

A business? He spoke as though his smuggling success was some legitimate form of trade.

"For example, I seem to recall when you and my son first met. You were living in Reims, were you not? Acting as a governess?"

"I..." He couldn't remember where she came from and who her family was. Wouldn't use them as threats.

"I remember well, but every so often my mind fails me." He snapped his fingers, and one of the guards stepped forward, a sheaf of papers in hand. "I've learned to take excellent notes, you understand." He took the papers from the guard and f lipped through them. "Ah, yes, everything is here. You're the niece of a *seigneur*, and your elder sister married a *seigneur's* third son. Your father has passed on, but your mother apparently maintains good health and resides in your childhood home. I wonder how your mother and sister have fared, what with the *Révolution* and all."

She gripped the edge of the table, her nails digging into the aged wood. "How dare you."

"When my informants tell me you plan to leave Calais, that you hide away money and slowly pack your things, I ask myself, where might my dear daughter-in-law go? And why might she go there? And then it comes to me, where you hailed from, who your people are. Then just as I feel a spark of compassion and think that perhaps it's time for you to return to Reims, I remember my sweet grandchildren. Grandchildren who are useful to me."

"I won't let you touch them."

"I'd always intended for Henri to run my enterprise after I passed on." He continued on as though her words meant nothing. "'Twas a natural decision, you see, with him being my only son. But now that he's dead, one of your boys shall have to take over."

The breath whooshed out of her, and the air surrounding her grew thick and heavy. He couldn't get to the older boys. They were safe in the navy.

Weren't they?

"So which shall it be? Julien or Laurent? Julien would be advantageous in that—"

"What do you want?" She spit the words between them. He winged an eyebrow up.

"That's why you brought me here, isn't it?" She toyed with the ends of the shawl lying in her lap. "To ask something in exchange for letting me move to Reims?"

He laughed, a soft, cruel sound. "Very astute, Brigitte. You always have been, you know. 'Twas why I was so in favor of Henri's marrying you from the first."

"I'd not have married him had I known he was a smuggler."

That cruel smile curved his lips yet again. "Which was why you made him such a perfect wife. You faithfully stayed home and bore his seed, not luring him away from his duties with words of love and flattery. Oui, you were perfect. Too dutiful to leave, yet too angry with his work to distract him."

"You're evil."

"It serves me well, does it not?" He took a sip of tea. "But let's begin negotiations. I have a certain task in mind, one that would perfectly suit a widow with three children to tend. You fulfill your assignment, and I let you and the children return to Reims. I'll even give you money to buy a house there. A nice little cottage near your sister, perhaps?" She drew in a long, slow breath. Only one job, and then she and the children would be free. The proposition seemed almost too good to be believable. But then, he hadn't yet said what he wanted in exchange. "If I do your bidding, Julien and Laurent return to me in Reims when they reach port. They don't come to you."

"Of course."

"And I won't kill for you."

Alphonse's smile turned from cruel to dangerous. "Don't worry, ma chère. I seek only a spy. And justice. For the man who killed your husband."

Justice from a man like Alphonse? The very thought made her shiver. But what other choice had she?

Chapter One

Near Abbeville, France, July 1795

The children. She was doing this for the children.

Brigitte Dubois surveyed the countryside. The brilliant blue sky where two birds twittered and flirted with each other, the lush green forest to her right filled with a host of insect sounds, and the rolling fields stretching beyond the farmstead ahead and into the golden horizon.

Serene. Peaceful. A pleasant change from the grimy streets of Calais.

She must have the wrong house.

She'd never before given much thought to the soldier who had dragged her husband away in the night to execute him for his crimes. Had never wondered where he lived, what he did, if he had a family. But farming?

She forced her feet up the curving lane, climbing the little knoll to the cottage. A man stood near the stable, stuffing vegetables into an old wagon.

Her husband's alleged killer?

Surely killers didn't farm the pristine countryside or load vegetable wagons on sunny afternoons. They skulked about in the dead of night, meting out death and destruction.

"Bonjour, Citizen." She neared the stable where the vegetables waited, stacked neatly in crates and sacks.

The man's forearms bulged as he hefted another crate, his shirt straining against wide shoulders and a torso thick as a tree trunk. He would tower over Alphonse's guards, and he was so thick of chest her hands wouldn't touch if she wrapped her arms around him.

Powerful enough to drag a man like Henri from his bed. Strong enough to beat her dead if he learned what she was about.

"If you're wishing to buy food, I sell it at the market, not here." The man didn't stop his work but reached for another sack.

"I'm not in want of food, but a post." Not that she wanted to work for a possible murderer, but truly, Alphonse had left her little choice.

He turned to her and paused, his hands gripping a crate filled with turnips. Harshness radiated from his being, with eyes so dark and ominous they were nearly black, and hair the color of the sky at midnight. His chin jutted hard and strong beneath a chiseled face, and an angry scar curled and bunched around his right eyebrow.

She wet her suddenly parched lips.

"I haven't a job to offer you. I only employ tenant farmers, and I've three men waiting for plots next year already." He slid the crate onto the wagon bed, then turned and hefted another. "Have you tried in town? The butcher might be hiring, and we can always use another laundress or seamstress."

Brigitte glanced down at her lye-scarred hands, unlikely to recover after sixteen months of taking in laundry and mending. Besides, Abbeville was a small town, not like the bustling port of Calais. The people here probably had a favorite widow they took their mending to. "What about working as laundress here? You said you have tenants."

"Aye, and several of them have wives. There're women aplenty for doing women's work and older men to laze about. It's young men we've naught of."

Yes, she knew. Perhaps the war with the Netherlands had been settled, but France still warred with the Austrians in the east, the Italians in the south, and the English on the sea. Which meant the country sorely lacked young men… Or rather, young, upstanding men. Her husband and the rest of Alphonse's smugglers had evaded enlistment.

As had the man before her.

That bore looking into. Why would a strong, healthy man be farming rather than serving his country?

Perhaps he'd gotten leave for some reason, or had already joined the army only to be injured and sent home.

But that still didn't explain how he had all his tenant positions filled and a waiting list of three farmers for next year.

And wondering these things would do little good unless she procured employment here and could seek answers. She forced her eyes back to the big brute of a man still loading the wagon. "What of you? Have you a wife to do your laundry and housework and cooking? I can bake bread and apple pies, cherry tarts and—"

"Non." The harsh word resonated through the air between them. "I've no wife, and no need of one."

Heat flooded her cheeks and she took a step back, even though the wagon already sat between them. "I wasn't asking for your hand, I was offering to hire my labor out."

She'd already tried to dig into his secrets from afar. She'd moved to Abbeville half a week ago, but talking to the townsfolk had gotten her nowhere. She had a meeting with Alphonse's man in three days' time, and nothing to report but the information Alphonse had already given her: officially, after Jean Paul Belanger's wife had died seven years ago, he'd gone to Paris and spent six years away from Abbeville, supposedly making furniture.

Furniture. In the middle of a revolution. Did no one else think that odd?

Alphonse did. And Alphonse also thought Citizen Belanger the lead soldier that had found Henri and broken up a smuggling endeavor over a year ago, while going by a different surname. Now she was here to find proof and present it to Alphonse's man.

"Where did you say you were from?" The large man shoved another sack of grain onto the wagon and turned, his eyes studying her.

"Calais."

He frowned. "The port on the sea?"

"Oui. Have you been there? You can see England and its white cliffs from the shore. It's a beautiful city." Or it was if you lived in the proud stone houses set back from the sea and not in a shack near the harbor.

The man's eyes grew darker—which shouldn't have been possible, as they had started out the color of midnight.

He knew what she was about, he had to. She took an instinctive step back. If he flew at her—

"I've been there once, and it doesn't bear remembering." Her breath puffed from her lips in shaky little bursts.

It was as she'd told Alphonse, she'd be no good at this information gathering. If she couldn't look the man in the eye and ask him a simple question without giving herself away, how would she uncover his secrets?

If he had any secrets.

If he wasn't the wrong man entirely.

On the eve of Henri's capture, the sliver of moonlight trickling through the window had been so dim she could hardly make out her husband's form on the pallet beside her. But she'd felt his presence, the heat from his body, the tickle of his breath on her cheek. He was home, for once, not off on some smuggling errand for Alphonse, paying some strange woman for a place in her bed, or drinking himself through the wee hours until dawn. He'd eaten dinner with her and the children, kissed them and crawled into bed beside her as though they were a normal family.

Then the soldiers came. They didn't knock, just burst through the solid wooden door and shouted for Henri Dubois. One man yanked him from their bed. A big man, so broad of back and thick of chest his body eclipsed any light from the window.

Strange that she should recall that of all things, the way the soldier's body had been so large it obstructed the shadow of her husband's form being dragged to the door. "Are you unwell?" Citizen Belanger watched her, his forehead wrinkling into deep furrows.

She shook her head, her throat too dry to speak.

"Citizen?" The farmer approached, stepping around the wagon and striding forward with a powerful gait.

"Non, I'm fine." She didn't want the hulking man beside her, innocent or not.

But he came, anyway, closer and closer until she stood in his shadow, those wide shoulders blocking the sun just as the soldier's body had blocked the light from the moon.

She pressed her eyes shut and ducked her head. What if this man had taken her husband? Would he drag her away to the guillotine, as well?

Her breaths grew quick and short, and the air squeezed from her lungs.

But nothing happened. She waited one moment, then two, before peeking an eyelid open. He stood beside her now, towering and strong, able to do anything he wished with those powerful hands and arms.

But concern cloaked his face rather than malice. "Are you ill? Need you sustenance?"

Sustenance? She wanted nothing from him—besides information, that was. She opened her mouth to proclaim herself well, except he stood so close she could only stare at his big, burly body.

"Here. Sit." He took her by the shoulder.

She lurched back, but his hands held her firm, leading her toward the house. Surely he didn't mean to take her inside, where 'twould be far more difficult for her to get away.

"Non." She planted her feet into the dirt. "I—I wish to stay in the sun."

He scowled, a look that had likely struck fear in many a heart. "Are you certain? Mayhap the sun's making you over warm. The house is cooler."

Her current state had nothing to do with the heat, but rather the opposite. Fear gripped her stomach and chest, an iciness that radiated from within and refused to release its hold. She'd felt it twice before. First when those soldiers had barged into their house and taken Henri away, and then the night Alphonse had given her this task.

Now she was in Abbeville, staring at the man she might well need to destroy and letting fear cripple her once again.

⸝.⸝.⸝.⸝.⸝

She's like Corinne. It was the only thing Jean Paul could think as he stared at the thin woman in his hold. She was tall yet slender, as his late wife had been, and had a quietly determined way about her. Unfortunately she also looked ready to faint.

He needed to get some food in her. He'd not have another woman starve in his hands, at least not when he had the means to prevent it.

"I should sit," she spoke quietly then slid from his grip, wilting against the stone and mud of the cottage wall before he could stop her.

"Are you unwell?" he asked again. A daft question, to be sure, with the way her face shone pale as stone.

She shook her head, a barely perceptible movement. "I simply... need a moment."

She needed more than a moment. Judging by the dark smudges beneath her eyes and hollowness in her face, she needed a night of rest and a fortnight of sumptuous feasts.

"Come inside and lie down." He hunkered down and reached for her, wrapping one arm around her back and slipping another beneath her legs.

"Non!" The bloodcurdling scream rang across the fields, so loud his tenants likely heard it. "Remove your hands at once."

Stubborn woman. "If you'd simply let me..."

His voice trailed off as he met her eyes. They should have been clouded with pain, or mayhap in a temporary daze from nearly swooning. But fear raced through those deep brown orbs.

She was terrified. Of him.

Why? He shifted back, giving her space enough to run if she so desired. The woman's chest heaved and her eyes turned wild, the stark anguish of fright and horror etched across her features.

"Let me get you a bit of water and bread." He rose and moved into the quiet sanctuary of his home. The cool air inside the dank daub walls wrapped around him, the familiar scents of rising bread and cold soup tugging him farther inside. But the surroundings didn't banish the woman's look of terror from his mind, nor the sound of her scream.

How many times had he heard screams like that? A woman's panic-filled cry, a child's voice saturated with fear?

And how many times had he been the cause?

Thank You

Thank you for reading *The Lady's Refuge*. I sincerely hope you enjoyed Isabelle and Michel's story. The Belanger Family Saga is the first series that I ever wrote, and a decade after finishing this very book (which was originally published as *Sanctuary for a Lady*), I'm excited to be able to share these wonderful stories with you. If I were to pick a theme for this series, it would be "Hope in the Darkness," because each of these books illustrates God's endless love and care for His children, even in the darkest of times. I hope you'll take the time to read the entire series. The next full-length novel is Jean Paul and Brigitte's story, *The Widow's Secret*.

Want a free Naomi Rawlings book? Sign up for my author newsletter and claim your free novel: http://geni.us/AqsHv (You'll also get special sales announcements and discounts, plus you'll have the chance to purchase an entire series from me at an incredibly low price—all for signing up for my newsletter!) If you find the newsletter isn't for you, you can unsubscribe at any time and still keep your discount books.

Also, if you enjoyed reading *The Lady's Refuge*, please take a moment to tell others about the novel. You can do this by posting an honest review on Amazon. I read every one of my reviews, and reviews help readers like yourself decide whether to purchase a novel. You might also consider mentioning *The Lady's Refuge* to your friends on Facebook, Twitter, or Pinterest.

Other Novels by Naomi Rawlings

Belanger Family Saga

Book 1—*The Lady's Refuge* (Michel and Isabelle)

Book 2—*The Widow's Secret* (Jean Paul and Brigitte)

Book 3—*The Reluctant Enemy* (Gregory and Danielle)

Eagle Harbor Series

Book 1—*Love's Unfading Light* (Mac and Tressa)

Book 2—*Love's Every Whisper* (Elijah and Victoria)

Book 3—*Love's Sure Dawn* (Gilbert and Rebekah)

Book 4—*Love's Eternal Breath* (Seth and Lindy)

Book 5—*Love's Christmas Hope* (Thomas and Jessalyn)

Book 6—*Love's Bright Tomorrow* (Isaac and Aileen)

Short Story—*Love's Beginning* (Elijah, Gilbert, Mac, Victoria, Rebekah)

Prequel—*Love's Violet Sunrise* (Hiram and Mabel)

Texas Promise Series

Book 1—*Tomorrow's First Light* (Sam and Ellie)

Book 2—*Tomorrow's Shining Dream* (Daniel and Charlotte)

Book 3—*Tomorrow's Constant Hope* (Wes and Keely: releasing 2021)

Book 4—*Tomorrow's Steadfast Prayer* (Harrison and Alejandra: releasing 2022)

Book 5—*Tomorrow's Lasting Joy* (Cain and Anna Mae)

Author's Note

I'm told that every author holds certain books closer to her heart than others. Please know that this book will always be special to me, partly because it is my first published book, but even more so because the story is so powerful. The tale seemed to grow into a living, breathing entity, and became more special with each minute I worked on it. I found myself loving the characters of Isabelle and Michel, entranced by their hopes and dreams and suffering through their pain.

Writers often have people ask them why they write. Just before this book was first published, I had a very powerful, influential person in the publishing industry ask me, "What kind of stories do you write?" I answered him simply and said, "I write the kind of stories that matter." And so I trust that this story matters to you readers as much as it did to me. My prayer is that God uses this story in your life to illustrate the depth and boundlessness of the forgiveness He offers, as well as the great price that forgiveness sometimes costs.

The French Revolution was a dark time in European history. Historians and political scientists today often ask themselves how a political movement with such good intentions—feed the poor and create a sustainable middle class—could go so very wrong and end up hurting the very people it was meant to help. I don't have the answers for you. I tried my hardest to convey the complexity of the

Revolution and the Reign of Terror, but I'm sure there are things I missed, and all errors are mine alone.

Thank you so very much for taking the time to read my book. I know that many of you lead busy lives with little spare time. Please understand that the time and energy you put into reading my novel blesses me.

Acknowledgments

Thank you first and foremost to my Lord and Savior, Jesus Christ, for giving me both the ability and opportunity to write novels for His glory.

As with any novel, an author might come up with a story idea and sit at his or her computer to type the initial words, but it takes an army of people to bring you the book you have today. I would like to thank my editor from many years ago, Elizabeth Mazer, for yanking my manuscript out of the slush pile and seeing some potential. I also thank my former agent, Natasha Kern, for believing in me as a new writer, taking time to teach me more about writing and publishing, and not giving up on me despite all the mistakes I made in my early years as a novelist. And finally I thank my critique partners at the time this novel was first published, Melissa, Sally, Glenn, and Anne, for trudging through this story with me. Numerous others have helped with this novel, through giving advice, answering questions and reading portions of this story. Thank you all for your time and efforts.

About the Author

Naomi Rawlings is the author of over a dozen historical Christian novels, including the Amazon bestselling Eagle Harbor Series. While she'd love to claim she spends her days huddled in front of her computer vigorously typing, in reality she spends her time cleaning, picking up, and pretending like her house isn't in a constant state of chaos. She lives with her husband and three children in Michigan's rugged Upper Peninsula, along the southern shore of Lake Superior, where they get 200 inches of snow every year, and where people still grow their own vegetables and cut down their own firewood—just like in the historical novels she writes.

For more information about Naomi, please visit her at www.naomirawlings.com or find her on Facebook at www.facebook.com/author.naomirawlings. If you'd like a free novel, sign up for her author newsletter: http://geni.us/35Yn

Made in the USA
Monee, IL
12 August 2022

11524120R00163